Mistletoe
in Juneau

USA TODAY BESTSELLING AUTHOR

DAHLIA ROSE

Print: 978-1-952210-34-1
eBook 978-1-952210-35-8

www.hallmarkpublishing.com

To my hero, my veteran and love, Robert 'Sarge' Pearson. You are stronger than anyone I've ever known, and I'm honored to be your wife.
Deployment sent you home hurt and bent, but it never broke your wonderful spirit.
This book is for you.
Army Strong! HOOAH!

Chapter One

E VEN BEFORE HALLOWEEN JACK-O'-LANTERNS CAME down and the Thanksgiving turkey was carved, New York City came alive with holiday magic. Twinkling lights and decorations graced the store windows in Manhattan, and at Rockefeller Center, the massive tree made the perfect centerpiece for Christmas in a city whose buildings reached for the sky. By the time New Yorkers heard the first merry jingle of bells or the hearty laugh of a mall Santa, they were in the Christmas spirit.

Thirty-year old Danni St. Peters loved the city. A Brooklyn girl born and raised, she could get from Canarsie to Clinton Hills by bus or train, and she always knew which street had the latest fashions or the hottest new restaurant. She'd built her career around that adventurous spirit and had made a name for herself. *Danni On the Run*, her video channel, had over two million subscribers—and that wasn't even counting all her other followers on social media. She was well known across the country and going worldwide.

"We're ready for you on set, Danni." The producer of

the morning show segment, a young woman wearing a headset, looked in the room as the makeup artist made sure Danni's face was flawless.

Danni met the producer's gaze in the mirror with a wink. "Thanks a bunch!"

"You look marvelous," a male voice added. "Are you ready to wow them with that Danni pizzazz?"

Austin Hammond, who had accompanied her to the morning show, stood at the door. His smile traveled to his eyes, making the blue even warmer. As always, Austin was dressed to the nines. His champagne-colored sweater was paired with dark dress pants and expensive, on-trend shoes. He'd left the jacket in the greenroom.

"Ready as I'll ever be," she said.

"Big smile." He made a smile motion with his hand, and Danni gave him a rueful shake of her head. Then she put a bright smile on and followed the producer down the hall.

Today she had an appearance on the entertainment channel's best-rated daytime show. Being featured on *The Aisha White Show* was another step up in her career. Aisha was a daytime drama actress whose career had taken off, and now she had her own line of clothes and shoes as well as the talk show.

Danni caught a glimpse of herself in one of the lighted mirrors offstage. Two barrettes pulled her hair back from her face to accent her cheekbones. Light bronzer made her teak-colored skin glow, like she'd just come from a beach in the Caribbean.

Danni stepped from the hallway into the shots of the cameras. When the lights hit her, she came alive. The audience clapped as she ran down the walkway, giving high fives and taking a selfie or two with guests before bounding up the two small steps that led to the stage.

"Danni, you look fabulous!" Aisha's bright eyes were kind and caught the lights of the set, and her wide smile instantly put Danni at ease.

"White pantsuit in winter—brave girl!" Aisha held out her arms for an embrace.

"You look amazing yourself, Aisha. That red dress is perfect on you, and I'm jealous." Danni hugged her lightly while they exchanged air kisses, and then did a little twirl. "I'm not a Hamptons girl, Aisha. We Brooklyn girls live a bit fashion-dangerously. Besides, I paired it with your red pumps and the look is fierce."

"Yes, yes, it's perfect." The audience clapped their approval while she and the host got seated on a pair of comfortable plush chairs.

"Danni St. Peters," Aisha said with warmth. "Your name is on everyone's lips. You have millions of followers who just eat up your every adventure. Tell us how it started."

Danni smiled. "It started because I was a dreamer. I didn't just want to read about places in a book—I wanted to experience them. So, three years ago, after saving for two years before that, I took my first trip to Paris... on a budget. And let me tell you, visiting Paris, surviving on croissants and cheese, and exploring the city was the best time I ever had. I stayed in a low-rent hotel, I made videos and livestreamed the different places I visited, and people loved it because they could relate."

Aisha said, "And you've gone much further than that. *Danni on The Run* is food, it's dancing...I loved the one when you tried hot yoga for the first time. Oh! And the food truck Friday in Charlotte, where you ate that loaded mac and cheese."

Danni threw her head back and laughed. "The food in that town is so decadent. *Danni On the Run* is going back for a second trip there for something called Queen Charlotte day, so look out for that in February."

Aisha leaned forward conspiratorially. "What about the man in Danni's life?"

Danni swallowed uncomfortably and looked toward backstage. What should she call Austin these days? They had morphed from manager and client to couple, and she honestly didn't know when it had happened. Now he practically beamed...and before Danni could say a thing, Austin jogged out waving at the audience.

Dude! she thought. *This is not your interview!*

But she tucked away her irritation, because as always, Austin didn't mean any harm in his actions. He was just...*excitable?* Yeah, that was the word.

He was the quintessential New York man, from the top of his blond head down to the loafers on his feet. His smile was perfect—white even teeth. Danni almost expected the little sparkle she saw in toothpaste ads. And Austin Hammond was accustomed to being in front of an audience. His family vacationed in Martha's Vineyard and played racquetball with the elite. He had tickets to all the best events, and he'd hinted they would need to coordinate their outfits for New York Fashion Week next year.

"Austin Hammond," Aisha said. "We all know who you are, and now we see why you have that gleam in your eyes."

With his hands placed on Aisha's shoulders, Austin kissed her on both cheeks. As he sat down in the chair next to Danni and held her hand, the host continued. "When did you guys meet?"

Danni opened her mouth to answer, but Austin beat her to the punch. "I met the lovely Danni last year at the Harlem Wine Festival. I saw her, and I knew she was the one."

Am I? And was Austin really the one for her? Even as confusion filtered through her mind, Danni kept her smile pasted firmly on her face.

"So, love at first sight, hmmm?" Aisha turned to her audience. "And they said romance was dead."

The rest of the interview consisted of Danni answering questions when she could. Austin also touted being her manager and anything else he could get out before the interview was over. She was tired by the end of it.

"That went wonderfully," Austin said, once they were offstage and heading toward the exit.

"It went," Danni murmured.

He frowned. "Not happy with it, honey?"

She cast a sidelong glance at him. "Well, you did all the commentary. You tell me."

"I gave the audience what they wanted." Austin grinned. "We are building your brand."

"I'm not a puppet. Austin, I can speak for myself," Danni said firmly. "It was my brand before you stepped in, and it will continue to be so."

"Don't be mad, babe, it went great," he said and patted out a little beat on his leg.

He never listens.

But he was only trying to help, she told herself. She was running on fumes—no food and plenty of caffeine—and it was making her oversensitive. She should quit being so hard on the guy.

She pasted a smile on her face as they stepped outside. "It went great. I'm just a bit tired. It's been a whirlwind of a year, and I honestly need a break."

"Ah-ah-ah, not the 'b' word again," Austin said.

A sleek black town car pulled up, and the driver came around to help her in. When they were settled in the back seat, he spoke again.

"This went fantastic. Did you see how they practically got out of their seats when I came out? It's what they want, babe—the most eligible, handsome man on your arm."

Danni said nothing as the car pulled away from the curb. Austin kept talking while she half-listened.

She was going to every event, every weekend—new restaurant openings, shows, clubs. When she'd first started out, she'd been able to choose what she did, but since he'd become her manager, she hadn't said no to a single invite. She no longer got her videos out after one simple edit. Now, it was tweak and re-tweak, take and re-take to get the perfect shot. The organizers who invited her wanted to be showcased in the best light.

Some of the clubs were not her scene. They were loud, hot, and crass, where egos were built on how someone dressed—usually, the more scantily, the better. That wasn't her.

She missed the days when it was just about her bucket list. The brochure for the butterfly exhibit she wanted to visit was still on her desk. Danni smiled, thinking about when she could actually go sit and film while butterflies flitted all around. Maybe they'd land on her hands or shoulders…

"Danni… Danni, are you listening to me?" Austin took her hand and patted it in concern. "Do you need to eat? Low blood sugar and Danni St Peters do not mix."

"Sorry," Danni apologized. "Slight headache. You're right though, I haven't had anything to eat since breakfast."

"I have protein bars, or should we stop and get you a quick sandwich? Danni, you need to take care of you, too," Austin said with worry in his voice. "You have to be on the ball. You still have that meeting for the makeup brand. If you get this campaign, you'll be worldwide baby, so you have to think about when you eat."

"Okay, Austin. I'll handle it... I know you're trying to help, but right now it's a bombardment of words." Danni sighed and leaned forward to tap the glass barrier between them and the driver. "Charles, can you take me to the Renaissance Hotel, please?"

"Yes ma'am." The driver made a left turn at the light.

"You don't have to see them until noon, and I can go with you." Austin smiled and picked up her hand to kiss it. "You need me to work this deal for you, honey."

Danni gently removed her hand. "Austin, I did this by myself before we met last year. Thank you, but this one I can manage on my own. I'm going to grab a quick lunch...alone, then freshen up for the meeting."

"Will I see you tonight?" His tone was subdued.

She shook her head. "I need to shop for my family get-together and go home to wrap gifts. I'll see you Sunday for dinner, how's that?"

He brightened. "I'll get Salvador to make us something fantastic at Ciao's."

Danni nodded. "Sounds perfect."

"Oh, that other show called, *The Scoop*. They still want you for next week."

"No. I won't be anywhere near that guy. He demeans people, and he glorifies misery. Don't even respond, and he'll go away."

"But—"

"*No*," Danni cut him off firmly. "I won't be fodder for his rumor mill."

Austin took her hand in his. "You're right, of course. That's not the image you're going for. I'll ask the street team for input."

When had she gotten a street team? Shouldn't she have heard about that? Still, she warmed pleasantly at his support. It wasn't usual for him to follow her direction when it came to her career, so it was wonderful when he listened and turned on his boyish charm.

"That's great," she said. "Thank you for seeing my point of view."

The car pulled to a stop outside the hotel, and she gathered her purse and the satchel that carried her laptop, tablet, and even a tripod in case she was inspired to shoot something interesting for her show.

She kissed him on the cheek. "See you Sunday. Go visit your parents, take them a gift."

Austin laughed. "Danni, you are so innocent sometimes. We haven't exchanged gifts since I was fourteen. They can literally buy anything they want."

She shook her head at his response. He blew her a kiss as the car pulled away.

Danni took a huge breath, clearing her lungs with the cold winter air, then walked toward the hotel and went directly to the posh restaurant on the bottom floor. The truth was, she could've seen him before her family's holiday get-together.

The dinner always happened early because her parents spent the holiday in Florida. It was the luxury they spent the entire year saving up for: a month in a warm climate to get away from the New York chill. This year, Danni had the perfect gift for them. Their month would be spent in a luxury condo instead of the cramped timeshare with two other couples her mother always complained about.

The waitress came over with a smile. "Good afternoon. Lunch menu?"

"Please," Danni said gratefully. "Can I have the

molten hot chocolate, extra warm, please?"

"And extra whipped cream?" the waitress hinted. "It's perfect to beat the cold."

"That sounds amazing. Put me down for that."

She studied the menu while waiting for her drink. The first time she'd tasted the hot chocolate at the hotel, she'd been surprised to learn it had red wine in the recipe. She'd loved the idea so much, she'd done a livestream with the chef as he made his signature winter drink. He explained how the heat evaporated the alcohol content of the wine, leaving only a rich flavor that enhanced the chocolate.

The waitress was quick to return with her beverage and Danni ordered the salmon burger with steak fries for lunch. After the first delicious sip, she impulsively pulled out her phone and started to record.

"Have you ever just missed reading by a window while the rain falls? Or going thrift shopping for that perfect pair of retro jeans? Lunch in the park with girlfriends, watching cute guys play Frisbee or flag football? I miss that. Sometimes the glitz and glamour takes away from the small things," she said into the camera. "Even this drink right now…it should be shared with someone who wants to snuggle up next to a fire, or watch a movie at home wearing mismatched socks." Danni gave a soft laugh. "Or maybe I'm just crazy, and I should be grateful for what I have?"

She stopped the recording, knowing she would never post it to her site. It was against the grain of what she posted now, and it was one more sign that she wasn't living her truth.

No, this recording was just for her. She would still enjoy the small things now, in the middle of this new, more glamorous life. Danni made a promise to always make time for herself, before she forgot exactly what that entailed.

After her meeting with the cosmetics company, Danni was jazzed. The representatives had loved her laugh and the clever little euphemisms she used when she talked. *Living life like a platinum record* was one of their favorite expressions of hers, and she saw one of the reps make a note of her wording.

But what if they went another route? She knew they were also talking to another influencer, one with more experience and more followers.

Stop worrying, Danni chided herself, knowing she tended to overthink things. What she didn't have would be made up with her personality, and she was ready to wow them at the second meeting.

Shopping therapy did her a ton of good. And her night only got better when she walked into her apartment, changed into her comfy pajamas, and piled her hair on the top of her head in a messy bun.

With festive music playing, she set up her artificial Christmas tree in the corner of her living room and decorated it. While the lights twinkled off the various ornaments and tinsel, she wrapped her gifts for her family. Honestly, she loved this part: making precise tight corners, curling ribbons, and figuring out how to use the paper on an oddly shaped item.

Danni smiled wide and wiggled her toes in the socks that featured dancing reindeers. She hoped they all loved their gifts. There had been a time when she'd only been able to afford small tokens of her love. Now she could spoil them and make their holiday bright.

Every time she thought about her family, it made her heart ache just a bit. The next day, she'd be at the customary family holiday dinner. Although she was happy, Danni was nervous about her lifestyle becoming the topic of conversation.

She'd always felt like a bit of an outsider growing up, and it was no different now. Her parents had set rules and choices they expected their daughters to make. Danni had started out gaining their approval with good grades and toeing the line of their strict imperatives. Quitting her job after college had really put a rift between them.

The dainty chime of her phone sounded, and Danni picked up the video call. "Hello?"

"Danni!" the voice squealed before the image came into view.

"Amy! Oh my God, Amy!" Danni cried out, instantly letting go of the dark thoughts in her head.

Her friend's face was a little fuzzy, but then Amy fiddled with something on her end and it became clear. The bright red hair and warm eyes of her best friend in the world, combined with her sunny smile, gave Danni a wave of fond memories. The two had been inseparable from grade school through high school. Amy had been a part of every adventure Danni had growing up.

Behind Amy, Danni could see a warm fire and big flakes coming down outside the window. "Man, that's a lot of snow."

"It's Alaska," Amy said with dry amusement. "I'm lucky I got through."

"How are you?"

Amy stood and revealed the round belly beneath her

oversized sweater. "I'm so good. Round as a Butterball turkey but good."

Danni's mouth fell open. "Wait, how come you didn't tell me about baby number two?"

A sense of disappointment filled her—not towards Amy, but herself. Had she gotten so focused on her career she forgot about the people closest to her?

"I sent you a message, best friend forever, but you are living the golden life," Amy said with a laugh. "You never responded."

Danni cringed. "Oh, Amy, I'm sorry. I meant to when I got home that night, but I was so tired I crashed. You know I would never forget you on purpose."

"I know," Amy said. "You can make it up to me, though."

"How? Do you need me to baby shop and send you boxes? I'll do it," she declared. "I just bought my family their gifts, and I don't mind shopping again. Remind me to tell you about the molten lava hot chocolate, Amy the taste is life, I tell you... L.I.F.E."

"First, I don't care how you do it, I want that recipe, because...chocolate. But what I really want is for my best friend to visit. You've never met Mateo, and Peter is three... I want you to be here for this birth and spend Christmas with me. I know your family makes their yearly pilgrimage to Florida. You can be here with us."

"I would love to, but I don't know if I can," Danni said. "I have so much going on here."

"This could be a new adventure: *Danni on The Run* takes on Juneau, Alaska," her friend hinted with a mischievous smile.

She laughed. "That's a great idea. But Austin is on me about more visibility. And I have another meeting coming up with this makeup line to be their spokesperson. I had the first meeting today."

"Wow. How did that go?"

"It was really good," Danni answered. "There's another woman, Sade Carole, vying for the same spot. Honestly, she may get it because she has more visibility, but one can hope. Which reminds me, I need to call Austin and let him know it went great."

"And there is the name Austin again. Who is this man I have never heard of because you don't call and dish?" Amy teased.

"He's my manager—boyfriend, I think. He's really cute and wealthy, and we've been seeing each other, kind of, for over a year." Danni plucked at the button of her pajama top as she spoke.

"Do you get all those butterflies in the tummy when you see him? Does his smile make your breath catch because you can tell how much he cares by looking in his eyes?" Amy asked. "You know me, I'm a big ol' romantic."

Butterflies. Did she ever feel that with Austin? Danni searched her mind, hoping to find one instance. She and Austin had just fallen into being a couple, there had been no big buildup, no anticipation of a first date.

"That doesn't really happen, does it?" Danni asked.

Amy laughed. "Of course, it does! Why do you think I'm living in Juneau with an Alaskan State Trooper as a husband? I think it was fate or destiny that Mateo was in Manhattan that day and we literally bumped into each other. It's been seven years, and I love him more every day."

"I don't think I felt any of that," she admitted.

"Maybe it's one of those slow-to-build kinds of relationships," Amy said. "Please say you'll come, Danni."

"How about I call you back tomorrow night and let you know?" Danni asked. "I have the St. Peters family dinner in the evening before the snowbirds, a.k.a. my parents, leave for Florida. Don't get me wrong I love seeing the family units and Christmas is my mom's time to shine, but it can be tense. My dad doesn't understand my career choice,"

"You know Edward and Sandra. They want the best for you, even if they don't know how to say it." Amy sighed. "I thought age would have mellowed them."

"Not a bit. My life choices, compared to my sister's, have not made them happy." Danni lay flat on the sofa and held the phone above her. "Combine that with the fact that I feel burned out lately. I hope they ease up a little, and we can just have a great meal and open gifts."

"It's your life, Danni. No one can tell you how to live it and then make you feel bad about it," Amy pointed out. "You really need to visit. A vacation in Alaska for the holiday—you'll love it, I promise."

"I'll let you know as soon as I get in," Danni replied. "Don't go into labor before then."

"I've got to bake this baby bun until Christmas Day, so you have time," Amy said with a laugh. "Talk to you later. It's seven a.m. here, so Peter will be up soon looking for hot cakes and bacon for breakfast."

"I love that kid already," Danni chuckled. "Bye, bestie."

"Don't let them make you feel bad," Amy called into the phone before Danni hung up.

The next afternoon her driver came to pick her up, and she watched passers-by through the car window.

Everyone was bundled up against the cold, rushing about with their gloved hands full of packages as they traversed the uneven sidewalks. The tall apartment buildings still stood near Tompkins Park as she passed by and then continued on Green Avenue and Gates, heading to her parents' home.

She passed through the street where her family had lived before her father had bought the brownstone. Two of the bodegas she'd frequented as a child to buy snacks and afternoon sandwiches were now trendy coffee shops. Her stomach clenched in anxiety as the car slowed in front of her parent's home. After the driver helped her with her gifts and piled them at the front door, Danni rang the doorbell and waited.

The door opened to reveal her mother. Sandra St. Peters was still beautiful for her age, and she liked to tease that their family has the great genes. Her black hair, now streaked with gray, was elegantly done as always. Her mother believed that you dressed properly every day in case of impromptu guests. Today, she wore her usual red for the holiday dinner: a scarlet pantsuit paired with a pearl necklace and teardrop earrings to match.

"Hey Mom." Danni smiled wide.

"Danni, you look good," her mother replied and kissed her cheek. "Come in, we're letting out all the heat."

"Let me grab these." Danni bent to take the first boxes off the top.

"Goodness, you came bearing all the gifts," her mother exclaimed. "Here, pass me those and you grab the rest."

The house smells so good! Danni thought as she stepped inside. It took her back to Christmases of her childhood.

She found the rest of the family in the sitting room, with her father in his usual chair. Edward St. Peters had gray peppered though his low-cut hair. Crinkles at his eyes when he smiled made her feel good about coming home. Danni knew he would smell like peppermint, because it was his favorite piece of candy for the holidays.

Grace, her husband Mike, and their three boys were there. Grace was a nurse—the path chosen for her by their parents, of course—and she'd married a man who was manager of an auto repair shop in New Jersey. They lived in a brownstone across the street from her parents.

Danni was group-hugged by her nephews. Her mother retreated to the kitchen to make sure dinner was perfect.

"Dad, happy holidays." Danni bent to kiss his cheek.

"Merry Christmas to you." Her father's smile was tight. "Got a lot of packages there. Trying to show us up?"

Her father's laugh didn't help alleviate the nervous tumble in her stomach. Was he kidding, not kidding? With him she could never tell. Her father had always worked hard for his family, and in his mind, anything that didn't take back-breaking labor and sweat would flitter away like confetti in the wind.

Her smile faltered. "No, Dad, I just bought everyone something I think they'd like."

"I know." His face softened and he patted her cheek. "You have a heart of gold, baby girl, always have."

He went back to watching football with his grandsons, and Danni focused on her sister. Grace, five years older than Danni, was just like their mom in looks and some mannerisms.

"Grace, you are looking good." Danni hugged her tight. "How do you keep that figure the way we eat?"

"Running around the E.R. telling doctors what they need before they need it," Grace said with a laugh.

"Well, nurses are the unsung heroes, so know your worth."

Danni turned just as her brother-in-law Mike embraced her and lifted her off her feet. "Mike, can't breathe."

"Sorry, you're skin and bones, lil' sis." He grinned.

"That's because you eat everything before I get here," Danni retorted. This was an ongoing joke between them.

"How did you get a biscuit?" Grace whispered and slapped at his hand. "Mom will kill you."

Mike's eyes twinkled as he bit into the biscuit. He was almost six feet tall and built like the trucks he fixed for the city. His sandy blond hair was always cut neat, and he had working man's hands. Her parents had automatically loved Mike; he had the same hardworking personality and ethics that the St. Peters family carried as their foundation.

Danni thought about Austin's twice-weekly manicures at an exclusive nail salon on the upper east side of Manhattan. He definitely wouldn't make the cut.

Luckily for Mike, he finished the biscuit before Danni's mother came back into the room. "We have twenty minutes before the scalloped potatoes are done," she said. "I say we open gifts while we wait."

Of course, Danni's nephews cheered loudly in approval. Jackson was the oldest: tall and lean, with kind brown eyes and a quick smile. David, the middle child, was excited about everything he read or saw. His laugh was as infectious as his big personality. Dontae was the baby of the bunch, and his quiet disposition didn't negate his very large vocabulary. When he spoke, people listened, and his dark brown eyes looked wise beyond his years. All three boys had a mass of light brown curls, each cut in a different style that suited their unique personalities.

Grace rolled her eyes as Jackson and David teased and nudged at each other. Danni's mother got Danni and her sister the exact same pair of earrings. They just looked at each other and smiled, because that was how it had been all their lives. From Danni, Mike got a new socket set for the garage, and the boys opened their gift from her —a new game console for them to share. In addition, they each got an individual handheld game system with a variety of games they could share.

"Aunt Danni, these are the best!" Jackson almost toppled her over with a hug.

"Yes, we were saving to get them the consoles for each of them since they fight about...." Grace shrugged and looked at her husband, who winked. "No worries, we'll get them something else. Thank you, Danni. You have effectively kept them out of my hair at home."

Danni instantly felt remorse. "I just figured they'd like it, and the store associate said it was what all the boys had on the list for Christmas."

Knowing how her father and mother used to penny-pinch to afford gifts, Danni should have thought about it more or called Grace to find out the best gift idea. She hadn't meant to steal their thunder.

"It's fine, Danni," Mike said. "We'll get them something to match what you bought."

For Mike and Grace, she'd gotten a weekend getaway at an exclusive spa in upstate New York.

"Our jobs are so busy..." Grace began and shook her head. "You know what, we are taking a trip! Thank you, Danni, we'll work out the logistics and the boys can stay with Mom and Dad."

"Oh, so three grown boys in a basket will be at my front door," their grandmother teased.

Mike grinned. "We'll definitely make time. Thank you, Danni."

"With these rambunctious boys, we need a break." Grace laughed and hugged Danni. "Thanks, Sis."

Her parents opened the envelope that held the reservation, and her mother read it out loud to her father. "A condo rental for one month, in St. Petersburg, Florida."

Her father looked at her and then his wife. "But we already have the timeshare, and we leave on the thirtieth."

"But you're always complaining about the people you share it with." Danni brightened her voice, even though what she really wanted to do was cry. "The timeshare will be there next year, and I thought this place would be a good gift. They have meals included, tours, and all kinds of stuff you can do for the entire month."

"We may complain, baby girl, but that's what we do," her mother pointed out. "We have fun anyway, and we end up liking the other guests. Sometimes it's people we knew from before. It's always a surprise."

Danni sighed. "Okay then, I'll cancel it."

"Don't do that. It may be fun to try something new," her father said looking at the envelope and then her. "Next year, Danni, think about doing a bit less. I need my baby girl to have a nest egg to fall back on."

"You always have such a sweet nature, and you give so easily," her mother commented. "We wouldn't be so worried if you had a more stable income."

"Let's eat," Grace said quickly before Danni could respond.

In the dining room, food was spread out on the table, from glazed ham and scalloped potatoes, to green bean casserole, roast beef, and rice. Danni missed cooking. There hadn't been time since...she frowned, trying to think back to the last time she'd actually made a meal instead of going to a restaurant.

After saying grace, her father as the patriarch took up the first dish and spooned a share on to his plate, before passing it down. That was their cue to fill their plates with food. Danni piled it on, even though she wasn't hungry, knowing that only nibbling would cause another comment.

"I have some news," Grace said. "Dr. Thorne put my name in to the hospital board to be head nurse, and it was agreed on today. I am now the head nurse for the Kings County Hospital ER unit!"

"Oh goodness, Grace, what a blessing! You deserve it," her mother said enthusiastically, and they all cheered.

"Anything new in your world, Danni?" her father asked.

Danni pushed the food around with her fork. "I just had a meeting yesterday to be the spokesperson for a cosmetics line."

He sighed. "I taught you better than that. We sent you to college so you wouldn't have to rely on your looks or these fly-by-night enterprises."

"This company has been around for over twenty years," Danni explained. "I'm very appreciative of business school, Dad. It helps me make sure my brand is on point and no one can cheat me of income."

"That wouldn't be an issue with a job that gives you a W-2 every year," her father retorted.

"I'm a self-contractor, I file a 1099-MISC," Danni snapped, frustrated. "I know you don't like my path right now, but why can't you give me at least an ounce of support?"

He looked at her. "I love you, Danni, but what will happen when this fizzles out? I taught you to make sure your money and your foundation is solid."

"I'll be fine." It made no sense trying to argue with him.

"Let's not fuss and enjoy the meal." Her mother tried to ease the tension.

While everyone talked around her, she barely answered and pushed her food around on the plate. At least she was saving money and investing it, just like he'd taught her to do. She and her sister met in the kitchen to clean up.

"You can't skip out early, Danni," Grace said knowingly. "I can see the look of escape on your face."

Danni glanced at her sister. "Can you blame me?"

Grace placed a covered container of scalloped potatoes in the fridge. "Mom and Dad are set in their ways."

"Easy for you to say. You're the one who's getting all the praise," Danni said. "And you act just like them and never once try to stand up for me."

"I do *not* act like Mom and Dad."

"*But when will we ever use this?*" Danni mimicked her sister's response to the gift for her and Mike. "Yep, just like them."

Grace tried not to smile. "First, that is not how I sound. Second, you show up with expensive gifts, things we have to save for, and that make us feel a bit insecure."

"You know I'm not like that," she protested. "I love all of you, and I want to share and do something nice for the people I love."

Grace moved to hug her. "I know, Danni-bear. I'll be better at defending you, I promise. Mike and I will make time to use the getaway package you got us and thank you."

"But will you have time? *We'll send the boys to Mom's...*" Danni teased in a squeaking, high-pitched voice.

Grace let her go long enough to swat her with a towel. "Keep it up, squirt, and Mom will find you locked in the pantry again."

Danni gasped. "I *knew* that latch didn't catch on its own!"

Grace smiled. "Whatever do you mean?"

They ended up laughing and finishing their chores before going back to the living room. Edward St. Peters put on his favorite music, that had them all on their feet dancing the Electric Slide. Soon after, Danni said her goodbyes feeling better about the evening because, beneath it all, her family loved her. She dutifully kissed her father's cheek while he patted her back.

The ride home took thirty minutes, and when she closed the door to her apartment, she leaned her head against the cool surface for a moment. Too many people, and the constant buzz of the city, was beginning to wear on her. It was ten p.m. in New York, and that meant it was six in Alaska. Danni sat down and pressed the number for Amy and texted two words.

I'm coming!

Chapter Two

E ARLY SLEET SHOWERS DIDN'T DETER Danni from the train that Sunday morning. Her parents would not be the only ones in her family heading to the airport that week: she'd be leaving on December first.

With her trip to Alaska set, she of course wanted new winter outfits to take with her. Amy told her a thicker coat would definitely be needed. How bad could it be, though? Her shopping expedition paid off. She found a cute boots and hat set that reminded her of elves with the green and white stripes. Even the mittens matched. *How adorable is that?*

Her next task was to meet Austin for brunch at his favorite restaurant. Telling him she was leaving for almost a month was going to be an uncomfortable hurdle, to say the least. Austin didn't react well to situations that didn't include him or that went against the plans he'd set in his head. Danni had been telling him for a while she wanted a break, but he had yet to acknowledge her words.

She shouldn't feel this way if she was meeting someone she cared about...someone who cared about her, too. She pasted a bright smile on her face as she was led to the table—the one that Austin's family had permanently reserved in the exclusive and ritzy restaurant.

"Thank you," Austin said to the host as he stood with a wide smile before he turned his attention to her. "Danni, you look amazing."

She looked down at her jeans and sweater with suede boots. "Compared to everyone else in here, I look very much regular."

"You look homey, how's that?" Austin pulled out her chair, and she sat down. "And that is one of my favorite things about you. You're down-to-earth."

"Well, thank you for the compliment." Danni smiled.

"It's not hard when it's you, Danni," Austin took her hand.

"You're being super charming today," she murmured and took a sip of her water.

"That's the kind of guy I am." Austin gave her that thousand-watt smile.

"How was the rest of your week?"

He sighed. "It was the worst. First, Mother made a surprise visit and showed up at the penthouse. Then Dad expected me to take over some of his meetings while they went jaunting around the city."

"But didn't you become the vice president so your father could cut back on the hours he spends at the office?"

Austin shrugged. "That's true, but it was a lot, and these people talked over me and didn't like any of my ideas."

"Maybe you should spend time learning your father's business so you can help him and not feel that way," Danni said. "You can hang out with me on weekends…"

"I'm your manager. How would it look if you do these events and I'm not by your side?" Austin looked horrified.

"Manager or boyfriend?" Danni asked. "And with either one, we do not have to spend every moment together."

"But that's how we are, Danni," he said smoothly as the server brought a bottle of wine. "We are joined at the hip, two peas in a pod."

"No thank you," Danni said to the server as they tried to pour her a glass. "Hot tea, please."

"Danni, come on. It's brunch."

She met his gaze. "It just turned two, it's too early for me, and I have to get home after this...to pack."

"Where are we going?" Austin said excitedly. "California, South Beach? I could use some sun."

"I am going to Alaska to see my best friend Amy before she has her baby."

He made a face. "That doesn't sound like fun, or buzzworthy for us."

Danni sighed. "Not us, me. I'm going to spend Christmas there. I'll be home before New Year's Eve."

"Danni, that's like a month, and you have events and at least two club openings." Austin opened an app on his phone and scrolled through to check her schedule. "Yep, exactly as I said. What about us? What am I supposed to do without you for a month?"

"You can work, hang out with your friends." Danni tried her best not to sound annoyed. "Seriously, I need this break, and I miss my friend. Have my back on this."

"What about the makeup company? If they call for a second meeting and you're not here, what then?" Austin met her gaze over the wineglass at his lips. "I have it on very good authority they're looking at Sade Carole as well."

His comment about her rival reminded her that not only did she and Sade compete for the contracts, they were also often at the same events. Sade had more followers, and her career was booming.

"If they call me, we'll video chat and I'll show them Alaska," Danni countered. "If it's for me, it'll be mine. If Sade gets the contract, then I'll move on and keep working my butt off."

"You still can't go."

Her irritation rose. "Even my father can't tell me what to do, and you are not him or my keeper, Austin. I'll do as I please."

"You have an interview in two weeks with Joe 'The Mouth' and *The Scoop*. You can't miss it."

She looked up from the menu. "No, I don't. I expressly refused that request."

"I accepted it for you. He is going to rocket you to the top," Austin said. "Wear the sleeveless red dress from when you cut the ribbon at Loca's...or actually, look at what Sade wore when she was on it and go further."

Danni's face flushed and her blood pressure spiked. How dare he go against her decision— one she'd been very clear on? This time she wouldn't bite her tongue and say it was okay. This couldn't go on any longer.

She placed the menu on the table. "Austin, I will not be going to any interview with Joe whatever his name is. I will not dress in ways that are uncomfortable for me. How can you expect me to change who I am for anyone...for you?"

"Danni..." Austin didn't say anything else; she could see in his eyes he understood he'd taken one step too far.

"My video channel and my life started out as an adventure, now it's... changed. Maybe I need to get used to it, but it's still my choice," Danni explained. "When I started this journey, it was because I was this Brooklyn girl living her best life and chasing her dreams. Now, I'm standing at club openings, and I can't even recall the last trip I took just for me." Danni took a deep, cleansing breath. She didn't like getting mad. "You never listen to me. You steamroll and keep going, and you never listen to a word I say."

"I'm trying to take your career to the next level."

"I never asked you to do that. I needed you to be my boyfriend. I wanted to have butterflies when I saw you." Danni's voice broke on the words. She gathered her coat and purse and stood. "I'm sorry, Austin, I don't know if this is going to work—you as my manager or you as my boyfriend. I... I need to think, and I can't here."

"Danni, babe ... you can't be serious." Austin tried to laugh it off as their interaction caught the attention of other guests.

"I am," Danni said. "Have a safe and happy holiday. And please help your dad. If he's asking you, he really needs you to step up."

Danni left him sitting there while she hurriedly took her packages from the host who had stacked them safely in the foyer of the restaurant. She turned to see Austin just staring as her words sunk in. Getting home was her only thought, because the tears that pricked the back of her eyes fought hard to get to the surface. A good cry was needed.

Amy had Mateo; was it wrong for Danni to want a love like that? She stepped outside, took another deep breath, and swiped at her cheeks, hoping the cold winds would dry up the few tears that had already fallen. She would do all her thinking with Amy...away from New York, Austin, and everything.

The weight on her shoulders seemed to ease and a

sense of freedom made her steps more assured. Danni focused on the excitement of seeing Amy and spending Christmas in Alaska.

Juneau, here I come.

"Sarge... Sarge, we have a..." The female voice on the dispatch radio hesitated. "What is the code for guys jumping in the ocean fully clothed?"

"Idiots," Declan Mathias answered. It amused him just a little that he left the military at the same rank and nickname.

"Polar plunge, and there is no call sign." The second voice was Mateo, Declan's friend and fellow Alaskan State Trooper for Auke Bay. "It's usually done for charity, but we didn't get any paperwork for permits or anything."

"So, my first assessment was correct." Declan pressed the button on the radio attached to his coat. "Meet me out there, Mateo, I'm thinking a party got too hearty. Jess, is it off the north pier?"

"Yes, Sarge, it is," she answered. "Maybe we should give it a call code."

"It doesn't happen often enough to make one," Mateo replied.

"I'm just going to call it a PP4," Jess announced.

"What's the four?" Mateo's voice was filled with humor.

"For...people being crazy jumping into the cold Pacific this time of year," Jess replied.

"Ah, well Sarge, we're going to a PP4," Mateo said.

"Copy, we'll take care of it." A smile spread across his usually stern face.

Declan looked left and right before pulling the Trooper's truck out onto the main road of Auke Bay. This was home, in its quiet winter perfection, but that didn't mean it couldn't become dangerous fast. Alaska was one of the last great pieces of wilderness, and it was easy to underestimate. Even the most professional hikers and military people sometimes got lost or ran into trouble. The water's freezing temperature should've been a deterrent against this erratic behavior. He was more concerned about their welfare than the overall nuisance of the call.

At the north pier, instead of a group of guys in search of an adrenaline rush, there was a wedding party cheering on and offering assistance to those who'd taken the plunge. He parked his truck just as Mateo pulled up. Declan zipped his own coat against the cold breeze while they walked out to the pier.

"Hey guys," he called out. "Are congrats in order, or are we trying to nullify a marriage the hard way?"

The bride turned with a smile. "Good afternoon, officer. The guys in the wedding party made a bet."

"Ma'am, you can't have an impromptu polar plunge in this area," Declan explained. "The water temperature here gets frigid fast, and right now it has to be below forty degrees. And with the riptides off this pier, one of your guests could get pulled out and freeze before they can find their way back to shore. Then we have to get the Coast Guard out here to perform a water rescue."

"It's all in good fun, Officer," the groom said with a grin.

"Trooper," Declan corrected him. "Please get your people out of the water and go back to your reception venue. I don't want to have to write you a hundred-dollar citation as a wedding gift."

"A hundred isn't so bad." The bride laughed. "What better way to celebrate our wedding? We came all the way from Fort Lauderdale for this."

"Per person," Mateo clarified.

That number erased the smiles quickly from the wedding party, and they all started to help the men out of the water. Declan watched them walk shivering back to the waterfront lodge where the reception was being held.

"That number made them re-evaluate this situation quickly," Mateo noted.

"I figured they weren't from Alaska, because people around here know better," Declan said as they walked back to the trucks. "Amy doing okay?"

"She's convinced the baby is setting up house in her stomach." Mateo laughed. "But guess what? Her best friend from New York is coming out for Christmas. She'll be here for a few weeks."

"Sounds fun." Declan pulled his knit cap down further around his ears.

"You should come—"

"No."

"You don't even know what I was going to say," Mateo grumbled.

"Yes, I do. Come over for dinner, hang out, meet the friend, socialize," he said. "It's going to still be a no."

Mateo rolled his eyes. "Fine, be a hermit, Scrooge."

"I will, thank you." Declan grinned. "Even though I'm practically on call for every committee for the Northern Lights Festival."

"That's completely different. These are people you know," Mateo argued. "Anyone new, you become a ghost and fade into the background."

How could he explain to his friend that new situations or people made him uncomfortable? There had been a period, after he'd been injured, when he wouldn't leave the house for weeks at a time. The job as a state trooper in Auke Bay pulled him out of that stagnant existence, but it was still slow going. He figured that new people, especially women, would either be put off when they learned about his prosthetic leg, or they'd get involved and he'd end up being hurt. Not if, but when, the relationship didn't work out. There was no way he was setting himself up for that. Never again.

Mateo went on to say, "I swear, they gave you camouflage technology when you were in the Army."

"You'll never know," Declan teased. "I'm going back into town to get the hottest cup of coffee."

"We should probably talk to Jess about creating new codes. This could go completely awry with her."

"Maybe. Hey, is the kitten family still living in the back cell?"

Mateo nodded. "Yep, there's a litter box and one of those cat climbing houses in the cell now. Mel and his brother were sleeping off their pre-Christmas celebration on the other side. Next thing I know, both of them are tucked in, napping with kittens."

"I'll talk to her." Declan shook his head. "You know what, leave her be. Maybe the kittens will get adopted."

"You have a soft, squishy heart, Declan." Mateo opened the door of his police squad car.

"Stop it," he muttered.

"All ooey-gooey and tender!" Mateo got in the vehicle before Declan could scrape snow off the car and throw it at him.

Even with the foolhardy choices people made in the

winter or the constant snow, Declan loved this state. He could even fish in the wintertime on frozen lakes, where his only companion was silence. Never once did he miss living in the lower forty-eight.

He was neither ooey or gooey, but he did have a heart, and in the center of it was the small community he policed. For a moment, he wondered about this best friend who would be visiting the Azure family, and then promptly put it out of his mind. This was their house guest, not his, and he would make every attempt to avoid this woman. There was always a bit of match-making going on in Auke Bay and usually someone tried to set him up. Declan wished they all would see he was okay by himself, and that love was nowhere on his Christmas wish list.

The few days before the beginning of December sped by. Danni didn't know what to expect in Juneau when she took the Air Alaska flight on the first legs of her journey. She was accustomed to John F. Kennedy Airport and the happy hustle and bustle of Christmas travelers, and the whole atmosphere made her smile. The airport was currently decked out with large Christmas balls and garlands of blue, red, silver, and green throughout the high-ceilinged structures. All the storefronts offered quick gifts for family and friends.

Impulsively, she bought a Mets baseball, T-shirt, bat, and a lion wearing the team logo for Peter. For the newest baby who had yet to make an appearance in the family, Danni got a stuffed pony with a cloth New York saddle. She also got T-shirts for both Amy and Mateo, and, by the end of her airport shopping, she had yet another tote to carry on the plane.

She hit Anchorage around nine New York time. Unfortunately, she had a layover until nine the next morning, which meant she slept in a very small hotel room adorned with moose wallpaper. It was clean and close to the airport, plus she was able to find dinner close by, so she couldn't complain. In fact, it was the perfect time for her followers to see where she was. Pulling her tripod from the small case, she set up her phone and hit *record.*

"Hey guys." Danni waved at the camera. "I bet you wondered if you would ever see Danni actually on the run again. Well, I'm in Anchorage overnight on my way to... Juneau, Alaska! First off, check out the wallpaper in my room! The tiny moose are so cute, and I had the best bison burger for dinner! I also had baked Alaska in...ta-da, Alaska!"

Danni shifted her position and leaned back against the headboard. "Tomorrow I take another flight to Fairbanks and then another flight to my destination. That's because my best friend Amy said she was making it as authentic as possible. I'm a little worried about what that means. But I can't wait to see her. Hey Amy! If you see this, I'm almost there!"

Danni laughed. "She's due to have a baby any day now, and we have so much catching up to do. So, my friends, for this holiday, I have a request. Spend it with people who make you laugh...people to make memories with, who will make this Christmas one that you can smile about for years to come. That's my wish for all of you...to have the adventures of a lifetime when Christmas magic is in the air. Danni out."

She used the tiny remote to turn off the camera and spent a few minutes on a quick edit before she posted it. Then she lay back with a smile and covered herself with a blanket. Outside, the colors of the lights from the snowman sign flickered on and off, lulling her to sleep with a huge smile on her face. The next morning, she was back at the airport and anxious to get to Juneau.

"Where's the rest of the plane?" Danni asked, looking at the small two-propeller plane she didn't expect to be so...well...small. She doubted the tank could hold enough fuel to get across the street, let alone make it to another city. And how did the propellers turn the... Nope, she wasn't trying to figure it out.

"This is how you get into Juneau, ma'am," the pilot said. "I'm Cooper, and trust me, this is safe. I can land it on an ice river easy-peasy."

"But I read that Juneau had a regular airport, I thought that was what Amy meant when she said this part of the trip was on her," Danni pointed out. "Wait. Are we landing on an *ice river*?"

"Your friend wanted you to have the pleasure of flying in the way Alaskans did it before they built the airport. We still do it because the small plane charter is cheaper for the residents than a plane ticket. And no, we are not landing on the river. I just mentioned I could."

Cooper looked to be around sixty-five, with a mass of wild white hair that jumped out when he took off his winter hat with ear flaps to scratch his head. "You're going to Auke Bay, ma'am, and that's a drive for Amy, in her condition."

"You know Amy?" Danni asked, feeling a bit more relaxed.

Cooper nodded. "Yes, ma'am, and she has flown with me dozens of times...safely. Like many of the residents of Auke Bay, I work out of and live there."

"Okay, but please miss all the bumps," Danni said skeptically.

"I'll try." Cooper grinned and grabbed one of her bags. "Four big bags for one lady. City people sure have a lot of stuff."

"And here I was hoping you'd have more plane," Danni said to herself as she followed him to what she hoped wasn't her doom. *Oh, Amy, what did you get me into?*

Cooper helped her into the front seat of the small plane and got in next to her. Danni breathed a sigh of relief that he didn't have to hold the propellers and give them a hard turn to get them started. Of course, she was being melodramatic. She had seen that in old movies. Still, this didn't seem much better when he flipped the buttons and the engines started with a loud roar. Cooper handed her a headset and motioned for her to put them on.

"Ready!" he called out.

"As I'll ever be," Danni called back and gave a thumbs up. She didn't feel as sure as she sounded.

The plane moved down the runway, slowly picking up speed until it gave its first jerky jump into the sky. A small squeak escaped her lips, but soon pristine beauty spread out around and below her. Everything was white, even the tall peaks in the distance. Below between the trees and snowcapped hills, trails of soft smoke puffed from the chimneys of the housetops. It wasn't the flight or the lift of the small aircraft that made her heart race; it was the scenery spread out below her that made Danni breathless.

Snow in the city was beautiful for only a time, before the dirt of the city streets and the dusty steam from subway grates made it gray and grimy. But nothing disturbed this winter wonderland. It smoothed down rocky slopes and covered the expanse as far as she could see. As they flew over the forests, Danni was captivated by fir trees and then the rocky beaches that separated ocean and land. Just as they passed the edge of a densely packed wilderness, a pack of animals broke out from the trees and ran across the snow-covered ground. An excited and amazed laugh escaped her. Danni had never seen anything like this in her life.

"The caribou are running today." Cooper's voice sounded scratchy in her ear. "That's the river they are on now—the ice is so thick you could sleep out there and not even know water ran beneath you. What do you think?"

"It's magnificent! Look at how beautiful it all is. There is nothing like this in New York City."

"That's why I live here. The last pure paradise is right here."

Danni continued to stare out the window, picking out snowmobiles in the snow and even people on horseback. The trip ended too soon; and she'd been so enthralled, she'd forgotten to be scared. Time always flew when you were having fun.

All she saw was snow. Yet, as promised, Cooper landed seamlessly and no worse for wear. Except when she opened the door, and the wind hit her directly in the face.

Danni gasped. *For the love of...* She feared her face had frozen instantly. The cold air in her lungs made her sinuses hurt. Her eyes watered, and she got a brain freeze akin to eating ice cream too fast.

"Nippy, isn't it," Cooper said cheerfully and took her hand to help her down. "Here, I got something for you.

Call it an early Christmas present."

He dug around in the back seat and pulled out a box from which he removed a knitted scarf. Cooper wrapped it around her neck and then pulled some of the fabric over her nose.

"My wife used to make these before she passed, for my clients who didn't know about the cold winds up this way," he said. "I kept up the tradition. I learned how to knit, and now I make 'em in the summer, sitting in my porch with my beagle."

"Thank you, Cooper," Danni said through the fabric, charmed and genuinely touched by her new pilot friend's story. "I owe you."

He patted her head like a father would a child. "Never you mind. I'm sure I'll see you around town and you can buy me a coffee, how's that?"

Danni impulsively hugged him. "It's a deal."

She took a breath, and he was right. The scarf did help. It also smelled like wood smoke and lavender. Danni could imagine him sitting next to wild blooms knitting away in contentment.

"Hmm, where are Amy and Mateo?"

"I think that may be your ride." Cooper pointed a gloved finger toward the nose of the plane. "I'll get you on over to the Sarge."

On the side of the runway was a truck with windows that seemed to have the remnants of rock salt spray and mud on the sides and back. "Alaskan State Troopers" was stenciled on the side. Danni studied the man she hoped was waiting for her.

He was tall and broad-shouldered, at least six-one, and dressed in uniform with a gun on his side and a large, thick Trooper's coat to keep him warm. His hat was pulled down around his ears, and he blew into his hand. He was clean-shaven, with ebony skin and soulful eyes the color of amber. He watched them with a completely neutral face. *Neutral but handsome*, Danni thought as they finally stopped by the large truck.

"Sarge."

"Coop," a deep baritone voice answered. "How was the flying?"

"We had a strong tailwind pushing us here, definitely snow coming soon," Cooper answered. "I got a Ms. Danni here... I assume you are her ride?"

"Yeah, I am." He turned his attention to her. "Trooper Declan Mathias, ma'am. Amy had a conflicting doctor's appointment, and they couldn't reach you. I volunteered to pick you up."

"Volunteered?" Danni asked with a laugh. "Let me guess, Amy wouldn't let you say no."

He smiled. "That's about right. Let's get your stuff in the back."

"There's a lot of it. This city girl didn't travel light," Cooper teased.

Sarge Mathias gave a small grunt, not much else, and as she followed them, Cooper winked at her. The two men got her four bags in the car easily and closed the back.

"Here's where I leave you, Ms. Danni. I'll see you around town," Cooper said.

Danni hugged him again. "Thank you for everything, Cooper. The amazing scarf will be my everyday accessory here. Do you mind if I talk about you on my video channel?"

The older man actually blushed. "You go right ahead, Ms. Danni. See you around."

Danni waved. "Bye."

Without a word, Declan helped her in the passenger

seat before he got in on the driver's side. He had left the car running so it was blessedly warm in the cab of the truck. He pulled away slowly and went over a hump of snow to the icy road, and the large wheels crunched over ice and rock salt. The silence inside the vehicle was deafening. Danni cast him a sidelong glance as he drove, and his eyes never left the road.

"So, does it snow here constantly? There are mountains of snow," Danni said, trying to make conversation.

"It does. It's Alaska."

"Been a Trooper long?" she asked.

"Long enough."

Two words. It was like pulling teeth, yet Danni would not be deterred. "I bet Amy must owe you a big-time favor for you to pick up someone you don't know. From New York, no less."

"Uh-huh."

"Planning on collecting?" Danni teased.

"Nope."

He *really* wasn't a talker. Danni let silence reign a bit longer before speaking again.

"Well, I'm Danni. Do I call you Sarge or Declan... Mr. Mathias, Sarge Mathias?"

He sighed. "Whatever you prefer."

That was, Danni supposed, her cue to stop talking. She stared out the window at the town they were driving into, but she didn't ask questions, even when they passed the big gazebo with the large tree in the center. She found herself wondering about the life of the quiet man beside her. Everyone had a story; what was his?

Finally, he turned onto a street with quaint houses and Christmas decorations everywhere, from snowmen and snow-women to lighted reindeer that glinted merrily. The entire area was so beautiful, and completely not what she expected. Another unexpected thing was how quickly the sun went down in Alaska. It was barely two, and it already looked like the sun was ready to set.

He pulled the truck into a driveway behind an SUV and turned off the engine. The front door opened, and her friend came out. Amy was very pregnant, and her husband stopped her with a gentle hand on her shoulder and then helped her down the few steps to the stone path so she could move to the driveway.

Her red curls still went everywhere, untamed and wild like Amy's personality. Her grin was huge while her husband looked at her fondly with obvious love and patience in his eyes. Danni forgot all about the uncomfortable ride and opened the truck door. She was short, but the truck felt too big because she had to dangle her feet out the door. Danni felt for the ground before jumping out, then made sure she was steady before running to her friend.

"Danni!" Amy squealed.

"Amy!"

Danni stopped in front of her and did the little dance from their childhood. Amy joined in and then they embraced. It felt so good, amazing, to be in the presence of the one person who truly understood her. Her worries in New York—even the tension with her family—melted away.

"We need to discuss your version of a true Alaskan way to travel," Danni said to her friend.

"Mateo did the same to me the first time here," Amy said with a laugh. "Besides, Cooper is the safest charter plane service around."

"I forgive you because I'm here and he gave me this scarf." Danni hugged Amy again. "I missed you so much. I didn't realize how much till right now."

"Danni, this is Mateo, my husband." Amy said when the hug ended.

She held out her hand. "Mateo, I have heard all about you and how you tamed this redhead and took her from New York City."

"We don't do handshakes here," Mateo said. He pulled her into a hug and practically lifted her off her feet.

She instantly liked Amy's husband, who seemed warm and genuine. He was a native Alaskan, and his dark hair and merry eyes made her comfortable.

"Thank you, Declan, for bringing Danni here safely," Amy said as Mateo placed her on her feet.

"Not a problem. How was the doctor's appointment? All good with the baby?" Declan asked. "Before I forget, Mom said to tell you the ginger tea you ordered is in."

Danni stared at him in shock. He actually could form sentences and talk to people. Maybe it was just her who put him off. Mateo unloaded her bags in the driveway.

Amy rubbed her stomach. "It's all great with this little jumping bean, three more weeks or less. I'll come by and pick up the tea. Your mom wanted to meet Danni, anyway."

Declan nodded. "I'll let her know. See you all later."

"Thank you for the ride," Danni called.

"Welcome," he answered without even looking back as he walked to the car.

They watched him reverse down the driveway before Amy looked at her luggage.

"Did you bring the kitchen sink, lady?" Amy asked.

"How many clothes do you need if you're in a town this big?" Mateo teased and held up two fingers to show the small space in between.

"What is with all of the Alaskan people I meet making fun of my luggage?" Danni grinned.

"Don't take it personally, they tease me for being too tall," Amy replied.

"I don't think I made a good impression on your Trooper Mathias."

Amy rubbed her stomach. "It's not you. It takes Declan a bit to warm up to new people."

"Ah, so I didn't cause instant dislike. Good to know." She gave a teary smile. "It's really so good to see you, Amy."

"Don't start crying or I'll be bawling. Hormones. Come inside and meet Peter." Amy linked arms with hers. "Before he takes the house apart and builds a new one."

Danni picked up the bag closer to her and laughed as Amy led her inside, leaving Mateo to handle the rest of her luggage. She was with her best friend for the first time in a long time. There was nothing more perfect than that. She wouldn't even let Declan not liking her ruin her Christmas holiday.

Chapter Three

ECLAN MATHIAS WAS THE HIGHEST-RANKING Trooper in Auke Bay, which wasn't saying much because only three of them policed a vast area. Juneau was the second largest city in the United States by area alone. He had to explain more than once that it wasn't a separate state, and neither was Sitka; they were both part of Alaska. He looked at the town he loved as he drove through the icy roads and it was like the perfect picture of Christmas. Many people couldn't handle the amount of snow Alaska had each year.

Spring was chilly up until around the end of May, and then the summer months were short, before the cold winds and snow started again by late September. But no matter what, it was gorgeous country. In the summer, the wildflowers and the pristine wilderness were incomparable. A winter storm was fierce, yet beautiful, and the wildlife didn't need to worry about the encroaching population taking the land.

Declan hadn't always felt the appreciation he had now. His parents had first moved here while his father was in the Army. He'd felt like it was a punishment even though his father's military occupation specialty, or MOS, was at Fort Wainwright. That was one of the reasons he had joined the military: to follow a tradition of the men in his family like his grandfather and then his father.

He accepted his own military designations far away from Alaska, telling himself that he loved living in the real world. Until his last deployment. He hadn't come out unscathed, and that was the reason he came home to Auke Bay. The world had seemed too big all of a sudden, too noisy and filled with too many people. In Auke Bay, he was just Sarge, or Deke to his mother. It was simple here, and he could breathe.

"Hey, Sarge," one of the residents called from his roof as Declan drove slowly by.

"Jimmy, get your son to help you with that. I don't need Mateo having to call medics out here because you fell off the roof," Declan ordered. Jimmy answered with a wave that meant he was going to do what he wanted.

In the center of town, the Christmas decorations set against the backdrop of snow and the quaint historic buildings were postcard-worthy. He parked outside the Baker's Dozen, the town's only bakery, and hit the button on his radio.

"Jess, I'm 10-7. Mateo comes on at eight and then you can do the same," Declan said into the radio. "Copy?"

"10-7... 10-7... 10-7..." The voice came back scratchy across the radio.

Jessica Nolan was a new hire by the county and was sent to Auke Bay as a place to cut her teeth in the new job. She was from the lower forty-eight, via Texas. In Alaska, deputies could work for a year before going into actual training. She was a sweet lady, around forty or so, ready to start a new life in Alaska, but she was having a hard time with the codes.

"That's out of service, Jess," Declan said with a smile.

"Thank you, Sarge. I mean...copy," Jess replied.

Declan turned his radio off and stepped out of his truck. Auke Bay was one of the safest neighborhoods in Juneau, but he still locked the old truck. He'd requisitioned a new car for Jess and an SUV for Mateo at the last council meeting and had gotten them. He loved his beat-up truck, and while there were newer styles out there, the classics were best.

The bell of Baker's Dozen rang merrily as he stepped inside. Behind the counter, his mother looked up at him with a smile. "Deke."

"Hey, Mama." He said in a teasing voice, went around to give her a hug. "How was business today?"

"Good," his mother said. "The community center Christmas party is coming up. I told them I would donate three orange and cream cakes, with the candied orange slices on top."

"Bringing out the fancy recipes," Declan teased.

His mother had left Fairbanks and bought the bakery after his father died, renovating it to the quaint style she loved. The upstairs apartment had become Declan's when he'd been honorably discharged from the Army. She lived in a neighborhood close by.

"Did you see what the kids from the university did?" She smiled. "I'm making them cookies. They deserve it after the exceptional decorating they did in the town this year."

"Mom, they are all eighteen or older. I don't think they want you calling them kids anymore," Declan said, amused.

She waved her hands airily. "Pish posh, they are

still babies to me. Look at Jeremy—he's so baby-faced and cute. I think the girls from the university come in to buy just to see him."

He laughed. "Great marketing strategy." He snagged a cookie that hadn't sold that day.

"You can only have one," she said. "I want to have enough for the shelter."

That was the great thing about his mom; anything she didn't sell was donated to the small shelter that was on Pointer Street. One of his missions was to never see people living on the street, especially in the freezing weather.

He and his mother had helped to get the shelter up and running. So far, it had enabled about three dozen people to either find resources in one of the bigger towns like Anchorage or get back home. People donated food and resources like blankets all the time. At this point in time there was a mother and daughter who now used the services of the shelter.

"How is the mom with the little girl?" he asked. Until they could find her help, she was their responsibility, and he took that as a serious task.

"Donna and baby Tia? I think they're hanging in there." She removed a tray from the glass case. "How was your day, Deke?"

"The usual. Mrs. Simmons thought a bear was in her shed again," Declan answered. "I picked up Amy's friend from the airstrip when Cooper landed this afternoon. Apparently, she's here for a few weeks for Christmas and the baby's birth."

"That was sweet of you to help them out."

"Not a big deal, they had an appointment."

"What's her name and is she pretty?" his mother asked with a coy smile.

"Don't start, Mom."

"What? I asked two simple questions, nothing more."

"Her name is Danni St. Peters, and she seems nice." Declan kissed his mother's cheek. He thought about Danni's wide eyes—the color of honey, in a heart-shaped face—and added, "Yes, she is pretty."

"I am going upstairs. And don't you get any match-making ideas. I'm happy the way I am."

"I have never interfered with your love life in all my years," she said with mock outrage.

"Uh-huh." Declan took the bag of cookies and a slice of cake she always packed up for him and moved toward the front door again. The stairs to his second-floor apartment were outside of the quaint two-story building on the parking lot side.

"Hey Deke," she called.

He smiled and his tone held affection. "Yes, mother of mine?"

"You think she's pretty." Her grin was broad.

"Goodnight." Declan shook his head. "Make sure to put the alarm on and please call me when you get home."

"Yes, sir." She saluted and laughed. "Just like your father."

He didn't say a word, but his heart swelled with pride hearing her say that. David Mathias was a great father and husband and was missed, but Declan was glad to see his mother living life. At sixty-five she was still energetic and even took Zumba classes. She'd been his rock when he came home, and he knew her meddling was from a place of love.

The stairs of the building always gave him a little trouble, especially when he was sore and tired. Declan had been up before four a.m. when an accident call came in from the highway that wove through Juneau.

It was close enough to the town limits that the Sarge needed to be onsite, and he just went right to work after. He breathed out an exhausted sigh, hoping his mother didn't see the pain on his face from his injury.

He secured his side arm first when he got into his apartment and after that he walked to his bedroom to take off his uniform. Even though he lived alone, weapons safety was a priority. One shoe off, then he pushed up his pantleg to remove his prosthetic leg. Even with the gel sleeve that he put on every morning before using the metal and plastic appendage, sometimes the soreness worked its way up to his back. One IED they didn't find in time had taken his leg and the life of one of his close friends. He suffered from PTSD and was plagued with nightmares, but compared to some he was good, and Declan knew he was blessed. From there, he could work on the rest in his life.

Massaging the cramp from his leg, he knew the only thing that would ease the soreness would be a soak in the tub he had bought specifically for his injury. That would come first, even before dinner. He took the crutches he kept by the bed to move to the bathroom. His mother's words made him smile. Yes, he remembered Danni and her perky attitude. How could he not? She practically talked his ear off as he drove to Amy and Mateo's house. He hoped she enjoyed her time in Auke Bay, and he hoped his mother wouldn't try to meddle.

Danni was a city girl, and Auke Bay had nothing compared to New York. Besides, what woman would want to be with someone like him—broken, gruff, and with one leg?

Declan frowned as memories made old wounds hurt while he filled his tub and put on the jets. He maneuvered himself to the edge of the tub and gratefully sank into the hot water, the heat instantly soothing. He had learned the hard way that a man who gave his all to his country, including a leg, didn't get the happily ever after when he returned home.

The next morning, Danni opened her eyes and saw the wood paneled wall instead of the art deco look of her own bedroom. Danni had learned from Mateo that most houses built in Alaska used peat moss and other materials to insulate their homes from the cold winters. He and his brothers had built this house themselves while he and Amy had lived in an apartment after they married. Thick insulation layered between the brick and the wood, while a neat little potbelly stove sat in the corner for extra warmth.

Their home was decorated with a mixture of rustic and contemporary. Her bed was one of those Swedish pieces that could be put together from the box, with a slatted headboard. The chest matched, and when she got into bed, the warmth of the thick comforter and another afghan made by Mateo's grandmother cocooned her. Everything he or Amy described fascinated Danni completely. She was completely and utterly content. *I'm so happy I made the decision to come here.* It was the last thought that filtered through her mind before sleep claimed her.

Before she got out of bed, Danni wiggled her toes in the thick socks she had borrowed from Amy. The warm flannel pajamas she'd bought in Manhattan had been a great purchase. Finally, she rolled from the warm cocoon of blankets and went to the bathroom to wash up and brush her teeth before going downstairs. She could hear Amy talking to Peter, and she hurried so she could go down and be part of the conversation. The fire crackled in the living room and cartoons were on the big screen TV that Peter could see from the kitchen table because of the open floor plan.

"A-Danni!" Peter yelled around whatever he was chewing and waved at her excitedly.

That was his name for her from the time Amy introduced them. His hair was a mop of dark red curls, a mix between his father and mother, and he waved his chubby little fingers. Instead of saying Auntie Danni, he chose A-Danni because, according to Amy, he gave people a name to suit what he liked. His preschool teacher was Miss Marcy, even though her name was Ms. Devon, but Peter assured them she looked like Marcy and thus he would call her as such. Danni didn't mind. She was an aunt and he liked her, that was all that mattered.

"Hey baby cakes," she said fondly to Peter and sat across from him. "What are you eating?"

"Honey hotcakes," Amy answered from the stove. "I'll grab you a plate. Do you want bacon?"

"Uh, yeah, it's bacon," Danni answered with a grin.

Peter giggled. "Honey hotcakes for a baby cake."

Danni chuckled. "Exactly. Let me guess, honey drizzled in the batter?"

"Even better: honeycomb, ground so we can use it," Amy said.

"No way!" exclaimed Danni. "I didn't even know you could eat it!"

"Look in the jar on the table," Amy encouraged. "We use all resources here in Alaska. While people in the lower forty-eight pay hundreds for this, the residents here add it to the harvested honey, and you can eat it when the jar is empty. I dehydrate it and put in in foods for Peter since he's so young and I don't want him chewing it. But the honey and the waxy comb has pollen from the flowers and plants around here. It's great for allergies, and I make it into a face mask every month for my in-house spa day."

"Please tell me I get one of these in-house spa days with you," Danni said.

"We definitely will." Amy laughed and flipped the three hotcakes in the pan.

"I need to get my phone and document all of this, take pictures of your process," Danni said. "Plus, the face mask—Amy, that's a viable business."

Amy held up her spatula in warning. "All of that work stuff is a no-no. It's your first day here, and you are on vacation."

"But..." Danni protested.

"No, we'll discuss it later." Amy brought a plate over and put it on the table. "Now we eat and catch up."

"Yes, ma'am." Danni winked at Peter. "Your mom is scary."

Peter grinned. "She makes me take baths."

Danni gasped. "Oh, the horror!"

"Don't encourage him, or you'll chase him around to get in the tub." Amy sat down with two cups of coffee, and as Danni watched, she added a piece of chocolate to both. "Try this decadence. Stir."

Danni stirred until the chocolate melted, took a sip, and sighed. "This is perfection. You have changed my way of drinking coffee forever."

"You're welcome." Amy laughed.

"Mommy, all done." Peter opened his mouth to show it was empty and his plate and juice cup was clear of any food. "Can I watch my shows now?"

"Yes, you may. Do you know which channel?" Amy asked.

"Two, zero, four," Peter repeated the numbers and ran off.

"How does he... can he work the remote?" Danni asked, amazed.

"Peter can out-think me. I think he trades stocks online without me and his father knowing." Amy sipped her coffee. "He and his tablet have secrets."

"I must learn from him," Danni teased. "Your town law enforcement seems nice. I mean, your Trooper Mathias... It was good of him to pick me up."

"Declan is cool. He's the one person in this town that everyone trusts," Amy answered. "I have never heard him raise his voice, not even when making an arrest. He doesn't just throw people in jail. Declan looks for underlying reasons and helps families in need. The last Boy Scout type...and a hero to boot, even though he won't ever admit it."

"Strong, silent type, I guess," Danni murmured.

"So, what did you talk about with our Trooper Sergeant?" Amy looked at Danni over her cup with a definite twinkle in her eyes.

"I can tell you there was zero conversation. The man said about three to seven words to me the entire ride," Danni replied. "Why, what did you hear?"

Amy laughed. "Nothing, you nut! I'm just letting you know, he's a nice guy, but he's been through a lot."

"Hmm, how so?" Danni took another bite.

"In the Army, he lost his leg after being deployed," Amy explained. "His fiancée dumped him because of it, and he moved back here."

Danni gaped at her. "I am floored. I couldn't tell he

was an amputee. He moves so easily."

"He also runs in the summer and does the Alaska Iron Man competition. He has this prosthetic that is completely space age when he does."

"How did you know about the ex-girlfriend?" Danni asked. "He doesn't strike me as the type to share when it comes to his life."

"You'd be surprised," Amy said. "But his mother owns the bakery, and when I moved here, we became friends. She adores Peter. You'll meet her, too."

"I guess I can understand why he didn't hold a conversation with me. I just felt he disliked me from the beginning. He is very handsome. Broad shoulders and amazing eyes."

"You saw all that, did you?"

Danni rolled her eyes. "Oh please. Anyone notices a handsome Black man like that."

"You said handsome twice." Her friend held up two fingers.

Danni deftly changed the subject. "This is amazing." She made a gesture that encompassed their surroundings. "You look so happy, Amy. Peter, Mateo, your home...you look so settled compared to when we used to run around the busy streets of New York."

"It's not always what we think we want. Life sometimes sends us what we need," Amy said. "I watch your videos. You seem to be living the dream."

"Am I?" Danni wondered out loud and cut a piece of hotcake. She chewed and closed her eyes as the honey flavor, combined with spices and vanilla, burst in her mouth. "These are so delicious."

"You don't like it?" Amy asked. "Your career, I mean, and thank you. I use real vanilla beans...why are you looking at me like that?"

"Are you real?" Danni touched her shoulder. "Real vanilla beans?"

Amy laughed. "Stop changing the subject. Aren't you happy?"

Danni sighed and chewed before speaking. "I am. I love that my whole career took off from my trip to Paris. But it feels like it's not my own anymore. Austin is always changing something or I'm always on the go at some event."

"Austin, your boyfriend."

"We broke up before I left. Well, I broke up with him. Kind of," Danni explained. "He booked some interview with that guy on the snoop talk show you see online and on TV. Then he told me to dress like my competition, and trust me, that's not me. If my family ever wanted a reason to disown me, that would be it."

"So, he's not listening, and it's not about your re-lationship?"

Danni shrugged. "I don't know, but I was tired of the stress."

"Grab your coffee and come with me." Amy stood and walked to the back door.

Danni followed her friend. Amy threw a thick blanket over Danni's shoulders and her own before they stepped out on to the deck. The landscape caused Danni's mouth to drop open in awe. Above the wilderness behind the neighborhood, a tall mountain reached up to the sky. The snow-capped peak settled between wispy clouds on a day that was blue and clear, even though it was cold. It was majestic and unlike anything Danni had ever seen.

"That's Mount McGinnis, and below it is Auke Bay Lake. In the summer, the sides of the mountain are lush and green between the rocks, and in the winter, I see this view outside my bedroom window," Amy said. "When I first moved here, it was a culture shock, but it was something I wanted because I loved Mateo with all my heart." She turned to look at Danni. "One thing I learned is that trying to change someone is like trying to move that mountain. It's not going to happen. But love makes it work, and you learn to compromise. If that's not happening and you're not happy, then you have a lot to think about when you get back to New York."

"You're right. I don't know what will happen with Austin, I'm trying to work that out," Danni admitted.

"Follow your instincts. They'll never fail you." Amy gave her a pat on the back.

"Stop being wise and sage," Danni grumbled. "You're my age." Amy laughed.

A noise made Danni look at the steps. A very large turkey stood there watching them. It gobbled again and flapped its wings.

"Uh, Amy, why...what...is that a turkey?" Danni asked.

Amy looked around her. "Oh, that's George."

"George..." Danni said the word slowly.

"I keep telling Peter he can't have people food." Amy chuckled. "He's our Thanksgiving dinner...from last year."

"I'm sorry to tell you, but your oven and butcher tricked you," Danni commented.

"Peter fell in love with him and pitched a fit about him being his best friend." Amy walked over to a bucket and took out a handful of grain and threw it out on the deck. "We ate spaghetti for that holiday, and Peter named him George. He has a nice warm little pen outside and the run of the yard."

"He's looking at me funny," Danni said warily. George

seemed to have zero interest in his food, but when she stepped, he followed her. "Is he like an attack turkey?"

Her friend laughed. "There is literally no such thing."

Danni moved to the door. "Tell him that. I'm a city girl. He can smell my fear."

She got inside before George could assess her weakness and strike. Amy followed, laughing. She took enjoyment from telling Peter that Danni was scared of George.

"But he's a turkey, A-Danni, he doesn't have teeth," Peter said. "Pterodactyls had teeth; now they are scary."

"Do you have a pterodactyl in Alaska I should be aware of?" Danni asked Peter.

He shook his head sadly. "No. I'll draw you one later, okay?"

Danni nodded. "Okay."

"We need to take him to preschool, and then I can show you around," Amy said. "I also need to get Harry to deliver our snowmobile, or Ski-Doo as it is also fondly known as. That way you can use it when the snow gets too thick."

"Don't you have snowplows that come through?"

"They can't keep up with snowfall sometimes, and around here, it's trucks with chains, ATVs or snowmobiles, especially when it gets deep," Amy explained. "Life keeps going no matter what, regardless of if it's two inches or two feet of snow. And that's on the low side of things."

"Two feet is a small amount?" Danni said, shocked.

"Wait for a snowstorm, you'll see." Amy put her hands on Danni's shoulders and steered her toward the stairs. "Go, dress, wear the long johns under your jeans. We'll be ready when you get back down here."

"You have to dress both you and Peter."

"We are a well-oiled machine, aren't we Pete?" Amy said.

He nodded. "Yep. But we could get to school faster if we could fly on a pterodactyl."

"This part is Mateo." Amy shook her head. "I'm the secret stock trading part."

Danni laughed as she went upstairs and changed, dressing in layers like Amy suggested and putting on her knit hat and scarf. Of course, she took her gloves. On impulse, she removed the fancy New York fabric and wrapped the handmade gift from Cooper around her neck. A gift from the heart meant much more to her than fashion at this point.

She also thought about what Amy had said, and for a moment, the picturesque image of Mount McGinnis filled her mind. Has she really been living or existing? Nothing felt more exhilarating than going to Paris on her own money, doing her own thing. Now it all felt scripted. Danni knew she had a lot to think about.

Chapter Four

L ATER THAT DAY, WHEN PETER was home from preschool and Amy got her errands done, it was time for dinner. Mateo wanted to take them out to the one buffet in town for some good old-fashioned cooking, so Amy did not have to cook. She was on maternity leave but still helping with the town's Christmas celebrations, including the school play. Night came quickly in Juneau. It was late afternoon, and it was already getting dark. Mateo was coming to pick them up to eat.

"Isn't this called brunch?" Danni teased as she went down the brick steps.

Mateo and Amy were putting Peter's car seat in the Sarge's department SUV and as her feet hit the concrete pavement of the path, a noise halted her movements.

Danni turned slowly and said a name. "George."

The turkey gobbled in response.

"Hi, turkey, umm buddy, yeah...good turkey, George. I'll just go this way." Danni moved tentatively, and the large bird moved too. "You run off and play or whatever it is you do in the yard... Amy!"

George attacked, not that she expected Amy to admit

it, and Danni took off running. George followed, apparently thinking it was a game. "Mateo!" Danni cried out and turned to see both him and Amy laughing. *Traitors!* She ran in a circle and then...oof! A face full of snow as she hit the front lawn.

"George, back to the yard," Mateo called between his laughter and herded their pet back to the yard. "Sorry, Danni. I forgot and left the gate open."

"I never laughed so hard." Amy helped her brush snow off the front of her coat. "If anything was to put me in labor, that would do it."

"I yelled help, people, help," Danni muttered. "Does it mean something different here?"

Amy hugged her. "Actually, you yelled Mateo."

The hug soothed her embarrassment, and they finally got into the car and slowly pulled out to Auke Bay's Main Street. The lights and the colors soon took her attention away from the turkey attack. The tree under the gazebo was massive and lit, and a festive banner hung from one building to another.

The streetlamps had vintage poles, and Amy had explained earlier that some of them were still gas-powered because electricity could be spotty at best with heavy snowfall. For Christmas, each had a snowflake-shaped lighted ornament that glittered merrily amid string lights, garlands, and the mistletoe that seemed to be everywhere.

When they stopped and got out of the SUV, Danni marveled at the Christmas train in a store window. It chuffed and choo-chooed and wound its way through the entire toy shop. Like a child, she pressed her hand on the window, looking at the toys carved from wood. The toy soldiers stood straight, and tall ballerina dolls posed in a perfect pirouette.

She looked down. Peter was right next to her in the exact same pose with childlike wonder all over his face. Danni smiled. She couldn't help it; she felt that magic in her heart again. It wasn't lost. They were so enthralled Danni wasn't aware of Declan's arrival until Mateo spoke.

"Hey Declan, thanks for switching shifts with me, buddy." Mateo clapped him on the back.

He nodded. "Not a problem. Should be a quiet night. You take it easy and enjoy your family."

"You guys, the tree under the gazebo and the banner, what's the festival about?" Danni asked, acutely aware of the man who stood close by. Declan had a commanding presence even though he didn't talk much.

"Let's go look at the ornaments," Mateo said.

"I should go..." Declan didn't get to finish because Peter took his hand.

"Come on, Uncle Declan and A-Danni, let's go!" He took Danni's hand, too, as they crossed the empty street.

"Do you want to find your ornament, Pete?" Mateo asked.

"Yeah!" the little boy exclaimed.

Close up, Danni could see many of the ornaments were handmade along with some that seemed fragile and vintage. She touched an intricately carved, stained-wood angel, with the wings' design in the pattern of snowflakes. Danni listened to Mateo and Amy as she walked around the tree.

"The Auke Bay Christmas festival has been around for generations, well before I was born," Mateo explained. "Each year a family with a new birth adds an ornament, to show the town has a new member and we are growing in size and we have one more heart in our village community. There were points when this town didn't have much of anything, so for families to survive the community shared all resources until the hunting and fishing season began again."

Danni was fascinated listening to his story of the town. Mateo continued his tale. "For Christmas, that was especially hard when there's not a lot, so the town leader came up with the festival with meager decorations, a small meal and carved toys. They made sure everyone was fed and the children were happy. It has grown over the years to what it is now, but the heart is still there. We make sure no one is without a meal and no child has an empty spot under the tree. Our community is strong because of our ancestor's vision, and any new resident to Auke Bay is embraced as family."

"This year is even more special because we'll be able to see the northern lights over the town," Amy added. "It can't be forecasted, but some of the tribal leaders have said this is the year, and they are never wrong."

"That's so very amazing." Danni smiled at her friend. "I'm glad I came."

Amy reached out and took her hand. "Me too."

"I found it!" Peter was bouncing up and down, pointing to a spot on the tree.

"Yes, you did," Mateo said, lifting his son so he could have a closer look. "I carved this one to celebrate Peter's birth. When I know if we are having a boy or girl, I'll carve theirs too."

"Mine is the honeycomb star next to Peter's eagle, and Mateo's is the reindeer carved by his father." Amy pointed to each one.

"Do you have one, Declan?" Danni asked impulsively.

"There," his voice was gruff, and he pointed further up the tree.

Danni followed his hand with her eyes and saw a

star with what seemed to be Army chevrons carved into the wood.

"That was my first Christmas in Auke Bay. In the center's my Army rank," he explained. "Now my Trooper rank."

She smiled up at him. "It suits you."

Declan cleared his throat. "Thanks."

"How do they know what goes where?" Danni asked. "I'm in awe of the care that has to go into knowing whose family is on the tree."

Amy laughed. "You would think, but that's the thing about a small community with everyone who knows each other. This is all done with love so it's not a chore to the community festival council, it's a blessing to have it every year."

"And all the mistletoe everywhere?" Danni asked.

"Ah look up, honey." Mateo pressed a kiss on Amy's lips, and she smiled at her husband. "There's this legend that anyone who kisses under mistletoe at the festival will fall in love and be together forever. So, we believe in padding the deck to help fate along."

Danni noted that Declan stepped conveniently away from the mistletoe to the one open spot by the entrance to the gazebo.

"Mateo's grandparents were married for over sixty years and his parents for almost fifty." Amy took his hand. "We are hoping for eighty."

Mateo laughed. "It's not a hope. We'll get that eighty years together."

"It's all so very different than what we grew up with," Danni commented as they left the gazebo. "I haven't been in the back of a cop car since that time with you in Central Park."

"Well, this is a story I've never heard," Mateo said

curiously. "Were the two of you the bandits of Brooklyn or something?"

Danni laughed. "Nothing that serious. We got one Saturday to ourselves and decided against our parent's approval to go to Central Park. Amy said she knew her way around, but we got seriously lost and luckily there was a cop when we finally found an entrance. He took us home in the back of the cruiser."

"But we had a fun day and ate hot pretzels," Amy pointed out.

"Yes, we did," Danni agreed.

"One more stop," Amy said. "We need to sign up at the bakery for the gingerbread house competition. And you can meet Susie, Declan's mother."

"You heading that way, Declan?" Mateo asked.

"Yeah," he answered.

The small group crossed the street again and walked down the sidewalk with Peter chattering away. After learning of his story from her friend, she wondered more about the stoic man with the wary eyes that revealed nothing about what he was thinking. He smiled for Amy, and it softened his face. Danni wondered if there would ever be a chance to show him she wasn't a flighty city girl who talked too much. She pushed those thoughts aside when they stepped into a warm store filled with the smell of fresh breads and had desserts that made her mouth water.

She nudged Amy. "There's dulce de leche cake."

"Okay, sweet tooth, we can buy a slice on the way out," Amy said, amused.

"Two," Danni murmured looking around and nodding. "Definitely two."

"Hey guys!"

A warm voice caught her attention, and an older

woman came out from the back with a tray of strawberry tarts. Danni couldn't help noticing the chocolate in the center of each tart and tried very hard not to lick her lips. Susie Mathias was a few dress sizes larger than Danni's own mother and had what Danni's family would call ample hips. Her hair was black, without even a strand of gray to hint that she was old enough to have a grown son like the Sarge. Her brown eyes were wide and filled with merriment, and the smile on her face was genuine.

"Hi Susie," Amy said.

"Miss Susie, guess what? We have a guest person at the house, and here she is!" Peter pointed to Danni.

"I see that, Mr. Peter," Susie said fondly. She'd put the tray into the glass case before coming around to hug Amy and Mateo and bent to embrace Peter. Then it was her turn. "I think you may be Danni St. Peters. My son mentioned Amy's best friend."

"He mentioned me...yes, I'm Danni, nice to meet you." She stuck out her hand, embarrassed he heard her stammered words.

"And look we found said son and brought him home," Amy teased.

"Oh no sweetie, I'm a hugger." Susie smiled broadly and embraced her. "Welcome to Auke Bay, the best little neighborhood in Juneau. Amy, thank you for finding my wayward child."

"Really, Mom," Declan's voice was amused. "And you wonder why I don't come in here."

"Oh, please, you are always in here snagging something or the other," Susie replied with a laugh.

"I already love it here, and now I have been eyeing your desserts," Danni admitted. She was practically drooling at all the lovely treats.

"Well, Peter gets cookies, and you get cake," Susie said firmly. "Don't worry, it'll be nice and cold in the car, so it won't fall apart."

"You'll need to give it to me, Susie," Amy said eyeing her. "This one is worse than Peter and will eat it before we get to the Bay Buffet for dinner."

"I am not," Danni declared, and Amy raised an eyebrow. "Okay, I am. Give Amy the cake."

"We also need to sign up for the contest." Amy rubbed her hands. "How many teams do you have this year?"

"I thought you might have decided not to enter since you're so close to the end of the pregnancy," Susie commented.

"No way, have you met Amy?" Mateo laughed. "She's been planning her gingerbread house since September."

"If you sign up, there are seven teams, and I would like an even number." Susie tapped her chin. "Danni, you can sign up!"

She waved her hands in front of her. "No, I have no clue about gingerbread houses or their construction, and you said teams."

"We'll find you a partner. There is always a spare someone standing around," Susie answered. "I'll throw in a tart with those cake slices if you say yes."

"Come on, you can do it," Amy cajoled.

Danni sighed. "You have appealed to my dessert love and sense of competition."

Susie clapped. "Yay! Don't worry about the partner, I can figure that out easy."

"Mom." Declan's voice held a hint of warning, and Danni noted the innocent look on Susie's face while he glared.

Danni felt her heartbeat pick up when he caught her staring. *Why does it keep doing that?*

Declan was dressed for work, except this time, he wore the actual Trooper's hat instead of the black knit hat with the emblem from the day she arrived. When his eyes settled on her, he quickly looked away again.

"Hey," he said quickly to his mother. "Do you have that thermos for me?"

"Yes, I do, let me get it." Susie cast a glance between him and Danni before going to the back of the store.

"Peter, stop running around," Amy said gently and turned her attention to Declan. "I know for a fact your shift doesn't start until later. We are heading to Bay Buffet, come eat with us."

Danni sidestepped Peter, and it brought her closer to Declan. She waited to hear his answer.

"Here's the thermos, full of hot coffee, and I made you a panini and some cookies," Susie said coming back.

"Thanks Mom, but you don't have to make me food," Declan said. "Um... Amy, thanks for the offer but I better get on shift early. Jess is still learning the ropes, and I don't want to leave her without someone at her back."

Mateo chuckled. "He's right. This morning she called a 10:10 at the grocery store, and I almost choked on my coffee."

"What's a 10:10?" Danni asked.

"Public nudity," both Mateo and Declan answered.

"Do I get cookies like Uncle Declan?" Peter asked.

"Yes, you do," Susie said with a smile and pulled a cookie from her apron. "And a small one before dinner."

"Yay!"

Peter ran between her and Declan, and his hand caught on her scarf. While twisting around so he wasn't caught, Danni stumbled. She felt herself falling, until two strong hands were on her shoulders, and she was pulled against Trooper Declan Mathias's chest. It all happened in an instant. When he looked down at her, that moment seemed to stop time in its tracks. He made sure she was steady before stepping away.

Is my heart racing because of almost falling or because of him?

"Peter be careful," Amy admonished, but Danni could feel her staring at them and not at her son.

She ducked her head, suddenly shy of the attention from her best friend, Mateo, and Susie.

"Thank goodness you caught me. After the incident with George, I didn't need to be on the ground again," Danni teased.

"I have to get going... G'night everyone." Without waiting for a reply, Declan turned on his heel, and the bell jingled at his exit.

"Well, that was exciting," Susie murmured before speaking louder. "Let's get you some cake and that strawberry tart, dear."

Everything went back to normal. Peter pointed to the cookies he wanted, and Amy bought cheesecake for her and Mateo. Danni was happy with her two slices of cake and her extra dessert, even though the price was signing up for a gingerbread house contest. She hoped they weren't expecting anything like Hansel and Gretel because while gumdrop and candy cakes sounded easy, Danni had a sneaky suspicion they wouldn't be. There would be many an online tutorial video in her future before the competition. Susie walked them to the door and placed a hand on Danni's shoulder to stop her a moment as her friends filed out.

"Don't mind him, he's been through a lot," Susie said apologetically. "Deke is navigating his new normal, and he's been hurt in life and in love. He expected someone to be there for him when he came home, and it didn't happen that way."

"There's no need to explain," Danni said gently. "We all have shadows of our past we need to work through. I hope he finds some kind of peace. I worked with a charity last year for wounded soldiers who came home with not just physical but mental injuries. They are all so brave to serve and lose a part of themselves for our country. It's honorable. You can see it in his face, and you don't ever have to apologize for him. It's not a fault in his character. He has to learn to heal his way."

Susie embraced her suddenly, and her voice held tears. "Thank you for that...thank you."

Danni was silent as they drove toward the buffet, thinking about what Susie said and so much more.

"I think I sensed some chemistry there," Mateo teased, breaking into her thoughts.

"Oh, I would say more than a little," Amy replied.

"What are we talking about?" Danni asked from the back seat.

"You and the Sarge," Amy said.

"He stopped me from falling on my face, there was no chemistry." Her face got warm.

Mateo and Amy looked at each other before saying simultaneously, "Chemistry."

Danni decided not to answer the teasing, but instead focused on the beauty of the town and listened to Peter jabber beside her. She had come to Juneau to be with her friend, nothing more, and no thoughts of 'what if' would be in her mind. When Christmas was over, she would go back to New York, and Declan would forget she was ever in his town.

Just because it was winter didn't mean his routine changed much. Two days later it was Declan's day off and he still managed to get in a run at least twice a week so the muscle memory of using his athlete's prosthetic didn't diminish in the long winter months. For an added layer of protection, he wore his Under Armor long johns beneath his thick gray sweats. The gel sleeve helped his running leg adhere securely below his knee but with the cold, sometimes even that didn't keep the ache away. Being an amputee meant Declan's leg did throb. It was a traumatic wound, after all. There was a criteria-of-care that he followed to the letter, but the soreness and pain still ran up his thigh. He tapered his run to accommodate for the snow piled up along the side roads of Auke Bay.

Taking the main thoroughfare would be easier on his leg. The hill that led to Mateo and Amy's house came into view, and Declan impulsively turned and jogged that way. Amy had taken to herbs, oils, and rubs since she moved to Alaska. She made candles and sweet-smelling jars of goop that women loved. She also made a leg rub for him that worked like a miracle on his sore leg and thigh muscles that took the brunt of the weight. Declan didn't ask what was in it, he was just glad it worked. While he was out for a run, he impulsively decided to stop by for a jar since his was gone.

When he went home to shower, it would be a welcome relief to sit at home without a prosthetic on and let the healing poultice do its thing. As expected, Mateo's SUV wasn't in the driveway, but the blue family van was.

Declan grimaced in pain as he walked up the driveway and then the stairs. The run back would be a slow one, but he wasn't going to let that stop him.

At the top of the steps, he leaned against the railing and rang the doorbell, expecting Amy to answer with Peter on her heels. Instead, her friend Danni opened the door with the young boy peeking out from behind her. Seeing her wearing a simple sweater with her hair up in a messy ponytail made Declan's breath catch in his throat.

"Hey Uncle Declan! Look A-Danni, it's my Uncle Declan!" Peter jumped up and down behind her.

"Yes, that it is," Danni said, amused.

Peter tugged on her sweater and sighed. "Well, let him in, he's wearing his space leg."

"Yes, I'm sorry, come in." Her eyes went down to his prosthetic, and Declan instantly felt uncomfortable.

"It's okay, is Amy around? She usually makes me a jar of stuff for my...um...leg." Declan wished he was anywhere but there at that point because if he saw pity in her eyes, it would be his undoing.

"She went to meet Mateo for a doctor's appointment," Danni explained and smiled gently. "Come in for a cup of coffee. I'm sure I can find what you're looking for in her stock room."

"Sure, thanks." Declan tried not to grimace as the throbbing pain increased. *Today was a bad day for a run. Too cold,* he told himself, and made a mental note to not to try until the next week.

"Here, sit at the kitchen table." Danni pulled out the chair.

"I can manage to pull out a chair," Declan said gruffly. His pride wouldn't let him admit that sitting sounded perfect right at that moment.

"I know, Sarge," she answered simply without even a hint of being offended. "I'll get you a cup of hot coffee to warm you up and then go hunting for that rub."

"A-Danni, my show is coming on soon." Peter hopped up and down.

"If I recall, Master Peter, you know the channel, and I already put your fruit and peanut butter snack right on your little table." Danni used a silly British voice that made Peter giggle. Declan had to admit she was good with kids, even making him smile as she put a hot cup of coffee in front of him and then dropped two pieces of chocolate inside. "For you, Master Sarge."

"She's nice, isn't she Uncle Declan," Peter said.

Declan ruffled the boy's hair. "Yes, she is. You'd better go get the TV on before the puppy superheroes run away."

Peter swooshed away with his hands out, pretending to fly. Soon, the large TV was on, and he sat quietly watching while he chewed his snack and laughed occasionally. Danni came out from the storeroom adjacent to the kitchen with a twelve-ounce mason jar held up in triumph.

"Found it," she declared. "It also helped that Amy is meticulous about labeling."

"Thank you," Declan said gratefully.

If she wasn't around, he might have taken off his leg to ensure he had some relief on the run home. But she was a new entity in his life and one that he wasn't sure about yet. He couldn't bear the thought of another reaction like Claire's when she saw his leg.

"Is the coffee any good?" Danni asked. "I'm still trying to get Amy's process just right, and I didn't forget to add the chocolate."

"It's great, thanks." Declan put the cup down. "That's

an Auke Bay thing, chocolate in our coffee for a little sweet."

Danni grinned. "It's how I'll be drinking it from now on, even when I get back to New York."

"And that's in a few weeks?" Declan asked.

"Trying to get rid of me, Sarge?" she teased.

"No," he replied and sipped his coffee.

"I'm supposed to be here until the thirtieth," Danni answered. "Fingers crossed the baby comes before then. I don't want to miss meeting him or her."

"Can't you extend your trip if she isn't born by then?"

Danni shook her head. "I wish I could, but I have work and then maybe another meeting, plus someone..."

"Someone waiting for you?" Declan finished the sentence for her.

Danni met his gaze. "Honestly, I don't know. Part of why I'm here is to work things out on my own without people pressuring me."

"I hope you find the answers you're looking for," he said. "It's hard figuring this whole life thing out."

"It really is," she said with a sigh. "I see the pain lines between your eyebrows. How bad is it?"

He looked up at her in surprise. *She noticed?*

"Not too bad. I can manage," Declan said.

"Can I ask how you lost your leg?" Danni's voice was soft and caring.

"I was an Army Crew Chief and I worked on the medivac Black Hawk taking injured soldiers and civilians back to the base for medical help. My last deployment had us in a province nowhere near the base and we were heading to a village. Where soldiers were pinned down and had sustained injuries." Declan closed his eyes for a moment, trying to tell the story and not relive it. "I dropped smoke before we landed to give the medics some cover when they got out and went toward where the soldiers were pinned down. I was on the gun and watched for muzzle fire so I could suppress and keep them safe."

"That sounds terrifying," Danni murmured.

"We don't think about it at the time," Declan explained. I was watching for gunfire and got an RPG instead."

"What is an RPG?"

"Rocket-propelled grenade," he answered. "In any case, my Black Hawk got hit and I was thrown out, landed on the rocks and sand...and then the jagged metal from the Hawk landed on me and my leg. They got me out but there was another few hours before additional help could arrive. My leg had a tourniquet and that is a time-sensitive injury. By the time we got back to the base, it was too late."

She covered his hand with hers. "I'm so sorry, but you made it home, and I am definitely honored to meet you. Thank you for your service."

A short laugh escaped him. "People always say that, and I think...please don't thank me. I was doing my service to my country."

She squeezed his hand. "And that's why men and women like you deserve all our thanks and our support. You didn't do it for the money or think you were owed a thing. To you all, it was for a country you love."

"Thanks... I mean for understanding that--- a lot of people don't."

Danni smiled, and a spark of merriment lit her brown eyes. "You'll see I'm not most people."

"I can already tell that." Declan drained his coffee. "I should get going. It's my day off."

Danni stood. "Of course, I didn't mean to keep you.

I like to talk and get to know people. Let me get a bag for that jar so you can carry it better."

Declan put on his gloves and followed her to the door with the jar in a brown bag securely in his hand. Danni opened the door, and he stepped out into the cold afternoon once again to make his way home.

"Danni." He turned suddenly. "Does it bother you… I mean…my being an amputee?"

She looked up at him, and Declan felt like he was drowning in her gaze. "It doesn't, and if it bothers anyone, it shows their character as flawed, not you. A leg isn't the thing that makes a man whole or how people should be defined. It's what's inside their hearts that counts."

"I appreciate that," Declan said. "See you around town, city slicker."

"Bye Sarge," Danni said with a light laugh and closed the door.

How could a simple conversation with a person he barely knew end with him feeling lighter? Declan didn't understand it, but he impulsively turned to her at the front door.

"Would you like a tour of one of the best places in Auke Bay?" Declan asked.

Curious, Danni put her hands on her hips. "Where is it?"

"Let me just say…chocolate." he hinted.

"I'm in," Danni said with a grin. "When should I be ready?"

"I'll be back around two?" he suggested.

"Sure, Mateo and Amy will be back by then," Danni smiled.

"I'll see you then" he said and added quickly. "Dress warm."

He chose a speed walk on the way home to keep his heart rate up but decrease the impact pressure on his leg. There were no real plans for the day, just home, quiet, until now. Declan told himself that he was just doing Mateo and Amy a favor by taking their friend to see Auke Bay. If he was being honest with himself, her words at the kitchen table set him as ease. *Seems like I'm going to spend my day with a city slicker,* Declan thought with a quick grin and picked up his speed heading home.

Chapter Five

THAT AFTERNOON, DRESSED IN HIS dark blue jeans and a warm flannel shirt, Declan threw his thick parka in the backseat of the truck before getting behind the wheel. It was almost two and being a military man, he prided himself with being on time. In less than ten minutes he pulled in behind Amy and Mateo's family mobile, as they called it, and headed to the front door. A sense of nervousness combined with excitement filled his chest. It felt like high school when Josephine Hughes agreed to go out with him.

"This is not a date," he told himself, reaching a gloved finger to press the doorbell.

Amy answered the door with a wide grin and a twinkle in her eyes. "Well look who's here, it's Declan."

Declan shook his head. "I assume Danni told you I was coming to pick her up."

"Yes, she did," Amy put her hands on 1and peered at him owlishly. "Where are you taking her that's the best place in Auke Bay?'

"Amy stop grilling the man, at the front door, in the cold," Danni's voice came from the bottom of the stairs and held a hint of amusement. "You're worse than my dad."

Danni wore a pair of blue jeans and a bulky thick blue sweater; the black boots were cut to the calf and Declan noted that the treads were good for the ice and snow. Amy probably loaned her a pair because the first boots she wore didn't seem Alaska-ready. Danni's hair was pulled back in a thick low ponytail. She pulled a warm hat over her ears. She wrapped the long scarf Copper made around her neck after putting on her coat.

"Ready to go?"

"Hmm?"

Danni smiled up at him. "Are we ready to go?"

"Oh yeah, I mean yes." He felt the warm rush to his face and stepped back so she could go down the steps in front of him. Declan also ignored Amy as she grinned while standing in the doorway as they walked to his truck.

"I'll get the heat on," said Declan.

"It's still kinda warm in here," said Danni, already buckled in the passenger seat. "Going to tell me where we're going?"

He flashed her a smile. "You'll see."

Declan left their small community in the heart of Auke Bay and pulled on to the highway. The road was clear with snow banked up on each side.

He drove past the harbor. "This is a great place to visit, in the summer it's filled with tourists. That patch of land right behind it is the county fair. You can't tell by it now, but grass actually grows there."

Danni laughed. "How long does warm weather last in Alaska?"

"Well, we have a really short summer about four months, and it goes by quickly. We are just getting rid of the last of the snow in May," Declan explained. "There's been many times that spring flowers have been buried under snow by an unexpected snowstorm."

"Ohhh, the poor flowers," Danni said.

Her empathy towards the blooms was another appealing aspect about her. He continued his explanation, "By the end of September we are back to cold temperatures especially further north near Dutch Harbor and heading toward Kachemak Bay."

"Wow." Danni's voice held fascination. "In New York, we are still having warm days in November."

"We have been seeing warmer temperatures in Alaska as well, guess the world is changing," he commented.

Declan got to their destination and parked at the storefront. "And here we are."

Danni looked at the sign. "No way!"

"Yes way," he teased. "Auke Bay's only chocolatier, and we are lucky, this is the very last weekend they'll be open until spring."

Danni bounced in the passenger seat and clapped her hand lightly. "If you ever want to know my weakness, it's chocolate."

Declan walked around and opened the passenger door. "I thought it was cake?"

"It's desserts," Danni jumped out of the truck in excitement and almost slipped. "Whoops!"

Declan caught her around the waist and kept her upright. "You need to be more careful."

The air was suddenly magnetic between them and Danni became breathless. "It's um...desserts in general, and especially chocolate."

"Then let's go see what in there you like, city slicker." His voice came out husky. Declan worried about his attraction to her. He tried to ignore it as he opened the door to Fifty-Eight Degrees of Chocolate.

"What an unusual name," Danni mused, looking at the elegant sign on the back wall.

"Auke Bay is fifty-eight point three degrees north," he explained. "And if you look over there you will see they make their own fresh saltwater taffy."

Her eyes widened. "Show me everything."

This was an afternoon that would be etched in Declan's mind forever. The look of excitement on Danni's face when she looked at all the unique chocolatier's designs. They allowed Danni to spread the chocolate in molds, then between the two of them they pulled saltwater taffy. Her laughter was infectious and more than once their fingers touched, making him feel more connected to her as each moment passed by.

When the sun started to go down, Declan escorted Danni home. She'd purchased a basket of assorted treats, including the saltwater taffy they made together. He pulled his truck into the driveway and for a moment they sat, silently enjoying the warmth. Declan was very aware of the woman beside him and the feelings that she caused within him in such a short time. He couldn't feel like this, not again. The ache in his chest grew insistent and he rubbed the area of his chest over his heart.

'Are you okay?" Danni's voice held concern.

"Yes, fine." Declan heard the gruffness in his voice, but he had to maintain the firm foundation he'd rebuilt to protect himself from pain and loss.

"Well thank you for a great day." The confusion in her voice was evident even though she kept her words light.

"Not a problem," he answered. "You should probably get inside before Amy and Mateo start to worry."

"Okay." Danni pressed a kiss on his cheek. "Good-night Declan."

"Goodnight."

The cold wind entered the truck when she opened the passenger door and Declan watched her walk up the driveway. He was confused. Declan knew he couldn't risk being hurt again after having barely recovered the last time. But somehow, he knew Danni could or would be his undoing.

****

The days seemed to linger which suited Danni just fine. Exactly one week after her arrival and a small snow-storm and a foot of snow, Danni was brave enough to venture out on her own. Thanks to a couple of lessons from Mateo on how to use the Ski-Doo, she had gotten pretty good at it and was able to get to the bakery on her own.

With Amy so far along in her pregnancy, Danni didn't want her running all over town on her account, so she took it on herself to explore. So far, she'd made trips to look around the historical society to learn more about Auke Bay and even the small bookstore so she could buy books about the area and a new novel she wanted to read. That was a luxury. How many times had she wanted to do so in her apartment, but her work sched-ule made it impossible? She loved cutting through the snow and watching the powdery snow be tossed while she was on the snowmobile.

Amy and Mateo gave their approval for her to drive the car, but Danni didn't think it was a good idea.

"What if your water breaks, and you need to get to the hospital?" Danni worried.

"I will not be driving myself to the hospital, and the dispatcher could reach Mateo easily," Amy replied.

"Push comes to shove, a neighbor can drive me, or I can have the baby in the house."

Danni balked at the idea. "Please don't say that."

Amy shook her head, amused. "I'm kidding. We'll be fine, and the baby is nowhere near ready to come yet. Go look around the bay. There's even a coffee shop next to the Coast Guard port."

"Okay, I won't be too long." Danni bit her bottom lip with worry. "Amy, are you sure..."

From her position in her recliner, Amy waved her away. "Go, have fun."

In the blue van that was the Azure family vehicle, Danni pulled slowly out of the driveway and made her way carefully to the highway using the car's built-in navigation system.

She maneuvered the car, making sure to drive a bit slower than the speed limit, because the roads could be icy, and she very rarely drove anymore. Danni found the road that the GPS called out and made the soft left turn, in only a few minutes she was parked by the Visitor Center. It was a short walk to where visitors could view nature's wonder. She marveled at the sight of the Mendenhall Glacier, which was an eleven-minute drive from Auke Bay. She longed to go into the ice caves, but she preferred to have someone with her who knew the terrain; so, she took her pictures from a distance.

Maybe I'll do the helicopter tour, she thought. Seeing the glacier from above would be an amazing sight. The ice blue of the frozen lake that surrounded the monolith of water was already imprinted on her mind. It was large and naturally breathtaking. From there, she changed course and went back toward the bay.

Danni made an impromptu stop at the Coast Guard port she and Declan had passed on their trip to the chocolatier. His name brought up a swirl of emotions that Danni didn't want to deal with right now. This was her adventure, and she wouldn't allow anything to stress her out including her very confused feelings. Taking pictures of the Coast Guard's famous boat, "The Liberty" only added to the perfect day. The boat, called a cutter or sloop, was a piece of history they kept pristine, and yet another memory to be filed away. Her adventures led Danni to the ferry docks, and the small quaint coffee shop was little more than a stand built on the side of the visitor's ticketing area. It faced the water, and as she sipped her hot coffee in one of the few small booths that were in the shop, Danni kept her fingers crossed she would see a whale.

Danni pulled out her phone and started a live video, narrating to her fans everything she was seeing and about her experiences in Juneau and the history she'd learned. Once done, she looked through the comments and answered questions before logging off. Sipping her hot beverage, she perused a travel guide of things to do. There was skiing, winter camping, and...

"Hi, did you get lost? Do I need to take you back to Mateo and Amy?" Declan's voice made her look up.

Danni smiled. "I'm not always lost, you know. I'm on an adventure."

"Are you now?"

Was that a hint of a smile at his lips? Danni took a chance and again acted on impulse. "Sit and have coffee with me. I promise I won't talk your ear off."

"Luckily"—he held up the coffee in his hand—"I'm on break." He slid into the bench across from her in the booth. "What are you looking at?"

She placed the brochure on the table. "Trying to decide if I should walk across the lake to the glacier or maybe go skiing. I was honestly sitting here hoping a whale would pop up."

Declan took a sip of his coffee. "The ferry is here but whale watching won't be until May. Too dangerous, and it's not the season for them. In the spring and summer, you can see them and their babies. It's one of the most beautiful things I have ever seen."

"Oh." Danni sighed in disappointment. "I won't be here in May."

"Still, if you look out to the water you may see a humpback or orca who hasn't left for warmer waters yet." Declan added, "Luckily, Auke isn't as harsh as Dutch Harbor when it comes to the sea and winter. They have waves in the Bering sea over thirty feet. When winter storms hit there, the crab fishermen take their ships into the harbor. Some of the ones who try to ride it out for a few thousand crab sometimes don't make it back."

Danni gasped. "That sounds terrible. Those poor men and their families."

Declan nodded. "We try to dissuade people from the lower forty-eight from coming here looking to make a quick payday. Life can be harsh if you're not ready for it." He took another sip of the coffee. "I never asked, but what do you do in New York? Teacher, nurse? Second conversation, and it's my turn to ask the questions."

"I'm kind of a social media influencer," she explained. "I built a video channel around a trip I took to Paris—I posted videos about ways to travel on a budget. It went from there, and now I'm paid for advertising, to host events, try products. I'm in the running to be the spokesperson for a makeup brand."

"Sounds very exciting, living in the limelight." He looked out to the water. "You probably can't walk any-where without people knowing you."

"It's not that crazy." Danni laughed. "You should try New York sometime."

He shook his head. "There's too many people, constant low hum of noise. I couldn't do it."

Danni felt sympathy for the man in front of her. "I can understand that. Did you always live here?"

"I left when the Army stationed me in California, then in Arizona for a while." Declan hesitated. "I got hurt on deployment, I lost my leg...came back here."

"Nothing in between?" she hinted gently, hoping he would open up.

"Nothing that seems to matter now." He looked out to the water again. "Look."

She turned in the direction of his face and at first Danni saw nothing. Then a spray of sea water went into the air before she saw the outline of a whale's body. It breached the water for a moment as if it was the last goodbye before it moved, following an invisible path to its pod. With the group, it would wait until the seasons changed once more before returning.

The upper half of its body emerged again, and she gasped in awe just before it disappeared again under the water. Her first look at a whale, and she missed getting video. It was only then she looked down to see she had taken his hand with hers, spellbound by the magic of what she'd seen and understanding she had shared the moment after all.

"Sorry," she apologized and pulled her hand away. For a moment it seemed like he held on just a bit.

He cleared his throat. "It's okay... I need to get going. I'm still on shift."

"I understand," Danni answered. "It was nice talking to you."

"Same," Declan said. "You'll have some interesting

stories for your fans when you get back to New York. They'll wonder how you survived in such a remote place."

"I'll tell them it was perfect."

"Get home safely," Declan turned to head back the way he came.

It seemed like she was always looking at his back as he retreated. They were making headway, but when she mentioned New York, his demeanor changed. Was it his deep wounds that made him wary of everyone or was it just her? Did she remind him of a past he was trying to forget? Danni watched the water a bit more before leaving.

Instead of driving straight home, she stopped at Baker's Dozen, one of her new favorite places. Susie was of course behind the counter, and her eyes lit up when Danni stepped inside.

"My new favorite regular customer," Susie said warmly. "What shall I get you today?"

"Red velvet cake for Mateo and Amy, four chocolate chip cookies for Peter, and today I think I will try the chocolate strawberry truffle cake."

Susie grabbed two boxes. "You are going to try everything I make before you go home."

She held up her fingers. "Fingers crossed. I'll need to join a gym."

"We have one at the University." Susie winked. "But a little weight never hurt any woman. We should be allowed to eat and enjoy life."

"I agree." Danni grinned and whispered conspiratorially. "I love food and cooking."

"Then do what you love," Susie encouraged. "Go to the market and buy some groceries, take over Amy's kitchen."

"You know what, I'll do that." Joy coursed through

her. "A little music, a glass of wine, and I'll make them my famous pasta. You should come."

"How about you bring me and Deke a plate tomorrow." Susie packed up her purchases neatly. "I have my own dinner plans tonight...with Cooper."

Danni laughed out loud in surprise. "So that's why I've seen him in the bakery literally every time I'm around. He's sweet on you."

It was Susie's turn to look shy. "I'm kind of sweet on him, too. Don't tell a soul. Deke doesn't even know. I worry about him so much..."

"I had coffee with him today at the ferry coffee shop and yesterday he took me to the chocolatier." The words spilled out because talking to Susie, even though she was Declan's mother, was easy.

"Oh really," Susie gasped and looked pleased. "How did that go?"

"We saw a whale today, and when we went to Fifty-Eight Degrees we pulled taffy," she said with a smile. "And we talked about New York and what there is to do here. He kind of shut down after that. Still, he talked, and he didn't look like I was annoying him."

"I wish he would open up more. After Claire, it's like he shut himself off from the world, even more than the injury..." Susie shook her head sadly. "It's his story to tell."

"I hope that he does. He's a good man," Danni wondered about all the what ifs. "My life is so simple here, it's like New York is so far away."

Susie smiled. "You needed this time away. I loved it from the time we left Georgia and were stationed in Anchorage. Not only do our spouses serve, we do as well, and sometimes men or women who marry into the military can't handle the life."

"How did you manage it?" Danni asked curiously. "Didn't you miss your home?"

"This place settled into my heart, and I don't think I could ever leave Auke Bay or Juneau for that matter," Susie smiled. "Christmas is my favorite time of the year in Alaska, it feels magical."

"I can see why." Danni took her packages and paid. "Let me get on the way before Amy sends Mateo to look for me. Besides, I'm making dinner tonight. Thank you for everything."

"No, thank you," Susie replied. "Be safe out there, Danni."

"I will, and tell Cooper hello for me." Danni rubbed the scarf against her skin.

She opened the door, and the wind blew the sign-up sheet for the contest on the corkboard that held business cards and flyers for babysitting. *Maybe I should go look to see who they paired me with?* Danni quickly put that thought aside. The sky was getting dim. There was time to go to the small market and go home before the short day turned to a long night.

There was Christmas music in the market and on the radio as she drove back to the house. A light snow started to fall as she retrieved everything she'd bought that day from the car.

"Goodness." Amy came slowly down the stairs, wearing the red sweater and beige tights she'd had on earlier. "What all did you buy?"

Danni grinned. "Food, wine, and dessert. Guess who's cooking tonight."

"Peter?" Amy teased.

"Ha-ha. He can help," Danni answered and emptied the bags. "Tonight, it's my turn to pamper you and the guys, my three absolute favorite people. George and I are still working things out. But first, we need music, you need hot chocolate, and I need Peter to dance it out with."

"By all means, let the feast begin." Amy pressed a remote and Christmas lyrics filled the air before she went to find Peter.

Danni hummed as she chopped the onions needed for the recipe before filling a pot with water for the pasta, and then pounded out the chicken breasts to the beat of the music that pulsed around her. In between the creation of chicken parmesan, linguini in red sauce, and fresh garlic bread, she held Peter's hand, danced, and laughed with her best friend.

Mozzarella cheese bubbled and melted on their chicken while "Rockin' Around the Christmas Tree" played and the lights from the tree and decorations gave the living room a warm, comforting feel. This was perfect. It was what was missing when she shared a meal with Austin. Danni couldn't recall him ever tasting a morsel of food she prepared with her own hands. This was comfort, and no judgment from anyone; just singing into a wooden spoon while her friend laughed and her nephew sang backup with his own utensil. This was the best holiday she'd had in a very long time. Being in Juneau with Amy and her family felt like home.

Chapter Six

"I'M STILL ME. LOSING A *leg doesn't change that fact.*" *A tentative smile pulled at his lips.*

"Declan…" Claire didn't smile in return. "I thought we would be traveling. Surfing in Cozumel, dancing in Paris."

He held out his hand from the Walter Reed hospital bed. His mom was on her way, but Claire had gotten there first.

"We can still do all of that," he said. "After a few months of physical therapy, I'll get fitted with a prosthetic leg. I'll still sweep you off your feet." But Declan could read the truth written on her face, and he dropped his hand back down to the bed.

She shook her head, her brunette hair tossing back and forth. "I'm sorry, Declan. There are more options out there for me than this." She stepped back. "I wanted a husband who could take care of me, not the other way around."

Then she turned and walked away. By the time his mother came in, he'd steeled all that away, even though his heart was shattered.

"Where's Claire?" his mother asked, looking around. "She said she would be here."

"Gone."

"To get coffee, lunch?" Her confusion was evident in her voice, and then the realization hit. "Oh, Deke. I'm sorry."

Never again... the words echoed in his head as he woke from a dream that reminded him why he didn't need to get serious about Danni. Declan sat up. He hadn't meant to fall asleep on his sofa but finally relaxing from the morning shift and being out on an accident call the night before had taken its toll. His body needed the rest. Tonight, Auke Bay's calls were going to the main Juneau police department.

In the eventuality of an emergency, he would be paged so he'd grab his things and head out. Till then, Mateo, Jessica, and himself would be 10-17 and at his mother's gingerbread competition. It was another reason why he loved this town. It was small enough that they rarely had serious crimes but that didn't mean something couldn't happen.

Returning home was the best decision he'd ever made. Thinking about the people, the traffic, the noises, crowds, and high rises boxing him in made Declan's PTSD even worse. It was like a clawing entity that stole his breath away, leaving him feeling weak. Only when he came back to Juneau had he felt some kind of peace. This was where he was meant to be.

Friday night and Declan knew he couldn't put it off any longer. It was the gingerbread house competition and if he didn't go down to the bakery, his mother would come up to the apartment. He took a hot shower and got dressed, pulling the dark blue jean leg down neatly over his prosthetic leg to the low black boot. He added his beige sweater and black leather coat. It was just downstairs, so he could get away with the lighter jacket because his destination was a few feet away. His mind turned to Danni, which it often had since their coffee. But her job, her life, everything about her screamed stay away.

He'd looked her up online, and the life Danni lived was everything Claire wanted. Parties, clubs, events, celebrities and even a whole man. It made him uncomfortable. *I have one leg, that doesn't suit the tux lifestyle,* he told himself as he locked his front door. Declan had avoided even talk of relationships since Claire left, and three years ago, her reasons why were perfectly clear. Her words were like a knife that sliced through his soul.

Being lonely didn't matter. The hurt was much worse when he saw the light go out in any woman's eyes when they found out about his leg. Danni didn't say a word about his injury, even though she knew about his leg. That was another thing, he wondered if it was pity. Being friendly because he was a friend of the family and an injured veteran did not a relationship make. By the time she landed in New York again, he would be a distant memory. All of these thoughts frustrated Declan. Life was simpler before she arrived.

His mother's bakery had been transformed into a smaller version of a chef's competition. Between him and her young employee, they had moved everything around while she directed. Her glass cases were now in the back. Luckily, they had wheels that locked in place when they were in use. Her tall, steel bread box with glass doors was now housing stacks and stacks of gingerbread bricks.

The metal worktables from the kitchen were lined up. His mom had back problems, so these were specially made to be at least seven inches higher than her waist; that way, she didn't have to bend so much. For each team, the table had four stacks of gingerbread bricks, bowls of gumdrops, candy canes, and an assortment of candies, piping bags with food coloring, and yes, a large tub of white royal icing. The flat foam boards were decorated on the outer edges while the center was ready for the gingerbread house creations.

Everyone was there, and the competitors were at their tables, talking. The spectators were along the edge of the wall in fold-out chairs that he had brought from the back storage shed. Jessica was there with her husband, Robert, who was a woodworker, Mateo and Amy wore matching green ugly sweaters... *they are disgustingly cute.* Peter sat by the window across from them in a chair with a cookie in one hand and a candy cane in another. *He's going to have a sugar high before bed.* Everyone had a partner at the table, and there was one empty spot next to... *Not... really... come on, mom!* It was Danni, wearing a champagne-colored sweater, jeans and black boots.

Declan moved closer. He could see she wore lace-up boots that were turned down at the top, revealing beige plaid to match her dress. Around her neck was the scarf that Cooper gave her. She wore it everywhere now, and that was endearing. *No, don't fall into that very cute trap.* On her head, there was a green elf hat with a silver bell on the end. His mother had mistletoe and holly hung everywhere, including over each table. *Oh, this is so obviously a set up!*

With a sigh, he looked at his mother who was standing with Cooper, and she winked at him. *Uh-huh.* He glanced over at Amy and Mateo as he took off his coat and stuck it on the shelf under the table. They grinned broadly, and Amy wiggled her fingers in a wave. *They're in on it, too!* In fact… Declan looked around.

If he'd been a paranoid type of person, he would've thought everyone in the competition and all the guests were watching him and Danni. Her eyes widened when she saw he was her partner, and she leaned back behind him to see Amy who gave her a thumbs up. With a sidelong glance, Declan noted that Danni gave her best friend the "I'm watching you" signal with her hands and they would talk later.

"Hey," Danni said shyly.

"Hi," he responded with the one gruff word.

"I guess we're together, I mean a couple, partners… uh, gingerbread buddies." Danni took a deep breath and ducked her head.

His mother came to the front and rang her bell. When he glared at her, she gave him that look. The one that said, *I'm your mom and you better play nice, because I know your secrets and I have your baby pictures.*

Declan rolled his eyes heavenward and mouthed, "What?"

Susie Matthias chose to ignore him, and he knew he would hear about it later when he helped to clean up and revert her bakery to normal.

"Hello, Baker's Dozen contestants!" she called out, and everyone clapped. "This is the fourth annual gingerbread house competition. Give a round of applause for last year's and the reigning monarch for four years, Amy and Mateo."

"Seriously? They win every year?" Danni asked in a low voice.

He watched his friends at the next table high five with a light belly bump. Declan nodded. "Every year. I don't know why we even try. Amy is very competitive."

"You're telling me, I grew up with her. Never play volleyball with her...ever."

Declan stared at her, and she smiled. Unable to help it, he smiled in return. *Do not fall for it,* he told himself and focused on his mother. *God, she's cute.*

"Remember, you have all the supplies you need, and we have more yummy bricks if you want to get elaborate and for eating," Susie called out. "Two hours begin now, and there's hot chocolate and extra-large marshmallows for whoever wants some."

"I want some and a cookie." Peter raised his hand. "Please."

Susie laughed. "For you, my favorite Peter...anything."

"Serves you right if he drives you crazy working off all that sugar later," Declan said with a grin to his friends at the table next to him.

"Don't hate, bro, it's not a good look," Mateo teased.

Declan turned to Danni, shaking his head. "This is the first year my mother guilted me into joining because someone didn't have a partner."

Her brown eyes sparkled with amusement. "If this isn't a set up, I don't know what is."

"They will never admit to it," he told her.

Mateo raised his hand. "Susie, we need more bricks if you please, for our two-story winter chalet."

Every other contestant groaned, and Declan shook his head. "We have no chance."

Danni laughed. "Especially since I literally have no clue what I'm doing."

"Don't look at me. I was just a crew chief in the Army, not an engineer."

"Helicopter engines not the same thing, huh?" Danni teased before picking up two bricks and set them down.

"Not even close," Declan explained. "Dropping smoke in hot zones or manning a gun doesn't need me to build. I have some medical training in case my medics need an extra hand, but mostly I made sure my Black Hawk was always ready to go on the FOB if they needed us to move fast. Hold the bricks together like this and I'll use the frosting like Mateo and Amy are doing."

She nodded, following his instructions. "FOB, is that forward operating base?" she asked tentatively. "I know you told me when you stopped by that you were hurt in a convoy, so I assume you were on your way to that type of base."

He was pleased she knew the term. "Yes, exactly that. How did you know?"

"I worked with the Home for the Heroes charity last year," Danni explained. "I picked up on a little..."

"That's a good organization. They contacted me after I was medically discharged. They have some good programs." Declan gave up more information than he realized and zipped his lips.

"Look, it's staying together!" Danni clapped hands in delight then swiped her hair from her face. Declan noticed she'd gotten frosting in her hair. *Definitely too cute for words.*

Together, they focused on the gingerbread project, but it was slow going with a few structural collapses. By the end, gumdrops and candy canes perched precariously on lopsided walls and the roof slid down to one side. A gumdrop fell off a window, and their laughs were echoed by his mother's light bell. Together, the sound was magical.

"Time is up!" Susie called. "Royal icing down. And now, the audience will vote!"

Declan saw the gingerbread masterpiece of Amy

and Mateo. All it needed was its own personal Christmas lights, and it could be an image in a cookbook. Of course, they were smug, and Amy did a very smooth victory dance even before judging was done. A pregnant woman who was still light on her feet.

"Well, you two tried your best…" Susie said with a smile as a candy cane fell off the roof. "Danni, you are covered in icing. How did it get in your hair?"

She grinned. "I have no clue, but it was absolutely fun and worth it."

"It looks a mess," Declan pointed out.

Danni looked up at him. "But it's our mess, and I'm proud of it."

She popped a gumdrop in her mouth and chewed around the smile on her face.

"Here, let me help you," he said gruffly.

There was a small container of warm water, the only thing that could clean up excess icing without a lot of mess. Declan dipped the cloth in and squeezed out the excess water before using it to wipe her face. How she had managed to get it in her eyebrows… He shook his head. Standing right next to her, and yet it was only she who was coated in the stuff. Her embracing the task with such exuberance only made her more appealing.

"That's the best I can do," he murmured.

"Thank you." Their eyes connected and held while the cloth was on her cheek.

"We have a winner!" Susie's voice broke the moment, and Declan stepped away. "Mateo and Amy have won the coveted gingerbread man trophy for the fifth year running." Susie called out the second and third place. "And finally, for best effort, Declan and Danni."

Their prize was a small gift card for the coffee shop in the ferry house. Declan gave it to Danni. For having so much fun and hearing her laughter, she deserved it.

"Let's finish up the rest of the food and hot chocolate," Susie called. "Or take it home, don't leave it here for me. I've got plenty of boxes in the back."

It was time to leave. All these feelings, being so close to her and having people around was starting to get to him, and he needed to keep his resolve strong. Being hurt couldn't happen. Declan wouldn't allow it.

"Mom, I'm leaving," Declan said when she came to their table.

"Without a kiss goodbye?" she asked. "A beautiful girl and mistletoe...it's kind of tradition."

"Not for me." He kissed his mother's cheek instead. "We'll talk later, call me when the party is over."

"Okay," his mother said in a resigned tone.

"Thanks for a fun evening," Danni said.

"Thank my mom, she's the one who puts this together. I'm just one of Santa's helpers," Declan replied.

He stopped long enough to congratulate Mateo and Amy before heading out the door. His mother would call when she was ready for his help. It was about an hour later when she sent a message to his cellphone. *Coast is clear.* It wasn't like that, well maybe it was, the people and then Danni were almost too much to bear. He went back downstairs to the Baker's Dozen and found that she was blessedly alone.

"Coast is clear?" he asked, amused. "Mom, are we secret agents now?"

"The way you tore out of here, one would wonder," she replied. "Amy was tired, and Peter was yawning, so they left with Danni soon after."

"Okay."

His mother sighed in frustration. "She is a perfectly lovely girl."

He raised his hand. "No, Mom, just no. I don't want to go through anything like that again."

"Deke, you can't judge everyone by Claire."

"Mom, Danni has a glamorous life in New York. Look around Auke Bay. We are quaint and low key with no cameras or fancy cars. There's no glitz here, just us. Right now, we are unique, because we're new. By the time she's ready to go she'll be over it and us."

"I wish you weren't so jaded," his mother said as he wheeled the counter cases back out. "Baby, you lost a leg but you're giving up your entire life because of one bad thing that happened in a sea of good."

"Let it go, please," Declan begged. "What would she want with a man who has one leg, who has to get up at night and remind himself he's not in the middle of a war anymore? I know when you lost Dad, you grieved. We both did. But look at you—you are doing good alone. Why can't that be me?"

"The only person who sees you as broken is you. I hope one day that changes." His mother gave him a smile. "And I am not alone. I let love back in my life because your father wouldn't want me existing in this world without the warmth of someone's arms at Christmas."

"Wait, what? Who's in your life?" Declan demanded. "You never told me so I can scope them out and run a background check. This isn't some internet thing, is it?"

"Give me some credit, son," his mother scoffed. "It's Cooper. We have been spending time together, and he is a lovely man."

"I'll have to have a talk with him and find out his intentions," he said, half joking and half not.

"Figure out *your* intentions, before you lose a chance at love. Now I'm going to put my bread ingredients out before I leave. Finish up and go on to your life of solitude."

"I love you, Mom," he called to her retreating back.

"I love you, too. It's my fondest desire to hear you say those words to someone else who deserves it."

He didn't respond. What could Declan say to a mom who wanted to see him happy? Nothing could be forced, not like this. He had to heal and move on in his own way. She saw something in Danni, but he couldn't risk looking deeper. When she got into Cooper's plane again and headed back to New York, his heart would be safe and unshattered.

"Ice fishing, how is that a thing?" Danni asked Amy.

The besties were in her bedroom on Sunday afternoon while she got dressed. Danni's days were filled with enjoyable adventures or spending time with Amy. Apparently, ice fishing with Azure men was on her list the Sunday after the gingerbread house failure.

"One pair of long johns then these overalls, and then a parka...how will I even move, let alone fish?"

"You'll be fine, and you won't get frostbite," Amy answered, amused.

"Should we discuss that I don't know how to fish?'

"Mateo and Peter will teach you and Declan will be there," Amy walked slowly to the bed and sat down.

"I don't see why they want me there," Danni murmured. "Declan runs so hot and cold. One minute, he's smiling at me...the next, he's gruff as a bear with a thorn in his paw."

"Should that be a lion?" Amy asked.

"I went with the geography. Alaskan bears," she said lightly. "In any case, he's confusing, and I left New York to get away from confusing for a while."

"Don't overthink it, unless you like him," Amy gave her a curious glance. "Do you?"

Danni shrugged. "I don't not like him...remember those butterflies and the way your stomach flips you were talking about?"

Amy nodded.

"I feel that, but then I have to wonder. Am I projecting to see something that's not there?" Danni pulled her thick hair back and used a wide band to hold it in place.

Amy stood to help her. "For now, it's only fishing, so how about we focus on that?"

"If I fall through the ice, it's your fault," she told her friend.

"I'll take that risk," With a quick hug, Amy grinned. "Let's go downstairs."

"With all these layers, I'm like one of those toys that wobble," Danni grumbled.

Amy went down the stairs and Danni followed, seeing the men waiting for her in the kitchen.

Mateo flashed her a bright grin. "Ready for your first ice fishing adventure?"

"No," Danni said automatically. "But I'm going to give it the old college try."

Declan took a sip from his mug, amusement glinting in his eyes. "We won't let you fall through."

Danni sighed. "Gee, thanks for that."

Five minutes later they were on the road, and twenty after that, she was sitting under a small wooden house on the ice, with a hole and her fishing line inside it. Two structures, one for Mateo and Peter and one for her and

Declan, protected them from the biting wind as they fished. She watched Declan use a hand auger to make the hole into the thick ice. When the water bubbled up, Danni had a moment of terror and with a small squeak, she put her feet up on the wooden bench.

"I'm sorry to tell you that if the ice was cracking, putting your feet up there would do nothing to help." Declan chuckled.

Danni frowned. "You're supposed to be reassuring me."

"Pretty much sure that the ice isn't cracking, how's that?" Declan sat beside her and opened a small container. "Now we bait our lines and drop them into the hole."

Danni tried to peer into the container. "What's in there?"

Declan held up a small wiggling fish. "These guys."

"Oh no, they are so tiny, they didn't have a chance to live!" Danni said in dismay. "Can't we use something like bread from our sandwiches?"

Declan stared at her with mouth agape for a moment. "No, because big fish eat small fish and then we eat the bigger fish. It's called the circle of life."

"Poor Timothy, look at him," Danni felt heartbroken for the fish.

"Don't name the bait."

"Let's free Timothy and his friends."

Declan sighed. "Danni, if we dump the bait in there, all the fish will still eat them anyway."

"I can't do it. I'm going to use chunks of bread."

Declan shook his head and started to bait his hook. "Stop!"

He sighed in exasperation. "What now?"

"Don't use Timothy...use one I don't know. When

we're done can we free the rest. Timothy and his friends deserve a fighting chance."

"Fine," Declan shook his head and grumbled. "Timothy."

She used a thick piece of her bread to bait her hook and mimicked how he dropped his line in the water. They sat quietly and she began to hum. When Declan glowered at her, she stopped.

"So, we just sit here, not talking, waiting on a fish to bite?" Danni stage whispered.

"Talking scares the fish away," he told her. "Now hush."

A few minutes of silence reigned before Danni leaned into whisper. "How do they hear us if the ice is so thick?"

"Danni," he growled her name.

She grinned. "Inquiring minds want to know... Oh shoot, shoot! Something is pulling on my line!"

Excitement filled her as she followed Declan's direction on how to bring in the line slowly. At the end was a massive fish that wiggled on the ice while Declan got it free.

'It's huge!" Danni danced around. "Amy told me to catch her a big fish she can fry up and look at what I did!"

"It's a pretty good size one," he agreed.

Declan dropped her catch into the cooler and when he stood, Danni threw her arms around him. He automatically held on to her, pulling her close into the embrace. The mood changed and her breath caught when she looked up into his eyes.

"Great catch." Declan's voice was husky.

Danni stepped out of his grasp and cleared her throat. "Thanks."

She had no problem being quiet after that. Again,

the feelings he caused when he was close made Danni think. By the time Mateo came to their fishing shack and knocked on the door, Declan had caught two fish to her one.

"Peter is getting cold, time to head home," Mateo said.

"Okay," Danni said in a subdued voice and Peter ran in to hug her.

"I caught a fish, A-Danni did you catch one?" Peter asked.

She forced a stiff smile to her lips. "I sure did, let's go to the truck and get warm, while your dad and uncle get our stuff together."

"Everything all right, Danni?" Mateo asked in concern.

"Perfect," she answered in a bright voice.

It was the tone she used when pretending to be happy even if she wasn't. The don't-make-waves voice, that reminded her of how many times she gave into other people's plans, even Austin's. Danni had no clue what to do, how to react because this was all new to her. Never for a loss of words, she found that forming a phrase to explain the maelstrom within her was impossible. How could she, when Danni had no clue what they were?

Chapter Seven

HOW COULD HE STAY AWAY from someone who seemed to be everywhere? December seemed to fly by and the entire next week was busy as the date of the Auke Bay Festival rapidly approached. After another snowstorm, the mayor changed the date to five days before Christmas because there was no doubt the town would soon be buried in snow. It was in only a few days, which meant everyone was working in overdrive to get everything ready. After his shift ended, he volunteered to help, assisting his mother with her hot chocolate stand and layering circles on the top to look like candy wafers.

When Declan saw Danni on Main Street, she was leading a group of preschoolers down the street like baby ducks so they could practice at the community center. Amy was getting bigger. *It won't be long now,* Declan thought.

Each time he was close to Danni, he felt things. There was a sweet ache around his heart that terrified him. *Leave it to you to start falling for a woman out of your state and league,* he chastised himself. Declan planned to keep his feelings under wraps. He couldn't get hurt or be pitied if no one knew.

Five in the evening, and it was already dark. He set up the wooden candy canes on the stage at the community center. He didn't mind either setting them up *or* painting but with Auke Bay residents one couldn't get away with doing one and not the other.

Tom the music teacher was practicing music on the old piano, Selma was on stage setting up the props. Amy was resting with her feet up and Mateo did her bidding from her base command at the house. He made sure all the seats had a program, mini baggie of snow confetti, and a tiny tea light. Everyone pitched in to make sure everything was perfect.

A revving engine made him and Mateo look toward the door. It stopped suddenly and the sound became muffled. A cry made him rush to see if anyone was hurt. Mateo on his heels. What they found was a Ski-Doo with pink stripes in a thick snowbank, and Danni standing in a slushy puddle looking at the machine forlornly.

"Danni, you okay?" Mateo asked.

She looked up, chagrined. "It got away from me."

"Please be more careful," Mateo said. "We don't want you getting hurt."

"That was not my intent, trust me. It was going great but then I hit a spot of ice under the snow, I think, and I spun. The snow was a pretty soft landing, but I stepped into a sloshy mess, and my feet are soaked."

"Mateo, take care of your machine, make sure there's no damage," Declan said and held out his hand to Danni. "Come with me."

His large hand enclosed around her petite fingers, and he instantly felt a connection. Trying to keep his thoughts to himself and keep a straight face, he led her into the community center and into one of the back rooms. There were two chairs outside the room and with his hands on her shoulders he sat her down.

"Wait here," he said.

Danni looked around the doorway as he rummaged through the shelves. "What is this place?"

"We have a type of shelter for people who move here and then fall on bad luck. Our precinct is small, no storage, so what can't be stored there, or donations, are kept here until we need them." Declan pulled out thick socks and a pair of boots.

"These might be a tad too big, but the socks will compensate." Declan pulled the second chair in front of her before sitting down. He held out his hand again. "Give me your foot."

"I can do it—"

"*Foot.*"

Danni sighed and lifted her foot. She spoke while he unlaced her boot. "Suede boots in a place filled with snow was a bad idea."

"Probably," he said under his breath and then added, "Your feet are freezing. Be more careful. This can lead to frostbite."

"I will." The sound of her voice made him look up. She was watching him, and Declan looked away so he could work on her other shoe.

"Declan, I..." Danni stopped talking and pursed her lips.

"What?"

"Nothing, thanks for the shoes. I hope my boots can dry out before I go home. I'll look weird with these on."

"We couldn't have that." Danni moved her feet and he got up. "Why are you here, anyway?"

"Amy sent me down for a progress check and to look around," Danni answered. "I'll have to ride home with

Mateo if Pinky is damaged."

His mouth curled in a smile. "Pinky?"

Danni put her hands on her hips. "Yes, and what of it? Peter and I think she looks like a Pinky."

He held up his hand and backed away. "Nothing at all. Heaven forbid I offend you, Peter or... Pinky."

Danni raised one of her wet socks as if to throw it. "Oh, you're making funny of me."

"Definitely not." Declan laughed, surprising even himself, and he stopped suddenly. "I have to get back to my..." He pointed to the area where the stage was. "The decorations won't paint themselves."

She gave him a mock salute. "Yes sir. I'll follow you and take the required information back to headquarters."

"It must be driving Amy crazy she can't fuss over every detail," he commented.

"Literally, she's holding my cake hostage." Danni sighed dramatically.

He painted as she walked around the set asking questions, relating them back to Amy who was so impatient she called. Mateo talked to his wife on Danni's phone.

"It's all good, honey." Mateo shook his head with a small smile on his face. "*Ax já* we got this, I promise *kusaxdn*... Okay, bye. The Ski-Doo is fine. I want to send you home before the snow starts again."

Danni laughed. "I'm on the way. Your wife is nesting, and I'm helping. I promise to calm her and keep her occupied the best I can."

Declan heard the conversation as he went out the door and placed the paint cans securely back into the shed. It was best to keep the paints or any flammable products away from the main building. The community center was an invaluable place in their community. The

tribes who called Alaska their home used it for meetings. It was a warm place when the snow knocked out
power and there were no firewood stores for people who
didn't have money.

The community held weddings there and cultural
services sometimes. Declan made sure he and the other
officers stayed on top of the upkeep, because, if needed,
it was also shelter in the worst possible weather. He
was locking the shed when there was a splat against
his coat, then another one. He turned to see Danni
forming another snowball in her gloved hand, and he
ducked as she let it fly.

"For teasing me!" she called out with a laugh. His
chocolate brown eyes were alight with merriment, and
she sent another packed snow missile at him that he
dodged.

"You want a war, do you?" he called back and scooped
up a handful of snow.

Declan threw it with precision, and she squealed
when it hit her shoulder and splattered apart. That was
the beginning of the brief but entertaining scrimmage
that ended with Declan being the winner.

"Uncle! Uncle!" Danni cried out in the midst of her
laughter. He could listen to her laugh all day. The throaty
sweet noise that was reminiscent of babbling brooks of
spring and the sweet bells of Christmas.

Declan laughed. "See, don't start nothing, won't be
nothing!"

"I reserve the right to revisit this and regain my title
of snowball fight champion." Danni brushed snow off
her coat.

He opened his arms wide. "Any time, I'm a big target."

"Goodnight big target, thanks for the game." Danni
got on the snow machine with a wide smile on her face.

He raised his hand in a wave and walked back into the community center while she slowly got moving with a more careful handling of Pinky. The name made him smile. Mateo was lounging around by his candy canes, with his legs swinging casually as Declan walked up. A grin was on his face, and he looked at his friend and Trooper curiously.

"What's wrong with you?" Declan asked.

"Did I hear you laughing? Even better, there was a smile on your face," Mateo commented.

He shook his head. "I'm allowed to smile."

"Are you?" Mateo teased. "Never saw it. I almost thought your face was cracking."

"Ha-ha."

"Looks like Danni has made an impression," he commented. "I have it on good authority that she and her New York boyfriend are no more."

"I did not need that information." He moved one of his wooden candy canes to its exact spot because Amy was a stickler and would notice any variation from her plan. "She hit me with snowballs, reminded me of growing up."

"Uh-huh." Mateo gave the noncommittal reply. "Nothing to do with her being gorgeous and, for some reason, her face lighting up whenever she sees you."

"Does it?" Declan turned in surprise.

Mateo pointed. "Ah ha, I knew you were interested."

Declan sighed. "What would it even matter? She's going back to New York, and I'm staying here. While it seems all fun right now, what about the summer when the mosquitos are like small jets and you can see a bear in your yard? There are no fancy lunches here, no malls for shopping and fancy parties or teas. It's just regular old Auke Bay with a Sarge who has one leg and hates crowds. If there were two people who were complete and utter opposites, it's me and Danni St. Peters."

"Opposites attract and it doesn't take a lot of time. Look at me and Amy."

He shook his head. "Can we not discuss this? It stands to reason she wouldn't be happy here, and I won't be moving to New York. That would be the eventual choice and a hard one for either of us to make. It would lead to resentments and another…"

"Declan…" Mateo nudged him with his foot.

He blew out a frustrated sigh. "I'm not doing that again, putting my hopes into someone who understands malls and shopping more than she would a man from Auke Bay."

"Mateo, I need a ride back. The snowmobile stopped at the corner," Danni said softly from behind him. When Declan turned, he saw the hurt and sadness in her eyes.

"I'll wait in the truck. If I could get the keys, please." Danni held out her hand. He could see she wanted to be away from him. It was a kick in the gut, and he immediately regretted his words.

Mateo jumped down from the stage and handed her the keys. "Do you know how to start it?"

She nodded and didn't smile. "Thanks, I'll see you out there."

"Sure thing." Mateo gave Declan a look that could only mean *apologize.*

Danni darted away in the boots that were two sizes too big. The warmth of their interactions each time he saw her and the fact she didn't seem to care about his leg endeared him to her all the more. Her genuineness made him feel even worse.

"Danni!" he called and caught up to her quick tiny steps at the door. He put his hand on her shoulder.

"Hey, listen, I'm sorry."

"Why?" she asked much too brightly. "You're right. I'm an outsider with nothing but baubles and malls in my head."

"Okay, I deserved that, but it's not what I meant."

"Then what did you mean?"

"This isn't how you live," he said. "We're a novelty..."

She raised her hand. "Never mind, just to let you know, Amy and her family aren't just some new fad for me. Nor your mother or even you, for that matter. I love the people here, how everyone embraced me and laughed with me. I may be an outsider but at least I don't judge people without truly knowing them. My family..." She shook her head. "I'm never good enough as I am for anyone, am I? I'm always going to be judged first and have to prove myself." She swiped at tears that slipped down her cheek. "Mateo, I'll be in the truck."

Danni rushed out, and he put his hand against the door and leaned heavily against it. "I'm an idiot."

Mateo patted him on the back. "Yes, you are, but hey, now you can figure out how to fix it."

"Wait, what do you mean?" he called out to his friend whose laughter was the only response. Yeah, he got it, insert foot into mouth, time to step out of his comfort zone and make her smile again.

But what could he do? As people left and he locked up, Declan thought. A slow smile spread across his face. He secured the door of the community center and made sure the keypad code had been entered. He drove the short distance to Baker's Dozen, and luckily, his mother was still inside.

"I need a really good cake recipe, as simple as you got," Declan said as he strode through the door of the bakery.

She looked at him curiously. "Why, I can make a cake if—"

He cut her off. "It's an apology, so I need to do it myself."

"But Deke, you can't bake," she pointed out, her lips twitching with a smile.

"How hard can it be?" Declan asked. "I can follow directions."

"All right then." She pulled a box from under her desk and rummaged through the neat index cards that held her recipes. "This one has a secret ingredient that makes it amazing. And it's as simple as it gets."

He plucked it from her fingers and went through to the kitchen. "Thanks, Mom."

"I have to go for a little bit and help Cooper with some Christmas shopping. Lock up when you're done." She took off her apron and looped it over his neck. "Godspeed, Deke."

"I can handle this," Declan muttered while looking at the card.

After gathering the ingredients, he mixed together the sugar and the mayonnaise. Mayonnaise must've been the so-called secret ingredient, and he had serious doubts about it, but he trusted his mom. He added the water and vanilla extract, then sniffed the bottle and added a bit more. *It smells good, so more flavor,* he told himself. The recipe didn't say to turn off the mixer before adding the flour and cocoa powder, and it got everywhere.

But finally, he had a chocolate-y batter that he scooped it into the cake pan and slipped it into the oven. *Turn on the oven.* He turned back around and set the temperature that was listed on the card. He'd made a bit of a mess. Mayonnaise, sugar, and in fact, all of the ingredients were on the stainless steel counter, and there was a definite flour handprint on the fridge door.

Making a mental note to clean it before he left, Declan set out the ingredients to make the frosting. The cake came out over thirty minutes later, and by the time he looked at the clock it was after nine. It was semi-cool, and he tried to use the frosting but it melted, so he added a second coat. He appraised his finished work. It wasn't as good as the actual cakes at Baker's Dozen, but it was the thought that counted.

Is it lopsided? Nah, it's fine. Declan looked around and knew he would have to come back and clean up after he dropped off the cake gift. He wanted to apologize before Danni fell asleep. The thought of having her go to bed with hurt feelings made him feel worse. He locked up the bakery and with his creation in a box and sitting on the passenger seat of his car, drove to make his apology, hoping this wasn't an even bigger mistake.

Danni opened the door when he knocked. The house was already dim except for the crackling fireplace. The television was on, and the house was decorated for Christmas. It reminded Declan he hadn't even put up a tree. *When was the last time I celebrated Christmas? Or any holiday?* He always took the work shift so his deputies could have the day off. They always made him a plate, and he was slowly becoming accustomed to fireworks that went off around the summer holidays. At one point he would have to drive into Fairbanks and stay in a hotel to avoid the commotion.

"Declan?" She wore thick pajamas and a penguin hat.

"Penguin?" He couldn't take his eyes off her head-wear, or her, for that matter. It was as unique as her personality.

She put her hand on her head. "Peter and I were

playing before. I forgot to take it off. How can I help you, Sarge?"

It was cute and refreshing that she didn't try to drag the hat off in embarrassment.

The formality of his title made Declan wince, and he held out the box. "I made this for you, to say I'm sorry. For what I said to Mateo. I didn't mean any of it, Danni."

"You did," she surmised. "You think we are from two different worlds. Maybe we are but I'm not the flighty person you seem to think I am. I may make videos and be part of the nightlife of New York and California but when I'm at home, I'm plain old Danni from Brooklyn, wearing mismatched socks and watching TV."

He smiled at the mental image. "Can I come in?"

"You have a chocolate cake, of course you can." Danni opened the door wider. "I'll get us some milk, and you can have a slice with me."

Declan hesitated before entering. "Everyone asleep?"

"Amy went to bed as soon as we got back." Danni went around the kitchen island to the fridge and removed the milk. "Regular cold milk or hot chocolate?"

"It's cake, cold milk." Declan sat down at one of the tall chairs in front of the granite countertop.

Danni pointed at him. "You, sir, know how to eat dessert."

After filling two glasses she took from the cupboard over the sink with milk, Danni sat down beside him. She opened the paper cake holder that was barely keeping the cake together to reveal his very lopsided cake.

"I'm sorry it's not better. I tried," Declan apologized. "I did not inherit my mother's expertise."

Danni took two forks. "It's perfect. It may not hold up to cutting. Let's eat."

He watched as she put the first forkful into her mouth

and chewed thoughtfully before speaking. "*Mmmm.* As a cake connoisseur, this is definitely not bad."

"Really?" Declan asked, pleased.

She smiled and nodded. "Most positively."

He never knew he would find such contentment eating cake straight from the box. Combined with talking to a gregarious woman and her huge merry laugh she had to stifle once or twice, wearing a penguin hat, Declan felt like he won the Christmas lottery at that very moment.

"Can I ask you something?" asked Danni.

"Sure," he asked around a big bite of cake. It was actually really good.

"When Mateo was talking to Amy, he called her *Ax já,* I hope I'm saying it right. Then he said *Kusaxán.* What do those words mean?"

"That is one of the languages of the indigenous tribes who make Alaska their home," Declan explained. "*Ax já* is sweetheart, and *kusaxán* means love."

"They sound beautiful when he says it." Danni sighed. "Then again, what they have is amazing. A love like that is what we are all looking for."

"Even you?" Declan asked. "How would it fit in with your career?"

"I guess it would have to be with someone who wants to embrace the life I lead, or someone so worth it, I can change it around." She took a sip of her milk. "I can't eat any more. This is really good, Declan, thank you."

"Does that mean you forgive me?" he asked. "I'm rough around the edges, but I don't go around hurting people's feeling for no reason."

"I forgive you...friends?" Danni held out her hand.

He shook it. "Great, I don't need Amy hunting me down and calling me a cad."

Danni laughed. "We wouldn't want that."

Declan stood. "I'll be heading out now. Thanks for the talk."

She embraced him suddenly. "Thanks for caring about my feelings."

He held her, a little longer than necessary, because for such a long time, nothing had felt so right. Declan stepped away, unsure of his feelings, not understanding what it was about this woman that made him forget all his rules and past promises.

"Goodnight, Danni," he said huskily as he walked to the door.

"See you tomorrow at the gala." Danni grinned. "I'm excited to experience exactly what the Plaid Shirt Gala is all about."

"Another video for your channel?" Declan asked.

"You know what? I have barely even remembered that, since I've been here," she admitted. "G'night, Sarge Mathias."

She closed the door, and as he walked to the car, his phone buzzed in his pocket. Within the warmth of his car, he looked at the text.

Declan Monroe Matthias! The MESS!

He sighed. One more chore before he could go to bed.

Danni didn't know what to expect when they left for the Plaid Shirt gala three days before the festival. First, she was dressed in a red and black plaid shirt and jeans, and the stuffed moose antlers on her head jingled every time she moved. And second, she was heading to a place called Moose Tracks in the backseat of her friends' car, and they too were also dressed in various colors of plaid.

"Red, yellow, and green, aren't we festive," Amy said joyfully.

"You're just happy to be out of the house at this point." Mateo squeezed her hand as he spoke.

For a woman in the last leg of pregnancy, she was surprisingly upbeat and didn't want to stay home. If she had opted out, Danni would have stayed home with her and Peter. But while he was being babysat by one of the female students from the university, they were going to party...or not party? Danni shrugged. She would know soon enough.

"I take it this is also an annual tradition as well?" Danni said from her seat.

"Yep," Amy confirmed. "But in our defense, if we like something once in Auke Bay, we make it a tradition."

Danni shook her head in amusement. "I'll make a note of that. Hey, maybe I'll start one."

Mateo glanced in the rearview mirror at her. "That means you'd be coming back yearly to partake in said festivities per our town bylaws."

"Is that really a thing or are you pulling my leg?"

"You could move here," Amy said sagely.

Danni sat back and folded her arms. "And there we have it, trying to coerce me into moving here."

"Can you blame me?" Amy reached back and Danni took her hand. "It's been great having my best friend back. I don't want to give that up."

"We're here," Mateo announced breaking the serious moment between the two friends.

Danni got out of the back seat while Mateo helped his wife from the passenger side. Waiting for the couple, Danni looked up at the lighted Moose cartoon sign that blinked merrily in the night. The Moose Tracks Bar and Grill was a one-story building with a wide, wooden front porch that was stained red. It reminded Danni of a log cabin except for the rectangular windows that featured the menu and of course stenciled Christmas decorations.

Danni had to admit that while New York loved and celebrated Christmas in more expensive and lavish ways, the quaintness of Auke Bay and the simple, sweet decorations that meant something to each resident drew her in. Here, Christmas wasn't commercialized. Community had a meaning to everyone, and as she lived with them and learned about them, it meant something to her, too.

When they entered, it was no night club with lighted ice bars and a DJ pumping loud music through massive speakers where she couldn't hear herself think.

Instead, the booths remained while all the tables and chairs were moved to line the edges of the large room. Inside was a Christmas tree that made her laugh because all the decorations on the fresh fir tree were of a moose in various forms of holiday activities. From skiing to wrapping gifts, there was a moose wearing plaid and enjoying the season. It was the most unique thing she had ever seen in her life.

Mistletoe hung everywhere with holly and fresh garland, and the smell of the entire place was wonderful and fresh. In all honesty, it was the first time Danni had seen a live Christmas tree complete with a natural pine scent instead of the stuff from a can. Moose Tracks was already alive with activity and a few couples were dancing to "Rockin' Around the Christmas Tree."

They were all faces she had come to know, and their festive greetings made Danni feel warm and at home. No matter what kind of viewership or notoriety she ever got from *Danni on the Run,* between all the faces of New

York she could still feel unseen.

Her eyes searched the room and settled on Declan. Her heart skipped a beat when she saw him in the corner talking to two guys and when their gaze connected. She raised her hand in a small wave, noting that he was wearing red plaid as well with his faded blue jeans. He raised his glass in response, and Danni turned away to find where Mateo and Any were sitting.

"Oh no." Mateo steered her from sitting down. "You're the first guest we have had at this shindig ever. You need to give the moose a gift!"

"The who, a what now?" Danni glanced at Amy dubiously.

Amy shrugged. "I had to do it."

"This isn't an actual moose you have outside or something?" Danni asked as he pushed her forward.

Mateo laughed. "If it was, you'd high tail it out of here."

"You are right." Danni looked up at the moose head that hang on the far wall. It wore sunglasses, and on the antlers were hats, earmuffs, beads. "Oh, I need to video of all of this."

"Not now." Mateo bent to murmur in her ear. "Live in the moment, *dlaak*."

She looked up at him. "What does that mean?"

Mateo's smile was wide. "Sister, and those sunglasses are Amy's. It's his signature look now."

Danni grinned. "Very chic."

Danni dug around in her satchel, hoping to find something she could place on the moose. What may seem silly was very important to the people of Auke Bay and her hand closed around a soft, rolled up bundle.

"Hey everyone, the moose is getting a new gift," Mateo called out. Danni then realized this wasn't just something she did and walked away. "Danni has blessed us with sharing the holidays in Auke Bay, and now she's embracing everything we know and love. Whatcha got?"

All eyes turned on her, and she was more acutely away of Declan's eyes most of all.

She cleared her throat. "Okay, so Amy and I have been best friends since we were kids, and she knew how much I wanted to travel. My first trip, I went to Paris."

"Ooh la la," someone teased.

"Shh, Drew, let her speak," said Amy.

"It's fine." Danni laughed and pulled the bundle out of her bag. "I was scared senseless to travel on my own, and to give me some courage, I put these in my bag. It's a pair of socks Amy gave me for my sixteenth birthday, and they have traveled with me ever since. So now I'm going to leave one here at Moose Tracks in Auke Bay and take the other one with me. Because I've found a second home here, and that's where she is."

Awwwww, the crowd cooed while Danni took one of the pink socks with unicorns and placed it over a single point of the moose's antler. There was a round of cheers, and when Danni made her way back to Amy, her friend was wiping away tears.

"I can't believe you kept those things all these years." Amy gave Danni a watery smile. "I bought them for ninety-nine cents at the bodega." Those words trailed off on a wail, and Amy was crying all over again while Danni patted her back.

"Would an ice cream float make you stop crying?"

"Yes," Amy hiccupped between her sobs.

"I'm on it." Mateo patted his wife's shoulder and went to the bar.

It took only a few minutes of Amy happily sipping on her very thick drink for the smiles to come back, and

Mateo also brought Danni a raisin beer. Unsure, Danni tasted it tentatively, and it was good! She usually hated anything beer-related, but this had a sweet flavor that reminded her of dessert, and Danni certainly loved that.

The party progressed, and she watched couples repeatedly kiss under the mistletoe, including Cooper and Susie. They made a cute couple, and as Danni flitted around from the food to the bar and talked to people, she saw Declan more than once. Somehow, they gravitated toward each other just as the DJ played "Have Yourself a Merry Little Christmas."

"Dance with me." Declan held out his hand.

With a smile and nod, Danni took his hand. He held her close, swaying to the soft tunes of the music.

"That was sweet, the Moose gift." His tone was a deep timber as he looked down at her. "You hold on to things that matter in your life, even if it seems simple to others."

Can he feel my heart beating? Danni wondered, but she pushed that thought aside as they danced.

"People think it's strange, but I have a box that has mementos that I treasure," Danni admitted. "I even have ticket stubs from the first movie I was allowed to go to alone. It's like landmarks in…"

"Your life," Declan finished for her. "I get it. Want to know a secret?"

She nodded as he swung her gently. "Sure, I'm also known to be a vault."

"I still have my teddy bear and blanket I slept with," he whispered. "I hope one day to pass it on to my first son or daughter. Until we settled here, being in a military family we traveled a lot, and they were a constant. I want them to feel that very same thing as they grow up."

"Can I say that is the sweetest thing I ever heard?" Danni melted just a bit at that admission.

"Stop it."

"Well, Sarge Mathias, I swear you are blushing," she teased.

The song ended, and he kissed her hand. "Thank you for the dance."

"You're welcome." Before she could turn to move, the music changed to a fast beat.

"Come on Danni, this is a line dance," Susie encouraged as she took position with Cooper.

"I don't know how to do any of this," Danni said. "This takes the coordination of a person who doesn't fall upstairs."

Susie laughed. "Deke has zero rhythm in his soul, plus our people are from New Orleans. If he can do it, you can do it."

Danni shrugged. "When in Rome."

She watched as more people joined the group who were now moving in tandem with the music. Who knew you could line dance to Loretta Lynn's "Country Christmas"? Soon she caught the beat and was actually not tripping over her own feet. Danni couldn't help the laughter of pure joy that escaped her lips.

Danni tilted her head back and let the sound escape, feeling freer than she had in a long time. Declan was staring at her with a small smile on his lips. That connection of their gazes said so much without words. They shared another slow dance to "Hard Candy Christmas," and while Danni never listened to the country music genre, each of these songs were etched in her memories for a lifetime. In the middle of the Plaid Shirt Christmas Gala, Danni wondered if this was what Amy meant about butterflies taking flight in her stomach. Was it the first hint of love? The thought alone terrified Danni.

What if it really is? What happens then?

Chapter Eight

SUNDAY BROUGHT WARMER TEMPERATURES, OR so Amy and Mateo said. Danni still considered thirty-five degrees stay-inside weather, but to them it was downright balmy, so she rolled with it. The house was warm, and beneath the tree, the pile of presents had grown. Danni loved her friend's tradition. Peter thought Santa Claus brought the huge main gifts for Christmas while Mommy and Daddy bought some too.

The day after the festival where Danni had the time of her life, everyone was home. The fire in the fireplace crackled and on the coffee table in front of them was an assortment of Amy's products and some new items Danni had helped her create. They came upon a business idea: trying recipes for skin care. It was something they had discussed doing long ago, being business partners. It could work even if she was back in New York.

They both wore bright pink flannel pajamas with the sleeves rolled up and white terrycloth headbands kept their hair piled high. The television played one of the 80's movies they grew up watching and three more waited in the queue. Mateo deemed it a good day to barbeque, while Danni was skeptical that anything was going to cook in the cold.

Amy assured her that Mateo and his family had been doing this for generations and their smokers were built specifically to withstand the wintery weather. Danni kept forgetting that Alaska had about four months of warm weather; of course they would figure out how to cook in the ice and snow.

She already planned to return the next year when the baby was older. Mateo promised to take her out with the family, and they would stay in the family tent. Amy explained that the tent was huge and warm. There was even a stove pipe that could go up in the center and a travel stove that kept the inside warm.

"Ready for spa day?" Danni asked.

"Ma'am, yes ma'am," Amy gave a mock salute. "Checking off the list. Honeycomb face mask?"

"Check," Danni answered.

"Honey and herbal face scrub?"

"Check."

"Eucalyptus sea salt foot spa blend?"

"Check." Danni help up a finger. "And before you ask, I have the pumice hand stones that Mateo got for us and smoothed down, plus nail polish."

"And finally, the clay hand dips and clover mint hand oil." Amy looked over her clipboard.

Danni gave her the thumbs up. "Check. Amy this is all going to be so amazing when we start jarring and listing them on my channel."

"With *Danni on the Run* telling the world about the products, we should have some cool sales." Amy winked. "Thank you for the idea and joining me on this."

"This is all you," Danni grinned. "The good thing is we won't really start until next year when you can harvest the products and in the small window for the summer months where you can make them. It's first come, first serve. The waiting list will be packed for the next year's stock."

Amy did her little pregnancy dance. "Perfect for me since I'll still be teaching. Honestly, while I love it, the pay isn't great here, and I needed a second income that wouldn't take me away from the kids."

"Let's do this." Danni rubbed her hands. "I'm excited to try all of it."

"Peter and Mateo are outside in the shed, finishing up the drawers and making a table while he barbeques. They both have snacks." Amy laughed. "I think we have all afternoon."

The duo began with the foot scrubs and then moved on to the hand masks. Between them, they nibbled on fruit and Greek yogurts while talking about anything and everything. Danni couldn't remember when she had laughed so much, reminiscing about growing up together and all the sleepovers. The face mask went on, first of the two-step treatment when one of their favorite parts of the movie came on.

"The dance on the desks!" Danni exclaimed. "Remember? We used to do this all the time!"

"We should do it now." Amy got up the best she could with her burgeoning belly and waved her over. "Come on."

Laughing, Danni followed suit and forwarded the disk in the Blu-ray player to the exact part they needed. Recreating their childhood like best friends always seemed to happen when they were together. They were engrossed in their own little world until Amy stopped and tapped her on the shoulder.

"What?" Danni laughed. "Forgot the moves already?"

"Um no, we have witnesses."

Danni slowly turned. Standing at the end of the living room was Mateo, Peter, and Declan. Poor Peter looked confused while Mateo was grinning, holding his cell phone up, and Declan was just amused. He leaned against one of the mahogany pillars with folded arms, taking in the scene before him.

"You better not have recorded anything, Mateo," Amy warned.

"I did, and I'm keeping it for all future forms of blackmail." Mateo laughed. "What are you two doing and with that goop on your face?"

"They look like Mommy and A-Danni ick monsters," Peter pointed out.

"This is our face mask, and we are…dancing," Danni said a little breathlessly. "We may have to use the witnesses as unwilling experiments, Amy."

Declan held up his hands. "Hey, I see nothing, I know nothing. That gives me immunity from this, right? It's Mateo's house, and he has the camera."

"You are guilty by association, so you go down with your crew, buddy," Danni teased.

Mateo moved toward the patio door. "Move slowly, Declan, and never break eye contact. They can move fast, these goop monsters."

Amy made a growling sound, and Peter laughed before screaming and heading out the door. The men followed, and Declan cast one last glance to Danni, sending her a wink before the men folk were safely outside.

"You didn't tell me Declan was coming over," Danni said as they moved to sit on the sofa again.

"I wasn't privy to that information, either." Amy took her water with sliced strawberries off the table and drank through the twisty straw. "I saw that wink and then your smile. You guys have hit it off."

Danni shook her head. "We're friends, nothing more."

"I felt that chemistry. It could be more," Amy pointed out.

"No, it can't."

"Why not? Because of Austin? Has he even called since you've been here?"

"He's texted and I've responded." She sighed. "Amy, I live in New York and Declan lives here. He sees me as this flighty woman who thinks of malls and shopping more than anything else."

"When did he say that?" Amy asked. "He doesn't know you like that to assume."

"The day you woke up and there was a half-eaten badly made cake on the counter. He made it as an apology," Danni explained. "But can I blame him? Everyone has some kind of perception of me. My parents think I'm wasting my life. Austin thinks I need him to make me a star. Now Declan thinks I'm a socialite. I accepted his apology but it's still in the back of my head."

"Well, I know for a fact, you are the most loving, caring person I have ever met," Amy announced. "I want to go throw a lemon at him in the yard."

A laugh sputtered out of Danni. "Don't do that."

"I can see it any time he's around, you like him," Amy said.

"I like dessert but that doesn't mean it's good for me." Danni sipped at her drink for a moment. "We are from two different worlds. It's not meant to be."

"And yet you can't pass by Baker's Dozen without buying some kind of treat," Amy said, amused. "I won't talk about it anymore, but I will say this. Things have a way of sneaking up on you when it comes to love."

"Hmmm, I'll take your word for it. I have never been in love."

Amy grinned. "I can't wait until you are, and I think it will be soon."

"Time to get this stuff off our faces and use the scrub." Danni chose to ignore her friend's words and went back to their afternoon of pampering.

They heard the electric saw and hammering along with the laughter and the men and Peter outside talking. By the time dinner was on the table, there was smoked chicken, corn from their small garden that had been frozen before fall, and macaroni salad. Declan didn't stay for dinner, and Danni pushed away the sense of disappointment when she didn't even see him to say goodbye. But she loved dinners with Amy and her family; they were always filled with conversation.

"Mateo, may I ask how the Inuit kiss started in your culture?" Danni used her fork to twist off a piece of chicken. "I've learned that 'Eskimo' is offensive to your culture, and I apologize if I ever used it around you."

"You never did. And you're learning and trying to be respectful, so that's what matters." Mateo chewed thoughtfully. "I could make up something all sage and wise, but it's really simple. In the winters especially further north as the tribes traveled, the colder it is, and the winters are very harsh. Places like Narvik and other areas had even more snow that we do, and the temperatures are so cold the only thing seen through the furs and thick clothing was the eyes and noses when we take off our face protection. Rubbing noses as a way of greeting between friends is also a sign of affection."

"Cute and practical," Danni said. "I love the snowstorms you have here."

"Oh, these are just little dust-ups," Amy said. "In

areas like that, you can't get out for months when the snow comes down. It's called whiteout conditions, and if you lose your way, it can be dangerous. The residents of some of these places have poles with ropes leading from building to homes so they can travel in the winds and snow if they have to. I'm hoping the big ones stay away until after you leave. Coop can't fly and has a heck of a time getting anything in and out of town."

"Or maybe she hopes you can get stuck for a while longer," Mateo teased with a knowing look. "I'm sure Declan wouldn't mind."

Danni rolled her eyes. "Declan doesn't care if I stay or go. He is an island unto himself."

"Declan reminds me of one of the legends of the Inuit people, *Tikta Liktak.*" Mateo's smile was always so knowing and gentle with a wisdom that belied his age. "He was a young warrior who was lost and floated away on an ice floe. With despair in his every step, he finally made it to a barren land where he was marooned and thought he would never see his family again. He fought the weather and a polar bear, so many different adversities, to make it home to the people he loved."

Danni stopped eating, drawn into the story. "How do you relate that to Declan?"

"He made it back to his own lands each time and Declan left again, became a warrior. Each time he came home, it was a triumph," Mateo explained. "The last time injured and unsure, he expected the one he loved to be there for him, and she turned away. It has to be a hard loss to bear. When he came back to Auke Bay, we embraced him because our lost brother was home, and he made this town and protecting us his life. But the heartache and the scars are deep. He lost a leg and so much more. We as his people can only be a balm...

to heal his heart, he needs love again."

Danni didn't know what to say. Mateo's eyes said exactly what he meant, and she had to look away. There was more to his story and hers, and maybe those worlds couldn't be combined. After dinner was done and everyone had gone to bed for the night, Danni laid on her bed staring up at the ceiling with so many thoughts running thought her head. Her cell phone dinged from beside her. It was a message from Austin.

How's it going?

On impulse she pressed his number, hoping that hearing his voice would give her some insight into choices that had to be made.

Austin answered on the third ring. "Hey Danni, how's Alaska?"

"Cold," she said with a smile and then listened to the background noise. "Are you at a party?"

"A little Christmas thing my parents put together every year. If you were here, it would be much more fun. When are you coming home?"

"Two more weeks," she replied. "I should let you go. I'm glad you're spending time with your family."

"I can't wait until you get back. Things will be different," Austin promised. "I may have a surprise up my sleeve for New Year's Eve."

"Can't wait," Danni feigned excitement. "Bye Austin, Merry Christmas."

"Merry Christmas Danni, miss you," Austin said before he hung up.

The need to speak to her parents suddenly overwhelmed her, and she called her mother's cellphone. Sandra St. Peters answered on the second ring.

"Hello?" Her voice was soft and always filled Danni with warmth.

"Hi Mom," Danni said with a smile.

"Danni, is this your number?" her mother said in surprise.

Danni laughed. "It's been the same for a while, Mom. How about you let Jackson or one of the boys program names into your phone for you?"

"I keep forgetting to do that." A big sigh came from the other end of the line. "I hate these phones. Let me and Dad figure out how to put this thing on speaker."

"Press the little speaker icon..." Danni shook her head hearing her mom and dad complain about technology.

"Danni can you hear me, it's Dad," her father practically shouted.

She held back a laugh before she spoke. "Yes, Dad, I can hear you."

"Now I know you're on a trip visiting Amy, how are you doing?"

"I really like it here, and Amy is going to have a baby soon." Danni recounted some of her events and things she'd done. They listened to her and asked questions, showing real interest in what she was doing.

"That sounds like a great trip, baby girl," her father said. "Maybe one day your mother and I will take a cruise to Alaska."

"You both would love it." Danni hesitated. "Mom... Dad, are you guys really disappointed in me?"

She heard a deep sigh escaped her father. "Danni, it is never my...our intention to make you think that. While I wish you had a more stable lifestyle, I can only be proud of the bravery I see in you."

"From the time you were little girl, you always had that fire in you to be adventurous," added her mother. "So, we worry, yes. But disappointed? No."

"Thanks, Mom." Danni tried to keep from crying at

their words. "I know you guys are probably packing to leave, so I'll let you get to it. Travel safe, love you both."

"Send us pictures of the northern lights and we'll figure out how to see them on this phone," Edward St. Peters said. "And we love you too."

After disconnecting she looked at the phone and dropped it on the blankets with a deep sigh. Her parents' words comforted her but there was a long way to go, and her mind shifted to Austin. Was Austin trying? Were they right for each other? That was another thing she would have to figure out. Talking to him didn't give her any answers or decipherable feelings—in fact, she had more questions. Danni rolled over and muffled a small scream of frustration into her pillow. *Can we rewind to the days when I danced to teen movies and crushed on cute heartthrobs please?* Adulting was harder than she ever realized when it came to her heart.

"Deke, do you need some help with that thing?" Susie Matthias asked.

Declan, hard at work on her large storage shed, he held back a sigh before looking over his shoulder. "I'm good, Mom."

In the warm months, he'd moved the structure closer to the main building that housed the bakery and his apartment. A family of bears had gotten into it, and of course, they'd eaten bags and bags of her chocolate melts, flour, honey, candy, and anything they could get their greedy paws on. The downside of living side-by-side with nature was that it sometimes walked up to the door and invited itself to lunch.

Declan added more insulation and reinforced the door with metal sheets. His mother would now use storage bins on the shelves. As well as holding in the scent of food, the structure was bear-proofed. Even if the animals tried, they would fail.

Everything had been contaminated by the furry burglars and had been thrown away, regardless of whether it had been opened or not. The kitchen was crammed with all her new goods. Declan got the last of the shelving in so she could have her counter space back. By the next day she would be happy and smiling again, because his mother hated clutter. That was one thing she had passed on to him; he was a man who liked things a certain way as well.

"When you're done, Coop is coming over to help us get things back in order in there," his mother said as she moved past him carrying a food bin and placing it on the floor. She had decided to start getting things in now so they would only have to be placed on the shelves later.

"Been hearing his name more often than not lately," Declan commented, and the electric drill cut off his words. "Mom, do not pick up those bags of flour. I'll get them with the dolly."

"I'm not helpless, Declan Monroe," she said with her hands on her hips. "I have been seeing Cooper for over six months, and yes, his name will come up more now that you know about our relationship."

"Aren't you moving a bit too fast?" Declan asked doubtfully.

"Deke, I am sixty-five years old. There is no slow when it comes to love," his mother answered. "You should take a page from my book and move with quickness toward Danni."

"Mom, don't start," he pleaded.

"I will start. Take her for a snowmobile ride to the glacier and drink hot chocolate, ask her out on a date," his mother fussed at him. "Or she will go back to New York thinking you friend-zoned her, when anyone can see you two have a connection."

"Friend-zoned? Where do you learn such language?"

"Hey, I have hip and cool friends from the university." She left and in minutes came back with another bin. "I'll have you know they think I'm the bee's knees."

"Not using that phrase." He chuckled.

"Would it be so bad to take a deep breath and jump in the deep end?" she asked.

"If it's going to drown me, yes." Declan put down the tool and tested the metal shelf before he turned to her. "She has a guy, maybe, in New York, and... I just don't know."

"There's a maybe in that sentence, and from what I hear from Amy, Danni doesn't get that zing when she's with him." His mother dropped that bit of gossip into the conversation.

"And does she get that with me?" Declan asked. Was it wrong to hope that Danni just might feel the same things that he did when he was anywhere near her?

"You won't know unless you find out for yourself." Her words were gentle. "Jump in, baby boy, and be surprised at the results."

"I don't know. I may not be good at any of this."

"Or maybe you are." She smiled. "I need to talk to you about something. I want you to take the house."

He looked at her in surprise. "You cannot be going up and down the stairs to the apartment, especially in the winter."

"I wasn't planning on it. Cooper and I are going to get married, and I'm going to live with him." Her eyes twinkled happily as she spoke.

"Way to drop a bomb, Mom!" Declan moved to hug her, and he looked at his mother with affection on his face. "Are you sure this is what you want?"

She put her hand over her heart. "He fills that empty place left when I lost your father. I will always love him, but this new love...it makes me feel whole again."

"Then I am happy for you. I only ever wanted you to be happy."

"And I am. That house was filled with love and happiness, now I want you to take it and make it your own." She patted his cheek. "Make a life and home there, a family...maybe with Danni?"

A laugh escaped him. "You will never quit matchmaking."

"Not when it comes to my son, I won't."

The bell over the front door jingled and a voice called out. "Hello, anyone here?"

"Back here, Cooper," his mother called. "Deke is almost done with the shelves."

Cooper came through to the kitchen holding his old worn hat in his hands. His smile reached the corner of his blue eyes, and Declan could see the love the old man had for his mother. How had he not seen it before? Cooper hugged his mother warmly before facing Declan, holding her hand.

"Sarge," Cooper said.

Declan nodded without a smile. "Coop."

"Susie told you our news?"

"In a roundabout way, yeah." Declan couldn't stand to see the nervousness on the poor man's face and broke into a smile as he held out his hand. "Congratulations.

Be good to my mom, because I have the keys to the jail."

Cooper shook his hand. "She will be my world, I promise."

"And none of that hot-shot flying when my mom in the passenger seat," Declan warned.

"Never," Cooper promised. "I won't be doing much more of that, only for fun. Come spring, my nephew is going to take over the business, and I'm semi-retiring except for some trips to some of the 'out the road' villages until they get accustomed to Vince."

"What do you plan to do in retirement?" Declan asked.

"Travel. We're going to Italy and Nepal next year in September," his mother answered. "And when we're here, he'll work with me. Cooper has a knack for pies."

"My rhubarb pie won first place in Anchorage last year," Cooper said proudly.

"Molly is going to manage the bakery while I'm gone." His mother kissed Cooper's cheek. The old man had actually trimmed his beard and hair. "But we are going to try to see at least one place on our bucket list yearly."

"When is the wedding?" he asked.

"We want something small, so in January at the community center," Copper answered. "Only a few weeks away."

"You guys have it all planned out," Declan said. His mother's bravery, her sense of self and happiness inspired him. Maybe he would take that leap...maybe.

"Let's get this kitchen cleaned out and all the stock back in place." Copper slipped his coat off and hung it on the hook on the opposite side of the wall.

"I've bear-proofed this thing so much that for them to get in it, they will need to develop safe-cracking skills," said Declan.

"Susie Esther Mathias, don't you touch those bags of flour. Either me or Declan will get them into storage," Copper said to his fiancée.

"Thank you!" Declan exclaimed and clapped Cooper on the back. "It's good to have someone to keep this stubborn woman in line."

His mother laughed. "If that happens, it will be a Christmas miracle."

"What about you, Declan, when are you going to ask the lovely Danni out on a date?" Cooper asked.

"Not you, too," he groaned. "Don't let my mother drag you into her matchmaking schemes."

"Hmph. Thank you, Cooper, for voicing what I have been saying," his mother said in a satisfied voice. "It works both ways, Deke. He can be on my side, too."

"That girl is one of the sweetest people I've ever met," Cooper declared. "She wears my scarf everywhere. It tickles me silly to see that she does."

"If I promise to think about it, will you two leave me alone?" Declan sighed.

"Scout's honor." Cooper held up his hand.

His mother smiled sweetly. "That's all I ask, dear."

"Funny, it sounds like so much more."

"Am I now?" she replied and winked. "Maybe your perception is really what you want and you're subconsciously pushing it off on me."

"Uh-huh."

Declan shook his head, knowing when the conversation wouldn't go in his favor. Together, the threesome worked together to return his mother's kitchen to its perfect state, and the atmosphere was comfortable as they chatted easily. All the while Declan wondered, should he, could he? One thing was for certain: his life had definitely changed since Danni St. Peters came to town.

Chapter Nine

I T WAS LIKE LIFE KEPT throwing opportunities his way to spend time with Danni. The Northern Lights Festival was the next day, and with the fluffy snow that fell softly in the afternoon, there was a buzz of activity in the town. Since his return to Juneau and Auke Bay, Declan had his own traditions. One was important to him because of Mateo and the people who lived in the smaller villages they fondly called "out the road." Some of the indigenous people who lived in these towns didn't have much at all in the way of material things. They hunted, raised animals, and farmed in the summer so that in the winter they had food.

They sold their crafts and different wares all over, from town all the way into Anchorage with people like Cooper taking items into towns and bringing back the money. It was an honor system, and it worked when good people were involved. More than once, he had to intervene when out-of-towners talked residents into a deal that ended up with the money being stolen. He was not one to stand by and see good, trusting people suffer, and if that meant flying into Anchorage or Fairbanks to see justice done, then so be it.

But for the holidays, they were not people who had a lot in the way of financial resources. Gifts for their children and family were made from the heart. That was where he came in; Declan and Mateo took turns becoming Santa each year, with a snowmobile trailer pack carrying presents for children and adults alike and covered with a red tarp. Yep, this was his year to be jolly and jovial, regardless of his introverted nature. They always picked the town in the center of the "out the road" villages that everyone could reach easily, and they celebrated. Even the local leaders, wise and old, attended to give their blessings, and that included the elder who was seen as the wisest person to many of the people.

This year his Mrs. Claus was out of commission. His mother caught a cold and actually hated snowmobiles more than anyone he'd ever met. Amy, who would've been his back-up, was so close to having a baby, they were all holding their breath waiting for the call. Needing to head out soon, Danni's name came into his mind. With his snowmobile packed for the trip, he headed to the Azure homestead.

On impulse he added soup, sandwiches, and hot chocolate. *Couldn't hurt, right?* Parking the snowmobile in the snow was easy, and he swung his leg over and got his footing steady before he walked up the driveway, carrying the bag that held the costume. Declan waited patiently after he rang the doorbell, and it was Amy who answered the door. *That's why it took so long.* Declan kept that thought to himself, knowing she had to be uncomfortable.

"Hey Santa, you are way early. Did you lose your calendar?" Amy teased as she stepped back to let him inside.

"Funny." Declan looked down at his red pants. "Can I come in?"

"Sure, coffee?" Amy asked. "I can't drink it, but I can smell it while I make it for Mateo and Danni."

"While I wouldn't say no to a cup, I was hoping Danni was up?" Declan asked.

"Sure, let me get her." Amy stood at the bottom of the stairs and called out, "Danni St. Peters, you have a visitor."

Danni came bounding down the steps, still in her pajamas. "What visitor? I literally don't even have them in New York."

"Well, here's your first." Amy pointed at Declan with a flourish of her hand.

"Oh...well. Good morning, I guess?" Danni's brows furrowed. "What can I do for you and why are you wearing Santa's pants?"

"Mom can't make the trip to the villages for the Christmas party, and I was hoping you wouldn't mind dressing up as Mrs. Claus and going with me? My other go-to for Mrs. Claus is standing right next to you, and she should not be doing anything but putting her feet up."

"If one more person says that..." Amy warned.

Danni stage whispered, "She's a tad cranky in the mornings with no caffeine now."

"I can tell," Declan said, amused. "So, up for an adventure?"

She smiled. "Sure...why not? Let me get changed."

He handed her the costume. "You'll be wearing this. Maybe Amy could help you with the wig, while you change? I have zero clue about that part."

"I have thermal long johns I wear under it that you can borrow and good boots," Amy said, grinning widely.

"Let's get you transformed into Mrs. Claus! Declan, grab some coffee and a flapjack or two. Mateo will be back down in a sec, he spilled syrup on himself. Here he comes now."

"Thanks," Declan answered. "I won't say no to his flapjacks, either."

Mateo passed them on the stairs and looked curiously at the two women as they went upstairs with the garment bag.

"What's that about?" Mateo asked Declan as he passed behind him in the kitchen. "Dude, do you want a plate?"

"Better this way." Declan folded the flapjack and took a bite before grinning around a mouthful of food. He chewed and swallowed. "Danni is going to be Mrs. Claus at the villages with me today."

"Oh really." Mateo fixed a plate for Peter and poured juice in a Star Wars cup.

"Stop with the voice," he warned. "I need the help, nothing more."

Mateo held up his hand and feigned innocence. "Hey, I'm not saying a thing."

Declan pointed his flapjack at him. "It's the voice you use, the 'oh so that's a new thing, look at you heh-heh-heh,' all-knowing way you say it."

Mateo burst out laughing. "You get all that from a tone in my words?"

"It's just a day trip," Declan said firmly.

"Do you have food?" Mateo asked.

"Yes..."

"It's a snow picnic, very romantic," Mateo cut him off.

"Why am I your friend?" Declan muttered.

"Because you're so grumpy, no one else would have you," Mateo said good-naturedly. "In all seriousness, my brother, have fun."

"Yeah, I plan on it."

Declan heaved out a sigh of nervousness. Was he making a mistake by asking her? It was too late now, especially when ten minutes later she came down in the red Mrs. Claus costume with the apron tied neatly around her waist. How had Amy gotten Danni's hair to fit under the wig? He knew better than to ask women their secrets. She definitely made a cute Santa's better half and Declan found himself smiling at her when she walked into the kitchen.

"Mrs. Claus, ready for duty." Danni did a little twirl. "I have my regular clothes to change in for the trip home."

"You look marvelous, doesn't she Declan?" Mateo said.

"She does. Thank you for doing this," he told her.

"You offered an adventure, who could say no to that?" Danni laughed. "Do I need to get Pinky ready?"

He shook his head. "It's some rough terrain, you'll be behind me. I have the snowmobile trailer hitched. It keeps us safer that way. We'll be going over some frozen river ice as well."

"Uhhhh, why do I feel like I did when Cooper said he could land on a frozen river?" Danni asked.

"Danni, the ice is so thick that for ice fishing we need an auger or chainsaw to cut through it," Declan assured her. "You'll be safe with me, I promise."

"Okay." Danni put her hands on her hips. "Don't let me become a popsicle, okay?"

"I definitely won't," he promised. "You have fifteen minutes to have breakfast before we get on the road. It's about two hours on snowmobile each way. By the time we head back, the sun will be setting."

"Take your phone," Amy encouraged. "It won't work

for calls, but you can get some amazing pictures of the sunset over the ice."

Danni pulled it out of her pocket. "Already got it."

"You better eat quick before Peter gets up and sees you two," Mateo warned with a laugh. "We don't need him to think we have a direct line to Santa."

"Good point." Amy put a plate and a cup of coffee in front of Danni. "Eat up."

It was twenty minutes before they actually got outside. Danni wore a thick coat over her costume and an extra pair of weather-proofed pants to go over the leggings. With the gloves on and the mask over her nose and mouth, the only thing Declan could see was the warmth of her brown eyes.

He helped her with the goggles before pulling the thick, fur-lined hood over her head. Declan got his own gear in place and threw his leg over on the snowmobile and got comfortably seated before he helped her get on behind him. He used the belt of his parka to give her additional ways to keep a tight hold on him. Silently, he showed her on one side how to make sure her hand went up and under to hold on like a harness, and Danni did the next side on her own.

"Ready?" His voice was muffled under his own face covering.

"As I'll ever be."

"Hold on tight," he called out.

Declan started the engine of the snowmobile, letting it run for a few minutes to get warm before he moved slowly away. He took it easy through the side streets of Auke Bay as he drove to the outskirts of town. When the snow got thicker, he increased his speed, and the machine glided through the snow easily, kicking up snowflakes from the snowfall. The skis on the bottom took them farther from home and into the wilderness. Whenever they hit a bump, she tightened her grip. Declan tried to navigate around any large mounds on the route to the "out the road" villages.

Mounds could be anything from just a large drift, to a fallen tree; the snow made it difficult to tell. Avoiding them was the best action to take, because he certainly didn't need them stranded in the wilderness. His satellite phone was charged in the supplies pack, but he would rather not be in a situation where Danni could be harmed in any way. Declan smiled behind his face protection. With Danni, he didn't feel so alone in a world that sometimes seemed too crowded. He also rued the day she would leave. He wished she'd stay, but he doubted he could voice what his heart truly wanted. Not to her.

It took her breath away. That was the only way Danni could explain being on the back of a Ski-Doo as it sped through the wilds of Alaska. She expected to be colder, but her winter wear was surprisingly good at minimizing the chill. The face mask, thick goggles and the fur-lined hood of her parka kept the snow off her face.

But nothing could compare to the way the landscape stretched out to the horizon on one side and the pure white snow with an icy tree line skirted the shoreline. They were on the river. Declan called it out to her, and she felt the change from snow-covered ground to pure ice with at least a foot of snow covering it. The bumps became one smooth ride, and Danni lifted her head to see white bunnies run from the sound of the snowmobile.

The laugh that escaped her caught and rushed away on the wind. This was the only place she could see wildlife up close. Little white birds took flight, and for a moment the snowmobile kept up with a small pack of caribou crossing the river. The towns came into view, and she could see the complete difference between their homes and the ones in Juneau, and well, anywhere in the world. The simple houses were made into duplexes or left as single-family dwellings. Almost everything was covered in ice, there were no streets signs or roads from what she could tell.

She was getting accustomed to the fact that Main Street in Auke Bay and some other streets were plowed, but that wasn't the case with these towns. Did they even have a main street? Very few decorations were outside, and Danni could tell the people lived simply. The community center was half the size of the one in Auke Bay. When they parked, Danni looked at the beige siding with three steps that led to a small patio area. Declan helped her off the snowmobile before he brought his leg over and stood stiffly stretching his back. He pulled down his own face covering and took a deep breath.

"Are you okay, in pain?" asked Danni, her voice full of concern.

"I'm good. Getting rid of the kinks from sitting in one position for two hours." Declan looked at her. "How did you like the first trip out of Auke?"

"It was exhilarating. Did you see the bunnies and the birds? Oh my God, and we were right next to the caribou, like we were a part of the herd."

"Did you know that caribou is what everyone calls reindeer," Declan said casually as they took the tarp off the boxes that were strapped down. "Those little birds are called Ptarmigan and sometimes you can't tell them from the snow. But it's a staple of eating here in the winter."

"You are kidding. I was close to reindeer!" She clapped her hands in delight.

"None had a red nose, unfortunately. He lives with Santa farther north," he teased.

Danni grinned as she took a box and walked up the small steps. "I thought you were Santa. I ran off with a charlatan."

Declan tweaked her nose. "A helper."

"The ptarmigan are so tiny, what can you make a meal of?" Danni asked.

"It's like a chicken breast, high in protein. In the winters here, we need that more than anything to stay warm and to keep up muscle mass. These small towns don't have the luxury of supermarkets, so what isn't shipped in by small planes like the services that Coop provides, they have to get from the land."

Danni looked around, then pulled her mask down to speak. "Wow, this is a very small town."

"A lot of the people around here live a nomadic lifestyle. Now is the time they would go to the winter homesteads where they can make their crafts and live by the culture that has been passed down through generations." Declan opened the door to the warm community center. "They keep the hearth lit here because sometimes it may be home or the jail until someone like me can pick up an arrest. Brody is usually here, the community officer who polices the four towns that share this center."

"Four? I thought this was just one," Danni said, surprised.

Declan chuckled. "We passed through two, and on the other side of this road are the other two. None have more than a hundred, maybe three hundred residents. That's why I started this little project when I came back to Auke. Toys and stuff like that are all good for kids, but the parents do need help. I have turkeys, hams, boxes to make Christmas dinners, milk, cereal, and things they wouldn't usually see until a trip to one of the main towns like Juneau or Fairbanks. Honestly, sometimes we even have to get shipments from Anchorage."

"It's such a different world," Danni mused. "I can step out my front door and find food and restaurants so easily, and here, what I consider normal would be a luxury. If I don't want to go outside, I can get my food delivered. It's surreal."

"It's Alaska."

"Sarge." A tall man ambled out from a back room. "I thought I heard the front door."

"Brody." Declan shook the man's hand. "This is Danni, my Mrs. Claus today."

Brody shook her hand. "Nice to meet you. That's a New York accent if I ever heard one."

Danni laughed. "And you sound like a Texan."

"Born and bred." Brody had to be around thirty-five, and his eyes crinkled when he grinned. "I gave up the longhorns and rodeos to take on a new challenge, trying to police miles and miles of Alaska."

"Brody used to be a Texas ranger, and now he lives in the house right next door. One man for four villages," Declan explained. "What time are we expecting people today?"

"Noon, so we better haul butt like biscuits and gravy to get set up." Brody put a cowboy hat on his head and walked to the front door, zipping up his jacket. "I'll help get everything in and then y'all can get prettied up in the back."

"He's wearing cowboy boots," Danni murmured.

"Even in the winter we can't get him out of that hat or those boots." Declan grinned. "You can put your winter gear in the back, then plug in the tree."

"Okay." Danni nodded. "I see he was setting up a table for food and drinks. I'll take care of that, too."

"That's my girl."

It warmed her to the core hearing him say that, and with a soft smile she hurried away to leave her things on one of the chairs in the back room and to quickly fix her hair, making sure that the parka hood and the wind didn't loosen any of the bobby pins that held it in place. Back out front she noted that Brody had put up paper chains and hung silver stars from the low ceiling.

He was certainly tall enough, she mused as she got to her hands and knees to plug in the wire that was hung from the tree. Danni loved how they all seemed to use fresh trees. Inhaling the pine scent filled her with a new kind of Christmas joy. It wasn't materialistic, it just felt good to be a part of something this magical for people who were happy with the simple things in life.

The multicolored lights flickered on and the colors bounced off the hand-carved decorations that were intricate and smooth. Danni touched a wooden hollow ball that had stars etched into it, with smooth lines joining them together. *How marvelous*, she thought and walked around the tree slowly. Like the tree under the gazebo in Auke Bay, she knew each of these ornaments were special.

Declan and Brody came back in, their boots thumping against the tile floor and from then the set up began. Food was placed on fold-out tables. She hadn't even known that Declan had trays of food in the trailer they had dragged behind the Ski-Doo.

His mother had, of course, packed it carefully so nothing spilled. She set up sandwiches and tiny cakes, items that would travel well and still be delicious and make a pretty presentation.

"The two crockpots are meatballs and the Auke Bay stew," Declan said. "If we put them in now and set it on high, it should warm back up pretty quickly."

"I don't know if they will," Danni said, looking at the half-frozen food. "Brody, is there a microwave in here?"

"No but there is at my place. Give them to me, and I'll have them back here in a jiffy, plug stuff in, and I'll discreetly get them poured in and turned on." Brody stacked one container on the other and went out the front door.

"Alaska has an eclectic set of transplants," Danni said. "I don't feel like so much of an outsider anymore."

"Imagine if you stayed," Declan said. She turned to look at him with wide eyes, and he turned away quickly and called behind him. "I mean, if New York didn't have everything you need."

"Yes, imagine that," she murmured.

"People should be coming soon, so Mrs. Claus, you are on," Declan said. "Play it up until it's time for me to come out. When you hear the jingle of the bells, you'll know what to do."

More and more she fell in love with Juneau and the people who lived within it, but her life was in the Big Apple, the city that never slept... But Auke Bay had Amy and the feeling of home that she always seemed to miss out on. There was the cosmetics company and the amazing contract. This was more confusing than anything in her life. Luckily, people started filing in slowly to the community center, taking her mind off of the confusing aspects of her life. Declan hid in the back, and she of course played up her part, so the children and their families entered into the warmth of the holiday celebration.

"Hello! My, my, I thought I had more time to decorate." Danni moved toward the group with her arms outspread. "Welcome to our holiday celebration. Does anyone know who I am?"

"Mrs. Claus," a small girl with a sweet, mischievous smile said and then darted behind her mother.

Danni pulled a candy cane from her pocket. "Aren't you a smart little girl? Can you be my helper this afternoon?"

After a nod from her mother, the little girl handed over her soft purple coat. Danni showed her the button to press, and the community center was filled with songs that embraced Christmas. Danni led them in games, giving out small trinkets in prizes while parents ate from the small buffet and made plates for their children to sit and have lunch.

Danni sat with them, talking to people and learning about their lives. Her new friend, the little girl in the purple snowsuit, was named Ahnah. Her father, Kallik, was a fisherman, and her mother, Meriwa, a teacher and artist who had the facial tattoos of her people.

"So, where is the school?" Danni asked Ahnah's mother.

She smiled. "You are in it. The children are either in walking distance or brought by snowmobile. I teach from kindergarten to the eleven-year-olds who will go to middle school. Then they will leave and go to a larger village for school."

"It took us a little under two hours to get here,"

Danni said. "How does that commute work?"

"We have homeschooling for those who choose not to go. Lesson plans can be sent by mail for an entire year," Meriwa explained as she fed Ahnah's little brother some stew. "For us, it would be Auke Bay. Many of us have families who live in the town or close by for the convenience, and the children can stay with family three or four days a week for school then return to the village for an education in the more traditional aspects of our heritage. We consider teaching them our skills, our ways, and how to survive an important part of their learning so our culture lives on within them."

"This is all so rich and diverse. I think I would've liked school here much better than in the city." Danni played with the toddler's little hand. "I hope I'm not rude for asking, but what do the tattoos on your face mean?"

The tribe in this area is Tlingit primarily, but I'm from the Iñupiaq tribes that are close to the Bering Sea. My husband is Tlingit, yet I honor the old ways of my people." Meriwa traced the lines on Danni's chin to match hers. "These mean that I became a woman and was eligible for courting and marriage. Our families still live very much steeped in our ways of life from the past. These lines get thicker with age and wisdom. It celebrates my accomplishments and more."

"They are beautiful."

Danni was in complete awe of the people of these villages who embraced such a rich and beautiful heritage. It was one of the reasons she loved traveling so much. Morocco, Paris, Italy, Greece and Budapest, walking through cobbled streets rich with culture and old churches that were quiet but filled with artistry. From food to dance, Danni loved to immerse herself in every activity to understand them more as a people.

Who knew that Alaska would be the place that filled her heart with a song she never felt before, and all she had to do was to come visit her best friend? The village elder was there. He looked on with a smile as the people who sought his wisdom in all things from disputes to the blessing of a new child celebrating Christmas. He gave her a nod and a wink as the musical sound of jingling bells brought her attention back to her job at hand. Santa was here, and he was ready to come to the party.

"Do you hear that?" Danni said in awe. "Come along, children, I think... Why, it must be! Santa Claus is finally here! Have you been good boys and girls?"

"Yes, yes, yes!" The children's shouts echoed off the walls of the community center.

"Oh good!" Danni clapped her hands. "Here comes Santa Claus!"

They screamed and clapped as Declan came out dressed in the red velvet suit with his torso stuffed with pillows.

"Ho, ho, ho, merry Christmas," Declan bellowed. His imitation of St. Nick made her laugh out loud. "I see so many good boys and girls with their families today. I wonder what we have for everyone. Let's go take a look! Santa has to sit down so I can talk to you all and ouch...my back is a little sore from working with the elves. Mrs. Claus and Mr. Brody will help me, does that sound okay?"

"Yes, Santa!"

The kids swarmed around him as he moved to the larger than normal wooden chair set up close to the Christmas tree. It was obvious that care had been put into making the piece of furniture. Learning about the people in the village, Danni had no doubt that one of the many craftsmen made it for occasions like this. Danni saw a side of Declan that she cherished.

His eyes were alight with kindness and twinkled merrily as he lifted each child on his lap, talked in whispered tones, and gave them a gift and a hug. His walls were down. Declan wasn't reserved, and Danni actually put her hand over her mouth in surprise when she heard the deep baritone laugh and saw his usually stoic face relaxed. It was like years melted away from his face, and the crinkles around his eyes made him even more handsome.

Children tore into gifts, and she thought about how, as a child, she and Gracie were grateful for any gift they got. It was all a luxury, from the dinners to getting a new doll for Gracie and for her notebooks, journals, and pens. Danni looked at the excited faces of the kids who probably walked or took a snowmobile over a few miles to get to the one meeting place all of the communities shared.

It was obvious the parents were relieved and appreciative of the large crate filled with food items as Brody handed them out. The crates contained more than just food for the holiday dinner; there was also things like flour and sugar. These were things they valued over money and would use to feed their families through the long winter months. It made Danni think of her own situation, how she'd built something out of nothing. It was all fragile and her life was the key.

Danni panicked and her breaths became shallow. What if she lost it all tomorrow, what if the makeup brand didn't want her after all? She couldn't go back to wondering how her rent and bills would be paid. Worse, what if she had to move back home to her parent's house and see the look of disappointment on their faces because their worst fears for her came true? She couldn't let that happen. Maybe a month was too long to take off when she could be working. *Should I have even come?*

A tug at her apron brought her thoughts back to the present. Looking down at Ahnah, Danni pushed the dark mood away. It couldn't ruin the commitment she made to do this and the promise she'd made to Amy. Things would work out one way or another, and she would continue working hard for her dreams. At the end of the gathering, Danni had a bag of candy for each child as the families filed out.

"It was very nice to meet you," Meriwa said. "I hope we see you again. Your soul likes it here in our slice of Alaska. Come back and nurture it often. You have made lifelong friends today, especially me."

Danni smiled. "I certainly will. I loved meeting you and your family."

The very last person to leave was the elder who moved with smooth, strong steps that belied his weathered and wise face. He took her hand and placed something in her palms before closing her fingers over it with his own.

"You are not an outsider, you are *ch'áal.* Even in the ice, the arctic willow grows." He smiled and patted her hand. "Merry Christmas."

"Merry Christmas," she whispered, and when the door closed behind him, Danni opened her hand.

The shaman had given her a necklace with blue, white, and black beads with little bronze spacers separating them. The pendant was a tiny hummingbird that was carved from silver. The gift humbled her. It was simple but beautiful, like her time in Alaska, where everyone had embraced her without reservation.

"He called you an arctic willow, essentially," Declan said as he walked over. "It's a high honor to receive a

gift from the elder. He considers you one of the villag-
ers now."

"Really?" Danni met his gaze and tears misted her
eyes. "I'm going to cherish that sentiment. The necklace
is so beautiful."

"Don't cry, it's a good thing. Here, let me help you
put it on."

"It's so special." She handed him the jewelry and
wiped at her tears before they fell to her cheeks. "Thanks."

Declan came around to face her, and Danni gently
touched the pendant.

"You look beautiful," he said with a smile. "He's right,
you know. You fit in without even trying."

"I appreciate you saying that, even though I thought
you didn't like me to start." Danni smiled wide.

"I like you just fine, but you sure can talk a lot
sometimes," Declan teased.

"Hey, I'm all nervous chatter." Danni pretended to
be offended.

"I'm accustomed to it now." He tweaked her nose
again. "Let's help Brody clean up and head on home."

"Declan, thank you for sharing this with me today."
She smiled tentatively. "It was wonderful to see this
side of you."

"Thank you for coming," he said.

She followed him to help clean up the rest of the
food, put away the tables, chairs, and the general clean
up after a party. It was about an hour and a half later
before they were on the snow machine skimming across
the soft flakes and heading back to Auke Bay. The trip
back felt much lighter with all the food and packages
gone.

Cutting through the snow with her arms wrapped
around him to stay secure on the Ski-Doo, she looked

at the sun which was now halfway down behind the frozen river. It had been a good day, one that she would remember for a lifetime. The urge to stay made Danni rethink her entire life, but could she give up all that she built for an uncertain future in Juneau, Alaska?

Chapter Ten

T HE RISE OVER AUKE BAY was a perfect place for Declan to stop the Ski-Doo and have some of the lunch he brought. They hadn't had time to eat while at the community center, and before they left, Brody graciously heated up the food for Declan on their way out of the village.

"I like Danni, she's sweet," Brody commented when he brought the food back as she got dressed for the trip.

"Yeah, she is," Declan said. "She's heading back to the city soon."

"Hmm, really? New York is just a few hours away," Brody mused.

"I think she's got someone." Declan heard the snap in his tone. Why did the interest Brody showed in Danni make him bristle?

"Does she now?" Brody grinned. "Maybe she will stick around. I mean there's so much more to the world than the Big Apple. Plus, she seems to have someone here, too."

"Merry Christmas, Brody, thanks for everything, call me if you need me," Declan said ignoring the not-so-subtle hints.

There was a stand of trees that kept the wind off their back, and he had always kept a dry store of wood under a lean-to he made. Declan liked the silence and sometimes he came out to that very spot in any season to sit by a fire and watch the sun set over the horizon. Sharing it with her felt right and as he helped her off the vehicle, Danni looked at him curiously.

"Why are we stopping?" She asked through her mask.

"Lunch," Declan announced. "I figured we could share a meal and watch the sunset from my favorite spot. You'll see something spectacular, so grab that basket and come on."

"Okay." She took the basket from the trailer and followed him through the snow. Their feet made soft sounds as they slipped through the packed snow. Declan left her by the lean-to and got the wood.

"Want to learn how to make a fire?" he asked, dropping the bundle onto the ground. Under the makeshift shelter the snow never hit the ground and beneath the canopy of trees it stayed dry and warm against the winter weather.

"Sure!" She rubbed her gloved hands while she looked around at the structure. "When did you have time to build this?"

"It's always here. I come out in the summer and fall, change out branches or add new ones to the sides, back and top to make sure it's safe and secure," Declan explained. "If anyone ever gets caught out here, they are welcome to use it until help can arrive."

Danni crouched down beside him. "How regularly does that happen?"

"More often than you think," he answered. "Mostly in the summer when people use ATVs and don't take the time to maintain them and the engine conks out."

He put kindling and smaller pieces of the dry moss down to start a fire. "Now the trick is to start a small fire with this stuff before adding the bigger pieces of wood. Now you light it."

"You are always so prepared." Danni used the lighter he gave her and together they watched as a small tendril of smoke curled up as the fire caught. "Look at me, I'm making a fire outside."

Declan chuckled. "You find joy in the simplest things."

"Isn't life supposed to be that way?" Danni sat back on the thick log under the shelter.

"Maybe so. I think I've forgotten how to be that whimsical." He piled the wood neatly until they had a roaring crackling fire and the warmth radiating off it could be felt.

"You still have it. I saw it today when you played the illustrious Saint Nicholas," she teased.

"It comes easy then. Life is... I'm trying to navigate it the best way I can," he admitted and sat beside her. Declan opened the basket that sat at his feet. "So, we have soup, sandwiches and hot chocolate."

"Still warm?" Danni asked in surprise. "I can't believe we forgot to eat."

Declan winked. "I had Brody warm it back up and the hot chocolate is in a twelve-hour thermos that keeps drinks hot. It even comes with an extra cup."

"Well bring it on," Danni said with a laugh.

He gave them both a cup of hot chocolate and then large mugs with soup. The sandwiches were of course for dipping, and they ate in companionable silence while watching the sun go down completely. The best part was always when the last line of orange combined with the twilight blue sky. The stars then popped out in the clear sky and were so close Danni felt like she could almost touch them.

"This is really good, thank you." Danni had finished the last of her meal and was now sipping from the thermos cup.

"Just a small thank-you for being my assistant today." Declan smiled.

"I had so much fun and took tons of pictures."

"My mom and Cooper are getting married," he blurted.

"That's so wonderful,"

"I don't know how I feel about it." He added with a sigh, "I still see her with my dad, but Coop loves her and she's happy, so who am I to complain?"

"My parents are still together so I can't imagine how you feel. We aren't as close-knit as you and your mom are, though," she said. "I always felt like I was on the outside looking in and didn't quite fit."

"But they love you."

"They do and I love them. My sister is just like them, I mean, living in the same cookie-cutter house across the street. I wanted to do my own thing, not the set plan they had for me. But my family thinks my career is a house of cards while they thrive in stability."

"You have to do what's right for you," Declan said.

"I know, I always just wanted to fit in with them, somewhere."

"You fit in here," he said gently. "Perfectly, like you always lived here."

"Everyone made me feel welcome," Danni held her hands out to feel the warmth of the fire. "But you and your mom have the best kind of relationship. When you talk, she listens. She doesn't expect you to be anything you're not."

"There's a downside that she thinks she knows everything." Declan chuckled.

"That's all mothers, Declan." She nudged him with her shoulder. "I have heard the words 'because I'm Mom or Dad' as a solution to an argument without either of them even listening to what I have to say."

"If I had a sister, I think she and Mrs. Susie Mathias would butt heads too." He used a stick to poke at the fire as he spoke. "When my mom came to Walter Reed after I got hurt, I think even the doctors were afraid of her. You don't say no to a Colonel's wife, and she traveled for forty-eight hours bouncing from connecting flight to connecting flight to get to me. She's that kind of woman, so I know if she loves Cooper it's real."

"When is the wedding?" Danni asked.

"New Year's."

Danni sighed. "I'm sorry I won't be here to see it."

He cast a sidelong glance at her and hinted. "You could extend your trip."

Her shoulders slumped a bit. "I can't. I have work obligations, and if I'm out of the game for too long, it moves on quickly. Plus, I have that contract with the makeup line I need to follow up on. Then there's Austin…"

Declan's heart dropped. "The boyfriend."

"Not really, we are on a break, I needed to think while I was here…" Danni shook her head. "He doesn't listen to me either. It's like everyone thinks their plans for me are better than the decisions I make for myself."

"The question is, what do you want, Danni?" Declan faced her. "Nothing else matters and people will have to accept your choices."

"There you go being a wise man again," she teased.

"Remember when I told you there was a surprise."

Declan inclined his head toward the horizon. "Look."

She turned to face the picturesque scene spread out before them. Christmas decorations in Auke Bay combined with the lights of homes peppered the night, creating a beautiful tapestry. The gazebo with the massive fir tree could be clearly seen. Beyond that the sky was a blanket of stars, and the horizon was illuminated as the first color of the northern lights danced their way into the night and slowly moved forward, outshining the constellations. He heard her gasp and Declan watched her face alight with wonder and joy as she watched nature's own light show.

A shooting star flashed across the scene and a wondrous laugh escaped her. Was fate making this all too perfect? He watched Danni glowing with happiness next to the campfire. Why did his heart squeeze with a painful sweet ache just from being around her? She turned to see him watching her and time stood still. Declan moved in and kissed her gently, watching her lids close as their lips touched. Quick and full of promise...

He pulled away to gaze into wide amber eyes that held so many questions. None he could answer, not even for himself. Declan sighed inwardly, knowing he had to break this perfect bubble they created.

He cleared his throat. "The fire is burning down. I should get you home before the temperature drops more."

"Okay... Deke," she teased and began to pack away the items back into the basket.

He threw some snow at her and she squealed. "That's what you get for teasing me."

"Come on, it's cute," Danni laughed. "I know your mom is the only one who calls you that."

"And Cooper...and now you," he answered with a smile.

"Thank you, I consider myself lucky." Her smile was pleased and that in turn made him happy.

Declan made sure the fire was completely out by banking it with snow and then they made sure the trailer was secure. He helped her back onto the snowmobile and headed the rest of the way into Auke Bay. Parking in front of Amy and Mateo's house, Declan made sure she was safe and sound without getting off the machine. His leg was stiff, and he didn't know if he had taken a step too far by kissing her.

"Danni I..."

"This was..."

They spoke simultaneously and stopped with a small laugh.

"You go first," Declan encouraged.

Danni moved closer and hugged him before speaking. "Thank you for one of the most amazing days of my life."

"You're welcome."

She turned to walk away but stopped and faced him. "What were you going to say?"

He grinned. "The very same thing. Night, Danni."

"Goodnight... Deke."

He made sure she got inside safely and with a small wave from the door Danni was gone. Loneliness washed over him all at once; today was the longest he'd spent in her presence, and he missed her already. What had he gotten himself into? Like the aurora borealis, Danni would be gone soon, except his heart wouldn't let him forget her.

Hello, Danni... This is Erika. I know you're out of town. Loving the travel pictures and videos! We'd like to talk more about the spokesperson opportunity. Can you sit in on a video conference tomorrow with me and the marketing team at three in the afternoon? That would be eleven in your time zone right now. We have sent a link to your email. We hope to see you there.

Danni heard the message at nine when she woke up and noted that it was sent the day before when she was at the "out the road" villages with Declan. Of course, she scrambled up, took a shower and drank a cup of coffee downstairs with Amy before going upstairs to put on makeup and make herself look presentable for video conferencing. The Northern Lights Festival would take place the next day and she was Amy's right-hand woman. That meant today was a flurry of last-minute ankle biters that needed to be taken care of. The call at eleven worked perfectly in this hectic schedule.

"Just a bit of eye shadow," Amy said from the door carrying a mug. "Since you've been using the eye cream, they are so much brighter and less tired looking."

"Gee thanks, bestie, for telling me my eyes were sallow," Danni answered from the mirror.

"Sweetie, when you got here, you were dead on your feet, and you had extra luggage under your eyes."

Danni stopped with her eyeliner and looked at her friend. "Was it that bad?"

"You are always beautiful, but you were tired." Amy moved into the room. "You got in late last night. How was everything?"

"Really good. I met Meriwa and her family and look, the elder gave me a necklace." Danni lifted the gift she wore around her neck.

"You're one of us." Amy sat on the bed. "And the

entire day with Declan Mathias, huh?"

She rolled her eyes knowing Amy could see in the mirror. "Just ask, will you."

Amy plucked at a thread on her sweater. "Fine, make me pull it out of you. How was your date with our town Sarge?"

"First, it wasn't a date. I was helping with community service." Danni turned on the chair that sat in front of the dressing table. "On the way home, we stopped at his...his...little shelter thing on the hill outside Auke Bay and ate since we hadn't eaten all day. Then we watched the sunset change to the northern lights."

"Sounds like a date to me."

"He kissed me," she announced, and Amy almost choked on her tea.

"What!" Amy leaned forward. "How was it?"

"Butterflies," Danni admitted. "I'm even more confused, because I feel something with him I've never felt before."

"This is it." Amy fanned her face to stop the tears from falling. "It's the falling in love I told you about, and now you have it, too!"

Danni moved to sit next to her. "Calm down, woman, before you have the baby on the bed, and I cannot sleep on it if you do."

"Oh please, nothing is going to get this baby out. He or she has taken up permanent residence."

"How can I be falling for a man who lives thousands of miles away from me?" Danni asked and flopped back on the bed. "My career is there, he is here, plus it was one kiss."

"Okay, close your eyes," Amy ordered. "Whose face comes to mind when you think about love?"

"Declan," Danni admitted and sat up. "That doesn't

mean a thing."

"If he asked you to stay, would you?" Amy prodded.

"I don't know..."

"Stop overthinking it," Amy said. "First thing that comes to mind. Declan says, 'Danni stay here in Auke Bay and be my wife'...and you say?"

"I don't know!" Danni got to her feet and paced the room. "There's so many variables in my life."

Her friend stood and gave her a sympathetic look. "Then you have to figure out if those variables are worth more than those butterflies that took flight when he kissed you. Go do your video conference, then we have to get to work."

"Are you mad at me?" Danni asked.

Amy cupped her face. "Never, weirdo, I want you to be happy and that's all that counts. You need to make you happy, no one else."

"Declan said the same thing," Danni sighed. "I just don't know what that is right now."

"He's a smart man, a keeper," Amy sing-songed as she left the room.

"I know it," Danni said softly and began to set up her laptop.

The video call started promptly, and Danni looked at the five familiar faces she had met just before leaving on her trip to Alaska. Erika, who led the team, wore a light blue sweater that contrasted against her flawless dark skin. Her smile was big and warm.

"Danni, good to see you!"

"Merry Christmas to everyone," Danni said with a little wave.

"We absolutely love the pictures and video shorts you've been posting from Alaska," Erika said. "I didn't believe the whole George the turkey thing until I saw the video of him!"

"That's the only time he let me record him," Danni laughed. "We have a tentative relationship being built."

Erika opened a folio in front of her. "Well Danni, as to why we wanted this meet up. We'd like to offer you the contract to be our new spokesperson! What a Christmas gift, am I right?"

Danni clasped her hand over her mouth and her heart raced. It was a few moments before she could speak. "Oh, thank you so much! It is, and I know it was a really hard decision between me and Sade."

"A few Christmas party incidents took her out of the running," Erika said frankly. "We want to project a sense of sweetness and wholesomeness for this line, and you are it. Might I say your skin looks amazing."

"My friend Amy is an herbalist and teacher here, and we have been creating some amazing face masks and body care products that we have been using."

"Please bring some samples so I can take a look," Erika encouraged. "Now, can you be home before Christmas Eve?"

"That's only a few days away." Danni pursed her lips for a moment. "I was going to stay till after Christmas..."

"We want to put a rush on the campaign and have the first images up on Fifth Avenue on Christmas Day," Erika said. "This part can't be negotiated. Danni, if you want this contract, we need you back in the city."

Disappointment filled her, and Danni knew Amy would be just as sad. But this was work, something she had been striving for, so there was only one answer.

"I can leave this Wednesday and be home in time," Danni answered.

"Great! To help you out, we will make your travel arrangements since it's so last minute." Erika looked pleased. "We have a great travel guru here and Joanne can get anyone anywhere in a pinch. Just send us your flight information for your return dates and we will get you all set up."

"Thank you for all of this and for choosing me," Danni said gratefully. "I'll see you all in a few days."

"Wonderful." Erika gave a big smile. "Welcome aboard, Danni St. Peters."

"Thank you all again," Danni said with a little smile.

There was a small round of applause before the call was disconnected, and she dutifully sent her information via email to Erika and then closed her laptop. Her dreams were coming true, and she was thrilled. Or was she? A tight fist closed around her heart because she would be leaving the one place where she felt welcomed and at home. She picked up her phone to make a call, trying to stave off having to tell Amy the bad news for a few moments longer.

Austin answered on the first ring. "Danni! I was going to text you later."

"Hey Austin, guess what? The cosmetic company wants to sign me—I got the contract."

"Yes! I knew it!" Austin shouted. "That's my girl. Why don't you sound happier?"

"I am." Danni swallowed the lump in her throat. "I have to come home earlier, like this Wednesday early. They want to start shooting ASAP."

"Fantastic! Charlie and I will be there to pick you up. Text me your info when you get everything changed. I had a surprise waiting on New Year's, but I can definitely up my plans. Don't worry about a thing, sweetheart. I have got you."

"Thanks Austin, I'll get back to you soon," Danni promised.

"Glad you're coming home. I really missed you."

"Same here. Bye, Austin."

Even as she said the words, she didn't feel them, not like the kiss. Her eyes opened wide because this meant she wouldn't be seeing Declan again. Amy's words echoed in her mind. *What if he asked you to stay?* That was before she had a big new contract, and giving up all she ever dreamed about for the unknown seemed foolish.

This could ensure Danni didn't have to worry about money, and her parents would be proud knowing her back account was secure. It was all a mess, and instead of feeling over-the-moon thrilled, Danni wanted to cry. She went downstairs slowly and found Amy sitting at the kitchen table. When she looked at her friend, Danni could tell she already knew.

"When do you have to leave?" Amy's voice was subdued.

"Wednesday." Danni's voice cracked with unshed tears. "They gave me the contract."

"Your dream." Amy tried to smile and failed. "I'm happy for you, but I can't even bear to see you leave. I missed you so much, I thought we'd have more time, and you'd get to meet the baby."

Danni wiped away her tears. "I'm going to be here for the festival, and I promise when things get easier, I'll come back. Like the spring or summer."

Amy smiled and her sob came out like a hiccup. "You better."

"Erika Wand wants me to bring some of our products for her to sample," Danni said. "This could be the opening to push our Alaskan Ice products."

"I like the name." Amy grinned. "I think we should run with it."

Danni hugged her. "Me too. I love you, Amy. I plan to visit as often as I can."

"We've already made progress from not seeing each other for years to starting a business and making plans for tons of trips here." Amy squeezed her and then wiped her own tears on her sleeve. "Okay, so enough crying. We are going to make these last few days the best ever."

"Yes, we are," Danni said. "I guess I should start saying my goodbyes."

"Declan should ask you to stay," Amy said, getting her coat.

"You can't force stuff like this. If it was meant to be, it would be."

"When you're right, you're right." Amy stood and stretched her back. "Let's go collect the little ducklings and Peter, then get them over to the center for final costume fitting and practice."

Danni bent to Amy's stomach and spoke. "Hey, you in there, time to come out and see the world. I want to meet you before I leave."

Amy sighed. "It's hopeless." She handed Danni the keys. "You drive. There is now zero room between me and the wheel."

It took them an hour to corral the children from the small elementary school and get them to the community center close by. It seemed the entire town was there in one capacity or another, from trying to sort out parking to working concessions on the inside. Main Street had become a winter wonderland, like a snow globe after shaking it when the flakes of white drifted down to the bottom. Except this was real, and even Santa's sleigh was sparkling clean.

The small park now had a skating rink with a hot chocolate station close by. Everything was lit with multicolored and white bulbs. The Christmas tree was the centerpiece, beautiful under the gazebo as people walked around. Danni thought she knew the beauty of the holidays from living in the city. But nothing compared to having actual snow that wasn't covered with city gunk only a few hours after it fell. In Auke Bay, there was the feeling of home and serenity instead of everyone hustling in and out of stores. She would remember this for the rest of her life.

No traffic went through the main street. It was blocked off for the holiday festivities. Inside, she helped Amy dress the children as little toy soldiers and sugar plum fairies. One boy was adamant he wanted to be a duck, so he got his wish because it was Christmas and hey, they would figure it out. Danni grabbed a bottle of water for her and Amy while the children went through their lines combined with the music coordinator. Susie and Declan were at the same table with Mateo.

"Amy told me." Mateo gave her a hug.

"Told you what? Is everything okay?" Susie asked, instantly concerned.

Danni cleared her throat. "Yeah, I got my contract from the makeup company. Downside, I have to leave Wednesday."

"Before Christmas?" Susie said, aghast. "I am so sorry, honey."

"Thanks, but I'll be back in the spring or summer. I just wanted to be here for Amy and the birth of the baby." Danni felt Declan's eyes on her.

"Congrats, I'm sure you will be great." Declan tried to smile and failed. "I'm going to check on things outside."

They watched him walk away, stoic, and he pulled the knit cap that went with his uniform over his head.

"He genuinely is happy for you," Susie said.

Danni gave a stiff nod. "I know. Let me get Amy her water."

If there was any way to feel worse, Declan made her feel it. The look in his eyes, the way his walls went back up as soon as he heard the news. Couldn't he see she was just as confused as he was? Neither were willing to step out their comfort zone, and her career meant a lot to her.

She couldn't be a spokesperson from Juneau, and the city was someplace that Declan wasn't willing to tread. Why did it matter anyway? Danni straightened her shoulders as she walked down the aisle between the rows of chairs on either side of the room. He made it perfectly clear she was a city girl, and he would always be a country boy who preferred the Alaskan wilderness.

Chapter Eleven

S HE'S LEAVING.
The words had filtered through his mind often since he found out the night before while everyone worked to put the final touches on the Northern Lights Festival. *I thought I had more time.* That thought also poked at his consciousness, but to do what? He tried to talk himself into taking that one huge step and daring to tell her his feelings.

What they were exactly was hard to put into words, and that thought seemed moot. Danni got her dream, an opportunity she couldn't pass up, and one he was unable to compete with. Admitting to himself that there was love forming and becoming strong in his heart was terrifying. To give it voice would leave him open to the heartache that always came with such feelings. No, it was best to let her go home to all she knew.

"We are the stars of Christmas, shining over our home in Auke Bay."

The kids on the stage who were dressed as stars and one duck said the words. Declan watched as she acted out each part so they wouldn't forget their words or marks. He smiled. It couldn't be helped,

Danni was as unique as each snowflake that dropped to the frozen ground. Soon she would be just a memory of a time when there was almost a crack in his armor. He was lying to himself. Danni had broken through every reserve without even trying, and now there would be an empty space. The next time she came to Juneau and Auke Bay, her life would have changed drastically. He would still be the Sarge doing what he did every day, and her face would be known across the world. Even more out of his league.

Unable to watch anymore, Declan felt the clawing need to be outside where the air was fresh, and the snow fell lightly. He could feel his anxiety trying to take hold and craved the solitude to shore up his emotions and lock them away tight. But how would it look if the Sarge of the town wasn't at the largest celebration of the year?

He took a deep breath, knowing that his mental re- action was because of the things he wished were within his power to change. Everyone would say, take the leap, the chance, but none knew exactly how he felt. They wouldn't understand.

Outside, the winter wonderland was complete, down to the jingle of bells and caribou that were tethered to Santa's sleigh. Thomas Hughes was the Auke Bay Santa, and he suited the part perfectly. Even in the summer, he had a long white beard, except his wife braided it in two long plaits so he could be cool. Then he looked like an old Viking warrior, especially when he was out on his boat. The caribou were his and all named after Santa's famous team.

The caribou were also tame, which made it easy for the children to pet them. Declan walked over in the midst of people enjoying the outdoor celebration. They always did preferred seating for families of the children first in the small community center. It would be recorded and shared with the rest of the community on Christmas Day. The snow and ice crunched under his boots as he stood by Rudolph and rubbed his snout. He was so tame that he always allowed Thomas to attach the red nose.

"Hey ya, Sarge." Thomas came around from behind the sleigh in his standard costume. "Merry Christmas."

"Merry Christmas, Thomas." Declan heard his own subdued tone and grimaced.

"You sound like a man who needs some Christmas cheer." Thomas studied him with kind eyes.

"It's there," Declan lied. "I see the boys are having a grand old time."

Thomas laughed. "Getting fat. They've already been given apples and carrots. I had to talk little Skye Crane from giving them candy canes. Told her it was bad for their tummies, but you know they would've eaten it, especially Blitzen."

The caribou shook his head and blew out a breath like he refuted the statement.

Thomas rubbed his head. "Yes, you would have, don't talk back. Donner was eyeing them too."

Declan couldn't help but chuckle at the interaction. "They all have their own personalities, don't they?"

Thomas nodded. "Just like us humans. Let me ask you, Sarge, are you okay? There's more people around than usual, even from the "out the road" villages."

"I'll be good." Declan looked at the older man. "Why?"

"Take it from an old marine veteran, I'd understand if you weren't." Thomas fixed the harness on his team. "It took me a long time to get accustomed to being around people again. How long has it been for you?"

"About seven years now," he answered, still petting the animals.

"Drop in the bucket, but you're doing good, especially losing a leg." Thomas pulled up a red pant leg to show his own prosthetic. "I get where you're coming from."

Declan looked at Thomas and felt the kinship between them. "Yeah I know you do."

Thomas smiled wide. "I also wear the harness on my hip because I messed that up too, so I wear jeans all the time to accommodate for that get-up. If it weren't for Beth and her patience, I don't think I would've made it. A good woman makes a difference, to soothe those bad dreams when they come a-calling."

"Since I don't have one of those, I manage the best I can," Declan replied.

"Heard about you and that new little miss, the city girl."

A short laugh escaped Declan. "How did you hear about any of that, living on that farm all the way out in nowhere?"

"I come into town, and Beth talks to her quilting friends on the computer," Thomas replied.

He shoved his hands in his pockets. "Well, there's nothing to tell. She heads home on Sunday."

"Then tell her how you feel, man, give her the option to stay." The older man clapped him on the back.

"There are a few problems with that," Declan admitted. "I don't know how I feel, so I can't ask her to give up her life and career for me."

"And what if she says no," Thomas finished for him. "That's the big one. What if you bare your heart to her and this city girl still leaves?"

"That too." Declan sighed.

"Sarge, I was an ornery old mule when I came back

from the war. Beth worked in a dress shop in Philadelphia, and I was just passing through, heading to Alaska. This state is made up of transplants who thought they could brave the wilds or by people like us who wanted the quiet from a noisy world. I saw her going to lunch one day, and I followed her into the little diner. We started talking. Six months later, I was still in that town, and I felt strangled, but I already loved her and made up my mind to stay and be with my Beth."

"What happened? How did you end up here?" Declan asked.

Thomas' laugh was jolly, and Declan swore he held his belly like Santa. "Well one day, she took my hand and said, Tommy—she's the only one that calls me that, so don't get any ideas, Sarge."

Declan's lips twitched. "I wouldn't dare."

"Well anyway, she said Tommy, what do you want? I can see in your eyes you're not happy here," Thomas continued. "Not with me, but here in this place. I told her Beth, my love is yours, but I need the wide-open spaces. I was heading to Alaska when I met you, but I vow this is where I will stay to be with you because I will stay anywhere you are."

Declan listened intently. "What did Ms. Beth say?"

Thomas grinned happily. "She said Tommy, don't you think while you would stay here to be with me, that I'd go anywhere to be with you? Three months later, we were heading to the acres we have now and built our home with our own hands. We raised three children there, and Beth loves it as much as I do. The moral of the story, Sarge, is how will you know unless you give the question a voice?"

"I'm scared to know," Declan admitted.

"It's like that for all of us who came home not knowing

exactly who we are. Certainly not the same men we were when we left." Thomas's tone was serious. "We left a part of ourselves there, but broken men can be healed. It's just how we choose to heal ourselves. Solitude and shying away from the hard situations ain't it."

The doors of the community center opened and people streamed out, the children bundled up after their performance to enjoy the rest of the festival. The first hints of green and reds of the aurora borealis danced through the sky, and at the pinnacle the mayor would speak from the gazebo and the university choir would sing.

"Better get ready, Santa. I see a bunch of kids coming to sit on your knee," Declan said.

Thomas patted his left leg. "The good knee. The cold has the other one a bit stiff."

"Talk to Amy, Mateo's wife. She makes me a balm that works wonders," said Declan.

"Come over anytime if you want to talk. Us veterans understand each other better than most." Thomas put on his red hat. "And I'll do that, Sarge, thank you."

Declan put his hand on the man's shoulder. "I appreciate the talk."

"Santa isn't just for the youngsters." Thomas' eyes twinkled, and as Declan walked away, he heard the echo of three simple words. "Ho, ho, ho!"

He moved back towards the crowd as parents holding children's hands ran toward Santa's sleigh and his reindeer, who stood patiently waiting for more treats. His mother and Cooper came out the front door, and then it was Amy, Mateo, Peter, and Danni. His eyes fixed on her, and when she met his gaze, her smile faltered a bit.

Declan always thought he was good at reading people, but now, when it counted, he was clueless and unsure of the next steps to take. Thomas had made valid points, but that was him, in a different time and place. Declan had lots to think about before she left on Sunday morning, and nothing would be solved tonight. Instead, he tried to conceal the tumultuous feelings swirling within him, hoping to God his smile hid his uncertainty.

The performances had gone off without a hitch, and Danni was ready to experience the rest of the festival. She made a video while she skated on the ice and show-cased Susie adding melted hot chocolate to the tops of her hot cross buns.

"The key to keeping anything warm and melted in these temperatures is a bain-marie," Susie explained as Danni use the video feature on her camera. "It's using a double pot technique where the bigger pot holds the water, and the second taller metal pot holds the choco-late. The boiling water will keep the chocolate in liquid form, so I can drizzle it on any of my breads or pastries."

"I have never tried this in my life," Danni said, en-thralled. "Want to tell my viewers what's the yummy something extra I can taste in the buns?"

Susie winked. "Orange zest in the glaze, and it pairs nicely with the chocolate."

Danni took a bite and chewed with a sigh before speaking. "It does. If you guys are ever... I mean, you should be online trying to see Alaska after all I've shown you. Auke Bay in Juneau has to be a stop, and Susie's Baker's Dozen has to be the first place you go."

She stopped the recording, and Susie gave her a napkin. "You have chocolate on your nose."

"How?" Danni laughed.

Susie shook her head in amusement. "How did you get royal icing in your hair and eyebrows at the gingerbread house competition?"

Danni laughed. "I'm exceptional that way."

"I am going to miss you," Susie said with a fond smile. "You brought something so beautiful to Auke Bay with your smile and personality. It meshed perfectly here with our hodgepodge of people, and I for one will miss it."

Danni came around the stand to hug Susie. "I'm going to miss you too, so much."

She looked around slowly, taking it all in and saving the images in her heart. Between the garlands and lights there was mistletoe, hung low enough for everyone to see, and more than once Danni wished she was standing beneath one of the green sprigs with Declan. From there, Danni went ice skating, something she hadn't done since she was a child. She held Peter's hand as he wobbled on his own skates. Amy watched from one of the benches, happily munching on French fries.

"Where did you get those?" Danni called as she went around slowly, holding both of Peter's hands.

"Look Mom, look, I be gliding now!" Peter called out.

"I *am* gliding," Amy corrected. "Don't you worry, Danni St. Peters, about my delicious wedge fries that are super crispy on the outside and are covered in parmesan cheese, chopped parsley, and truffle oil."

"Seriously!" Danni urged Peter to the side. "Want fries, Petey-Pete?"

"Extra ketchup," said Peter.

They moved close to where Amy was sitting, slowly and gingerly on blades before Danni helped Peter back into his snow boots. She had for some reason taken to wearing the horrid two sizes too large boots Declan had put on her not too long ago. Two pair of thick socks, and they worked just fine.

"Those things are terrible," Amy said.

"I like them," Danni said, pulling the laces tight.

Amy pulled a fry from the bag and waved it. "That's because Declan gave them to you."

"Where be the fries, woman?" Danni chose to ignore her words.

"Where are the fries." Amy grinned and popped one into her mouth. "Over there, the Moose Tracks stall has them."

"Be right back," Danni said.

She was filled with so much energy and excitement, she practically danced, humming along with the Christmas music that played. She looked up and noticed the northern lights came through the sky like fingers. They danced and weaved in the ink-black night, more colorful and vivid than the last time she saw them. The night she watched them on the hill with Declan.... *Ooof!* Arms enfolded her against a large chest, and she looked up through her hair to see Declan's amused face.

"One of these days I won't be around to catch you," he murmured.

"But for now, you are." Danni smiled. "I haven't seen you much."

"Been doing the law enforcement thing. You know, making sure everyone is safe."

Danni stepped back. "I kinda got the impression you didn't like my news about leaving Sunday."

He shrugged and glanced away. "You have to do what you have to do. It's your career."

"Yes, I guess so." Danni sighed. "I'm going to miss it

here. I can't wait to come back. I'd stay in a minute if…"

"If what?" he asked.

She shook her head. "Nothing. The logistics are crazy, maybe when I have more money, I'll buy a house here to vacation."

"I guess we're a good tourist spot," Declan muttered.

"You know that's not what I meant." Danni frowned. "Amy, Peter, Mateo, all of you mean a lot to me."

"Hey, I get it. You're in the big leagues now, so why would you want to stay here?"

"Because it's amazing, that's why," Danni retorted. "I'm going to grab our fries before Peter starts yelling that he's hungry."

"Enjoy the food." Declan moved to walk past her.

"Sarge Mathias," Danni said sweetly.

He turned. "You only call me that when you're irritated with me."

"Me, no… never." She batted her eyelashes innocently. "I just wanted to say, I have seen everyone here for their true selves, and I care for them all. Some are just more pigheaded than others."

She walked away with him staring after her again, and Danni refused to let the interaction ruin her mood. Her heart ached, because of a combination of things, Declan being one of them. They were back to him thinking she was a city girl who would get bored with everything, even after the conversations they'd had.

One step forward and two steps back. It was crazy how life and people worked. Danni ordered fries and hot chocolates because it was too cold for anything else, and with drink holders in one hand and the bag holding the hot fries in another, she walked carefully back to her family. They were her family in more ways than one, and it didn't take blood for it to mean it for her.

"Hey, some of those for this lil' guy?" Mateo walked up holding Peter's hand.

"It surely is. Where are you two off to?" Danni asked. "Small hot chocolate and bag with blue sticker, it has extra ketchup."

"We are going to go see Santa and sit on a reindeer." Mateo smiled. "The mayor will be speaking in a few, and our special guest is bright in the sky. Grab Amy and come to the gazebo in about ten minutes."

"Will do."

Mateo and Pater walked away with Peter reaching for the fries first. Danni got back to Amy and gave her a cup before sitting next to her.

"I saw you barrel into Declan," Amy commented and took a sip. "Thanks for this, the little one is in rare form tonight."

"Maybe the bun is ready to be out of the oven," Danni teased. "She only has a few days left."

"She. We keep calling her that." Amy looked whimsical. "We always said we would raise our kids to be best friends like we are."

"And we will when I have some of my own," Danni agreed. "They'll come with me too."

"Danni, please don't go," Amy said.

"I wish I didn't have to," Danni said. "I need to work and show my parents I can do this."

"It's your life," Amy pleaded. "I know how you grew up, and yes, you vowed to not live like that again. You wouldn't here, our business could grow."

"I can't live with you forev1er, and at some point, my followers would want to see something more," Danni pointed out gently. "I'll be back, I promise. We won't go another seven years."

"I know." Amy sighed. "It's the hormones."

Danni put her arm around her friend's shoulder. "You can't keep blaming them."

Her best friend leaned her head against Danni's shoulder. "It's me but they're a good excuse for now. I wish I could marry you off to Declan and keep you here."

Danni chuckled. "I think we need more of a reason than that to put a ring on it."

"Stop being practical, it's not becoming," Amy grumbled.

"I'm to have both you and me over to the gazebo in a few. Let me eat my fries," Danni said.

"Can I have one?" Amy said in a tiny voice.

"You just had a...." Danni held out the bag. "Go for it."

Amy grinned. "You love me."

"I do, weirdo," Danni said with a smile.

They finished her fries, they because Amy had more than one, and together made their way to the gazebo. Amy kept rubbing her back, and Danni looked at her with worry. But Amy smiled and winked as if to say *I'm okay.* The Mayor of Auke Bay went up to the mic that was set up on the steps and tapped it lightly. Everyone winced when it made a high squeaking sound. The Mayor was a taller woman with brunette hair, and evidence of her native heritage was on her face. *Yay for being progressive,* Danni thought. More people milled over as she began to speak.

"Merry Christmas, happy holidays, and welcome to the Northern Lights Festival of Auke Bay!" she called out and the people cheered. "You all know me."

"Do we, who are you?" someone called from the audience, and everyone laughed.

"Funny, Drew," she answered. "For those who don't know me, I'm Ollie Mason, the mayor. Good enough for you, Drew? Tonight, we celebrate the blessing of living on one of the last vestiges of perfect land in the United States. And our little town is so perfectly situated with the mountains at our back and the ocean to bring us food and the sea breeze."

Clapping and whistles punctuated her words, and Danni looked around at the smiling, happy faces of the residents of Auke Bay. They would be etched in her memories forever, and her eyes widened in surprise when she noticed Declan stood beside her. She hadn't noticed him come up to their group, and now he stood with them as the snowfall became heavier.

"The holidays always draw us closer," the mayor continued. "It brings those we love home and sends us new people who we embrace as our own." Her eyes settled on Danni, and she instantly felt the warmth of the mayor's words. "While we celebrate the Northern Lights Festival, every so often, Mother Earth sends us her lights to shower us with her blessings, like tonight. So, while we listen to the University choir, let's watch her light show with those we love. Because Auke Bay is home, and for Christmas, it's the most beautiful place on earth."

The first few hums from the choir started, and every face turned to the sky. Cold flakes landed on her face, and no one seemed to care. Danni certainly didn't, because above her the light show danced in the sky. Listening to *Have Yourself a Merry Little Christmas* being sang ever so sweetly made the ambiance magical. She felt a large, warm hand close over hers, and Danni laced gloved fingers with Declan.

That connection made it more real, but it wouldn't be enough to keep her there. Her career and life were a solid foundation and being with Declan was like walking on thin ice and hoping it didn't crack. For an instant their gazes met, and it seemed like time slowed. Declan slowly slipped his hand away, as if he didn't want to let go.

He didn't look back as he weaved his way through the crowd, but Danni watched his back as he walked away. At that point, life seemed so unfair. Why couldn't she have everything she wanted? Why did she have to choose? How could she, without knowing? *Listen to your heart.* The words filtered through her mind, but sound decisions were made with logic.

The night came to an end as families flitted away, the cold becoming too much to keep them out any longer. They were moving to their car when Amy stopped, and the expression on her face was a mask of shock then excitement.

"Mateo, we are gonna need to make a pit stop at the hospital." Her voice trembled slightly. "The baby is ready to make an entrance."

"Now? Now!" Danni swore that Mateo's voice rose a few octaves higher. He was carrying a tired, mumbling Peter.

"What do we do, should I boil water?" Danni asked and they both looked at her dumbfounded. "What? I have no clue what the process is here."

"We all go to the hospital," Mateo said firmly. "The bag is in the car, and there are blankets for Peter as well. My family can come, but it'll take a few hours..."

"I can take care of him," said Danni.

"The waiting room is comfortable, great sofa and sitting chairs, for families who have to come in from the villages and need to rest," Amy said as she leaned against the car.

Danni took Peter and got him in the car seat while Mateo helped his wife into the passenger side of the family van. Declan was helping his mother and Cooper, and they noted the family taking longer than usual. The trio came over while they were getting ready to leave.

"Is it time?" Susie asked.

Amy nodded. "Heading to the hospital now."

"I'll get Brody from the village to cover for you," Declan said and shook Mateo's hand. "Congratulations, my brother."

"Hey, he isn't doing a thing but holding my hand, congratulate me," Amy said with a breathless laugh. "Honey, we have got to go."

Mateo hopped in the car, and Danni couldn't help but grin as they drove off Main Street and headed in the direction of the University.

"Good job, baby, you know I wanted to meet you before I left." Danni almost bounced in excitement.

"We aim to please." Amy's tone was dry, and she rubbed her stomach.

A wide smile was pasted across Dani's face as they made their way through the town. Even if she had to leave, she would get to meet the newest member of the Azure family before she went back to the city.

Chapter Twelve

T HE EXHAUSTION HIT HER ONCE she settled into the waiting room. They had arrived at the hospital, and while Amy was taken to one of the labor rooms, they were ushered into a small family waiting area. Danni got a very sleepy Peter into the bathroom and made sure he brushed his teeth.

She wiped the remnants of the festival off his face and hands before changing him into the warm pajamas that was in the bag. Amy had thought of everything, and the bag even had one of his stuffed animals he liked to sleep with and a small pillow. Danni set him up on a love seat, covered him with a blanket, and he was asleep in seconds. That's when she yawned widely, wishing she had her thick socks and pajamas as well.

"Would you like a warm blanket?" a nurse passing by the room asked.

"Can I really?"

The young woman laughed. "Yes ma'am, we like to make sure everyone is comfortable, like he is. I'll even rustle up a pillow for the recliner. You can pull it closer to him and rest while you wait."

"Thank you, bless you, you are a paragon among people." Danni wanted to hug her but that might have been a bit too forward.

"I'll be right back," the nurse said, amused.

Minutes later, she was under not one but two warm blankets with her feet tucked beneath her and her head on a pillow. She pulled the plush sitting chair close to the loveseat where Peter slept so she could be right there to watch over him in case he needed her. From what Amy had told her, bringing a child into the world could take more than a few hours. Danni wondered how she would handle having a child of her own. Would her life allow for it after she started the hectic work and appearances of being a spokesperson and running her own brand? She fell asleep with those swirling thoughts until a gentle hand shook her awake. Danni opened sleepy eyes to see Declan, Susie, and Cooper. The elder from the "out the road" villages was there, along with two other older people. The features and friendly eyes revealed them Mateo's relatives.

"How are you doing?" The deep timber of Declan's voice was soothing.

Danni stretched. "Okay. Peter is knocked out."

He smiled. "So were you."

"What time is it?" she asked.

"A little after two."

Danni sat up. "It's been five hours already."

"We didn't want you to wait alone," he explained. "My mom of course has food and because she's here, well, that explains Coop. These are Mateo's parents, Isla and Pana. The elder is here as a custom for each new birth to bless the baby."

"Not too long ago, Mateo came out and said the doctor said she'd been in labor with all those back pains she was having, so she's progressed a good way," Danni updated everyone.

"She will be born before the moon leaves the sky," the elder said with wisdom in his voice and then went to sit in a corner.

After exchanging greetings with Mateo's parents, they also found a place to sit and wait. Declan pulled a chair next to her, while Susie and Cooper with their basket of goodies started trying to care for everyone in their own way, with food.

"Are you hungry, dear? Maybe a hot cup of tea?" Susie asked.

"Tea would be good, thank you." Danni smiled at the older woman. "Are you sure I can't wrap you in bubbles and take you with me?"

Susie poured a cup from the thermos and handed it to her. "Coop and I will visit. He's never seen New York."

"Thank you for being here," said Danni.

"Where else would we be?" Cooper took Susie's hand. "We're all family."

How quickly they had accepted her as one of their own, without reservation or a hint of doubt. Thinking about her life, Danni could recall every time she struggled to fit in at home, at school, in college and just about everywhere else, except Auke Bay. From the time her feet sank into six inches of snow and Cooper gave her a scarf, she was accepted. She rubbed the material that had become a fixture in her life and an accessory to every outfit against her face.

"You and that thing," Declan said, amused. "I swear, we can pick you out of a crowd with that blue and pink scarf around your neck. It's one of the long ones, too., Maybe he should cap these at a certain length."

"It's one of my favorite things on earth, even if I have

to wrap it twice around my neck so it doesn't drag," Danni replied. "Are you off duty?"

"Brody came in and took over. Jess will be in at five, all is quiet," Declan answered. "So yes, after that round-about way of answering your question, I am off duty."

"I think I shall miss our scintillating conversations most of all," Danni teased. "We worked our way up from one-word sentences to this."

He grinned. "What can I say, you pulled it out of me. We are going to miss you, Danni."

Then ask me to stay. "I'll miss you all too."

It would take another two and a half hours before Mateo came out with a huge smile on his face. "It's a girl."

Danni noted the sun hadn't come up, and like the elder and she and Amy dreamed, the baby was a girl. They all crowded around him, offering congratulations and hugs. About an hour later, Amy had been wheeled into her room, and they all witnessed the village elder blessed the family in their native tongue while Amy held the baby and Mateo held Peter.

"Everyone, meet Luna Sparrow Azure." Amy's smile was wide. Danni was in awe of her best friend who just had a baby and was sitting up in bed holding the tiny bundle with curly black hair.

"There's your little sister, Peter," Mateo said gently.

"She is very small. Can she play trucks with me?" Peter asked and yawned.

"Not quite yet, buddy," Amy answered. "Give her some time to catch up to you, but you'll have to be kind, patient, and gentle with her."

"I promise," Peter said somberly, yawning even wider.

"He needs to go home," Mateo said. "I'll take them..."

"No, you won't. We can take them home so you can

stay with Amy," Declan said. "We can transfer the car seat to my truck, and I'll be sure they get to the house safely."

"Thanks, man. Let's go do that now."

Declan and Mateo left, and the group of well-wishers followed, leaving Danni and Peter alone with Amy and the baby. Peter was already curled up in the ball on the chair, ready to fall asleep when Danni sat on the side of the bed with her best friend.

Danni lightly touched the baby's soft curls. "She is so beautiful, Amy. I'm glad I got to be a part of this and meet Luna before I leave."

Amy smiled at her. "I am, too. I am so blessed that you are here with me. You know you're not just my best friend, you are my sister."

Danni sniffed as tears threatened. "I know, and you're mine... I wish."

"I know," an emotional Amy nodded and whispered, "I know."

"All done," Mateo said as he came into the room.

Declan held up the bag. "I packed up the stuff in the family room."

"Let me get the sleepy boy home," Danni said, standing and taking her coat.

"There's all kind of pancakes and stuff frozen in the fridge," Amy told her while Mateo dressed their son in his warm parka and snow boots. "I'll be home tomorrow."

"And I leave the next day." Danni felt a little numb at that thought.

Amy patted her hand. "We'll be fine, sweetie, we always are, you and me."

"Ready to go Petey-Pete?" Danni asked.

He nodded. "My bed misses me."

Danni laughed. "I know, mine too. Bye guys, see you soon."

They trailed behind Declan, and she got Peter secured in the car seat before he helped her into the tall truck. Declan slid into the driver's seat and started the engine. He maneuvered out of the parking space to the road. They drove in silence as Danni stared out the window, looking at the sun slowly changing the color of the horizon.

"You don't seem happy," Declan commented. "To be going home, I mean."

"I am. I guess it's all still sinking in," Danni said. "I'll hit the ground running when I step foot in the city. Austin has some surprise."

"Are you guys back together?" Declan asked.

She glanced at him. "No...no, we're not. We were better as friends."

"Does he know that?" He turned on to the street that would take them to the Azure house.

"He does in a way, but Austin doesn't really listen, so I may have to sit him down and have the talk." She frowned. "Again."

After a long pause, Declan said, "I hope you figure out what you want in your life."

"You too," she murmured, thinking, *You're a very confusing man.*

At the house, she unlocked the door while he carried Peter inside and upstairs. After she undressed the little boy and tucked him in, Danni went back downstairs where Declan waited by the door.

"Lock up when I leave."

"I will. Thanks for getting us here."

"It's not a problem." He shoved his hands in his pockets and hesitated at the open door. Danni waited for him to say more. Danni rubbed her arms and shivered against the cold wind. "I'd better go."

"See you later, Sarge." Danni watched him walk down the steps to the truck.

Danni made sure the house was secure before making her way upstairs to the room she had slept in for the last few weeks. It was all exhausting: the day, Declan, and trying to figure out what she truly wanted. The lack of sleep and the roller coaster she was on took its toll, and a headache started at her temples.

If there was one thing she could take away with her time with Declan, it was that she and Austin were not meant to be. Amy said there were butterflies when a person fell in love, a heartache that was like a sweet pain, and a pulse racing in excitement when that perfect someone was near. It was time to admit, at least to herself, that she was—madly, completely, and irrevocably—in love with Declan.

But the Sarge of Auke Bay ran hot and cold, and there was no way she could stick around for that. Maybe it'd just been wishful thinking that she'd seen the same emotions in his eyes. If only he'd give her a sign, say the word, anything to make her take that leap of faith. Declan was mired in his own doubt, and the heartbreak from the past may be one thing he could never overcome because he too was terrified of the unknown. She left New York knowing she had to return to her life and work there.

Now, as the time was moving closer with each second that ticked by, Danni understood what it meant to really want to stay in a place that felt like home. She climbed the stairs with heavy legs, exhaustion making her body feel like it wasn't her own as she got ready to sleep for a few hours. Between the thick warm covers, sleep took hold quickly with Auke Bay and Declan in her thoughts, then her dreams.

On the Wednesday before Christmas, morning came all too quickly. Danni woke up and stared out the window, disappointed that it wasn't overcast and snowing so she would have to stay one more day. In the midst of packing, she spent as much time with Amy and her family as possible. Peter broke her heart when he sat in her lap and looked up at her with wide, innocent eyes.

"Why do you have to leave? I like you here," he said. "I'll make George be nice."

She hugged him hard, trying not to cry. "I'll be back soon, I promise."

"But how will Santa find you?" Peter questioned. "It's pretty late for him to switch places now."

Danni gave a watery laugh. "He has that magic stuff, Petey-Pete. That big blue box under the tree is from me. I want you to video call me when you open it."

"I promise," Peter said.

Danni held the baby, smelling her downy hair and watching her sleep as she rocked her while Amy rested in bed. "I swear if we could bottle baby smell, we'd be millionaires."

"Wait till you see what comes out the other end, just from milk alone," Amy said. "No one wants that bottled."

"That's on you and Mateo." Danni grinned and then crooned at Luna. "You are just the best sugar plum fairy in the world. Tell your parents I said that."

"Did you eat? It's a long trip back," Amy said.

"Yes mom, I had flapjacks and country ham," she answered. "Are you going to be okay?"

"I'll be taking it easy for a few days. Mateo's mom

will come and help as well," Amy answered. "You've got to head out, Danni, the weather changes at the drop of a hat here."

"Yeah, I know." Danni sighed.

"Hoping for a storm doesn't mean one will happen," Amy teased.

"Get out of my head," Danni said, handing her the baby and then hugging her around the shoulders. "I'm going to miss you so much, chick."

"You'll be back soon." Amy leaned her head into the crook of Danni's arm. "We have Alaskan Ice to work on, and when I'm on my feet, look out for all those video calls."

"And I'll be able to see everyone."

"Maybe someone will keep you here next time." Amy smiled. "It's there, even if neither of you say it."

"We'll see." Danni chose not to think about what Amy was inferring. If she was ever going to leave Auke Bay, she couldn't face that truth. "Bye, my loves."

"Bye Auntie Danni, we love you." Amy waved her fingers before holding up the baby.

Danni waved, trying not to cry, and headed downstairs where her luggage awaited her by the door. Mateo was bringing Peter to the landing strip, so Amy didn't have to watch the little guy. Mateo already had her bags in the family van and the three of then descended the stairs to the driveway. A soft gobble, then more, louder and faster, made Danni turn. Mateo had left the back gate open again and there stood her nemesis, George, looking at her curiously.

"Bye George, stay out of trouble," Danni said.

He turkey-talked again, but instead of chasing her, he walked up and bobbed his head in her direction before going back to the yard.

"Will you look at that? You and George are now friends," Mateo said, scratching his head.

"He's not so bad," Danni said as she got into the passenger seat while Mateo secured Peter. "Do we have time to stop by the bakery so I can say goodbye?"

"Of course we do," Mateo said. Peter was content playing a game on his tablet for the ride. "I have to say, Danni, I wish you were staying in Auke Bay, but then I'm not the one who matters, am I?"

She lightly punched his shoulder. "You matter."

"Nice deflection but you know who and what I mean." He chuckled.

"It can't be forced. I can't make someone see me through different eyes. I'd be doing the same exact thing I accuse my parents of, expecting me to be something I'm not."

Mateo blew out a frustrated sigh. "The both of you are stubborn."

The now familiar ride to Baker's Dozen took only a few minutes, another thing she loved about Auke Bay. She could almost imagine walking to Main Street in the summer for a cool drink and to see what dessert with fresh fruit Susie would have. They all got out, and of course, Susie had a cookie for Peter before she embraced Danni.

"Oh, I'm going to miss you haunting my store for desserts," Susie teased as she held on to Danni.

"You can always ship me my desserts."

Susie put her hands on her hips. "Oh no, I can't make it easy for you. I hope that they lure you back soon."

"You can count on it." Danni kissed her cheek.

"Well, here is a care package. You can snack on the plane." Susie handed her a small box with the Baker's Dozen emblem.

"Merry Christmas, Susie," Danni answered and with a small wave she followed Mateo and his son back outside.

"Danni!" She turned and saw Declan coming around from the parking lot. "I thought I missed you, then I saw Mateo's car."

"I was just leaving," Danni said.

"This is for you...a Christmas gift, so to speak." Declan put a small box in her palm.

"Thank you. I didn't get you anything."

Declan hesitated. "You didn't need to. Having you here was enough."

When he said things like that, it was even more confusing. She wanted to scream at him. *Tell me to stay, say you love me, say anything!* But he didn't, and in the end, to keep from crying, she turned her face away.

"Thank you for this, for showing me my first whale and the northern lights by campfire." Danni's voice was husky, and her eyes filled with unshed tears. "For making a gingerbread house and changing my shoes when they got soaked in the ice puddle. Merry Christmas, Declan. I hope you find your peace, someway, somehow."

She got in the car quickly and pretended to talk to Peter in the back seat so he wouldn't see her furiously blinking away tears. She was an idiot, falling in love with a man who couldn't or wouldn't open himself to love. *Danni St. Peters, you never take the easy route, do you?* She glanced out over the dashboard to see Mateo and Declan exchange a few words but couldn't hear what they were saying. Declan gave a stiff nod and walked back without another glance.

"Everything okay?" Danni asked, wondering why Declan's face looked like storm clouds.

"All is well," Mateo answered. "Let's get you to the airport. Luckily those cosmetic people are bringing you home in luxury."

"Yeah, I guess," Danni sighed. "It is weird I prefer Cooper's Cessna?"

"Not at all," Mateo smiled.

At the airport, she said goodbye to two of her favorite people.

"Don't forget to video call me," Danni told Peter, knowing if she cried, he would be confused, and his tears would fall. "And when I come back in the summer, you promised to show me the best place for berry picking."

Peter nodded. "Daddy will take us. I love you, A-Danni."

"I love you too, Petey-Pete," she whispered and kissed his head.

"Bye, baby sis." Mateo enfolded her in his great big hug. "He's a fool, and I told him so."

Danni smiled. "Good looking out, big brother."

Even the beauty of Alaska as she flew away from Juneau couldn't fill her with joy. Her heart was aching, and sadness filled her very being until she had the overwhelming urge to be alone and cry in her bed. On the plane she finally took the small box Declan had given her from her backpack. She opened the silver tinsel that covered the small box and lifted the cardboard lid. Inside, set on blue velvet fabric, was an intricately carved crystal snowflake. She ran her finger over the piece before taking the quarter-size figurine between her fingers and holding it up to the light. It was beautiful, a perfect memento of her time in Auke Bay and of Declan. *One last goodbye.*

Three days before Christmas and she was heading home, alone, without her friends. Her sister's family would be in the midst of their own celebration. She hoped and prayed that the cosmetics company would keep her so busy that she fell into bed every night exhausted. She'd made tough decisions. She and Austin would never be a couple, and their work relationship would have to change.

With Amy, she had made great headway on their brand. She held the reins to her career, and Austin making questionable decisions for her was a thing of the past. It would be a hard fight but what else did she have to do? Her career would be her life because this love thing hurt like heck

Danni wished it would be like some great romantic comedy where he came running through the terminal looking for her to declare his love, but it never happened. The incurable romantic in her was sorely disappointed, while the realist in her said life didn't work like that. She lowered the crystal snowflake and held it in her hand before putting it back in the small royal blue box. Losing the hope in the magic of Christmas that Auke Bay had given her only made her heart ache worse.

Chapter Thirteen

"Y OU'RE A FOOL TO LET her go." Those were Mateo's words before he drove Danni away that morning.

"How can one man be so blind to what is right in front of his face?" Cooper had asked.

"You're going to let your past define your future, and you're a poorer man for it." His mother's lips had become a disapproving frown. "We taught you better than that, Deke."

Didn't they think he knew that? He had counted every hour since Danni left. Seven, since he saw her that morning. He knew every second that ticked by into minutes and then into hours. He'd hoped she would... No, he couldn't put that on her.

Asking her to give up her career and life on an unknown was selfish and when the time came, he couldn't get the words to form in his throat. It tore his soul out when she thanked him for the time they spent together, and the tears in her voice made him want to comfort her and declare his love.

Yet he watched Mateo drive away with the one person

who made him feel like he wasn't just existing in this world. And he did nothing to stop it, not even daring to try. Everyone's disapproval only added extra weight to his already heavy heart. Driving around on his route, doing a job that usually brought him peace didn't much help.

He saw Danni in the small things, like the snowball fight they had outside the community center. She wanted to free the tiny fish bait because her heart was so big. Or watching snowflakes fall on her face as she looked up to the sky. Declan ended up at Mateo's house, and for some reason got out of his car and knocked on the door. Amy, still in her pajamas, answered the door and stood behind it so it would block the wind.

"Come in quickly." She ushered him inside. "I've got the baby in the portable bassinet in the living room."

"The temp has really dropped out there. I think we are going to be snowed in soon," said Declan.

"Then Danni made it out in time," Amy said. "Grab some coffee."

Declan made himself a mug of the warm brew and came into the living room where the fireplace blazed a cozy fire. He looked into the bassinet. Luna was swaddled in a pink blanket with penguins all over it. She slept with her tiny mouth open, and unable to resist, Declan ran his finger over her tiny ones. She opened her hand.

"Has she gotten bigger since we saw her in the hospital?" Declan asked.

"Probably not," Amy said. "Mateo and Peter went to the store to stock the house with food."

"I came to see you, actually." Declan sat on the sofa while Amy used the recliner close to the bassinet.

"Me... Why?"

"Clarity, I guess. You're the only one who hasn't called me some variation of fool for letting Danni go." Declan took a sip from his mug.

"Oh, I agree. You are a complete idiot for letting her go, but she is too for leaving," Amy answered. "Both of you need to find your footing. Declan, Danni is nothing like your ex-fiancée, I think she's proven that. Danni needs to stop searching for security in her career and the acceptance of her family."

"Wow." Declan sat back. "You will always be as blunt as a hammer with the truth."

Amy raised an eyebrow at him. "Would you have me any other way?"

"I guess not."

Amy sighed. "I understand both sides. You were hurt, get over it. You're not the same guy, and Danni doesn't care if you lost a leg. She will love you harder than anyone else possibly could. Then there's Danni. When we first met, her parents had just moved into the brownstone. They didn't have a lot, barely enough furniture for all the rooms. But it was theirs, and the St. Peters were proud. Danni's family didn't have a lot, she was fourteen and working a few hours at the bodega to have spending money. She understood the feeling of poverty a lot of people face here, and she doesn't ever want to feel like that again."

"So, she pushes herself with her career even if it doesn't make her happy, because failing can't be an option."

"Yes, and she is seeing that, but...." Amy paused. "Danni can't leave a sure thing, her security blanket so to speak, for the unknown."

"Me," he said.

"Ding, ding, ding, give that man a prize." She clapped

her hands lightly. "Declan, what do you want, admit it right now. First word that comes to your head."

"Her," he said softly and then sat up. "I love Danni. I want to show her she can have a career and still be here with me. I want to watch the stars with her and take her to the glaciers and see them through her eyes. She experiences things so vividly, she laughs, and my heart just skips a beat and I smile. Danni is the one, and I hope to God it's not too late to show her that."

Amy leaned forward. "Five days before Christmas, what are you going to do?"

"I'm going to go bring our girl home," Declan said with a wide grin. "I need to go and get Coop in the sky. Don't get up, Amy. I can see myself out."

"What about flights and stuff?"

He gave her a wink as his heartbeat fast in his chest. "I may be a veteran, but I still have some favors I can call in. All I need to do is get to Fort Wainwright."

She waved him away. "Then why are you still standing here? Go bring her home!"

With a laugh, he opened the door to leave as Mateo and Peter came in.

"Hey, where are you heading to?" Mateo asked.

"To get Danni from New York. Hold down the fort until I get back," Declan answered and went out into the cold brisk wind. "Your wife is a godsend."

"I know that!" Mateo called after him. "Go get the girl."

The first stop he made was to the bakery, and he walked into the door with his intent clear. "Mom, I need your resources, flights out of Juneau are booked rock solid."

"For what?" his mother looked up from her task.

"I'm going to find Danni and bring her home."

"Oh, sweet merciful heavens! I don't know what got

into you since you left this morning, but I am all for it!" His mother let out a small scream and did a dance. "Okay, go pack a bag. I'll get Cooper on the phone and then I'm calling your dad's friend in Fairbanks to get you to Wainwright. I assume you want to be on a C-17 heading to the lower forty-eight."

"And this is why you're my mother." He kissed her soundly on the cheek. "Make those calls, Mom."

"Thank you, Jesus, Santa, or well, anyone for making this happen." She picked up her phone and began scrolling for numbers.

Declan didn't think about the people, he wouldn't let his anxiety keep him from telling Danni he loved her. This was her home. He could see on her face how much she loved Auke Bay. If she said yes, he would show her for the rest of his life what it was to be truly loved. He packed quickly in the black military backpack he kept in the closet, enough for two days. By the time he came back downstairs, his mother was waiting at the door.

"Cooper is fueling up and will be ready to go," Susie said. "When you get to Fairbanks, a Captain Coleman will be waiting to get you to Anchorage. He still has some connections and can get you where you need to go."

"Thanks, mom. Love you, see you in a few days." He threw the bag in the passenger seat and climbed in his truck.

"Good luck, son!" Susie called to him. "We love you!"

Declan made the drive to Cooper's hangar in record time and like his mother said, her soon-to-be husband was waiting.

"Bout time." Copper grinned.

"You just get me to Fairbanks, Cooper. I have a mission to complete." Declan levered himself up into the small plane and sat down. His leg had already begun to ache, but he would manage, and his focus was set. He would do it right this time and hoped that it wasn't too late.

"Sun's going to be down soon," Cooper commented. "Will your father's friend be able to get you to the base tonight?"

Declan spoke into the headset. "If Captain Coleman is still the man I remember him to be, he will."

The flight took an hour because of the weather conditions, and by the time they landed, Cooper made the decision to stay in Fairbanks overnight and then continue on once the forecast improved.

"I hate that you have to sleep here tonight," Declan said as he got his backpack.

"It's okay, Deke, my friend Junior can put me up, he has before," Cooper said. "I hope you don't mind me not calling you Sarge anymore?"

"You took up my mom's nickname." Declan chuckled. "It's fine, Cooper, you're family."

"I know I'm not your dad, but I will love your mother till my last breath, and I'll be here for you, too. If you ever need someone to listen, I'm that guy."

Declan clapped him on the back and then pulled him in for a quick hug. "Loving my mom is all I can ask, but the other part, well, that's a bonus."

"See you soon, and hopefully with Danni." Cooper gave him two thumbs up. "It's almost Christmas, and we are all hoping for a miracle."

"Me too," he breathed out and swung his pack over his shoulders.

He made the short trek in record time, and after communicating with the tower, Captain Coleman was cleared for takeoff and did so seamlessly, a skill gained from years of flying in the military. The sky was so dark the snow seemed to be appearing out of nowhere, but Captain Coleman got him on the ground safely. A few strings were pulled to get him on a C-17 heading into New York to get soldiers home before Christmas. The military got its recruits home by any means necessary. Declan didn't mind travelling with the newbies; he used to be one.

The engines of the C-17 Globemaster were loud, and the wind from the powerful engines hummed in the cabin. This was the only way to ensure he got to New York only a few hours behind her. Of course, there was a bit of protocol being broken in giving him a seat on the aircraft, but it wasn't unusual for the brass to help a veteran. Hopefully he was coming home before Christmas with Danni sitting next to him. *Please don't let me be too late.*

He removed his prosthetic to give his leg a reprieve from its confines. With a sigh, he leaned his head back as the plane shuddered its heavy body into the sky.

"You okay?"

A voice called out over the engine noise, and he opened his eyes. Declan turned his head and noticed the young man no more than twenty offer him a granola bar.

"I'm asking if you're okay," the young soldier said.

"I'm good." Declan took the bar. He hadn't eaten since breakfast. "Thanks."

"You a vet?" The man ripped open his own snack. "I'm Matt, going home to see my family and my girl for two weeks. Then back to base."

Declan forgot how chatty some newbies could be. "Yeah, I'm a veteran. Sergeant Major Declan Mathias, retired. I'm an Alaskan State Trooper out of Auke Bay now."

"Dang, a real SGM!" the boy's eyes got wide. "You

lose your leg in deployment?"

Declan nodded. "The last one, about seven years ago."

"Still hurts," Matt guessed.

"Sometimes. Mostly tired and stiff right now."

"Any advice for me?"

Declan hesitated before answering. "Look out for your brothers and sisters-in-arms, they are your family too. Don't let a person's color, race, or religion make the decision for you, look at their heart. Make good choices, even when it comes to love."

Matt gave a salute. "I'm on it, Sergeant Major, and thank you for your service. Why are you heading to New York?"

Declan grinned. "To get the girl."

Matt grinned and gave Declan a fist bump. "Legit."

With a smile, Declan ate his granola bar and leaned his head back and closed his eyes. Being on the Globemaster brought back memories, but at least now he was able deal with them. For the first few years after deployment, it had been hard, physically and emotionally.

But with the love of his family and the people of Auke Bay, he healed the right way. Now if Danni said yes to loving him, this could be the balm to soothe a heart that never really mended. He could close his eyes and see a future with her where each Christmas brought them closer because they fell in love under the northern lights.

Home. How did it feel so foreign in only a matter of weeks? Danni walked off the Air Alaska flight and out the gate into the hustle and bustle of John F. Kennedy airport. It was packed with people trying to get on flights before Christmas Day, and many who were visiting loved ones. There were no excited family Christmas dinners waiting for her, not like she would have had at Amy's house. Her parents were in Florida, and although Grace would invite her over for dinner, it wouldn't be the same.

It was almost midnight when she finally got all her luggage and made her way out of the airport. First thing Thursday—well, it was already early Thursday morning—Danni would be back to the grind. There was already a guest spot on a cooking show scheduled and she hoped they would let her talk about the new Alaskan Ice brand of skin care. That same afternoon she would be signing contracts and getting to work. Danni tried to focus on that, hoping it would stave off the sadness. She already missed everyone in Auke Bay. And any time she thought of Declan, her heart ached.

"Danni! Danni!"

She heard her name being called and turned to see Austin standing there, holding a big bouquet of roses. He was of course handsome in his version of dressing down: men's couture jeans, a cashmere sweater, and a leather jacket. *I wonder if he ever wore plaid.* A small smile crossed her lips as she thought about the Christmas party at Moose Tracks.

"Austin, I would've taken a ride share home," Danni said as he kissed her on the cheek.

"Nonsense. Charlie is waiting outside, and we can talk shop on the way to your apartment,"

"I'm exhausted," Danni said with a sigh. "It can all wait until tomorrow. I just want to go to bed and crash before I need to be up at seven to be on Chef Johanna's show."

"I'll talk, then. You can sit back with your eyes closed." Austin handed her the flowers. "These are for you."

The sight of them gave her a twinge of unease. "Very pretty, thank you."

He took her luggage while Danni held the flowers, and they went through the large glass doors that led to the outside. The city air was cold, but not as cold as Alaska. Danni knew she had to stop comparing two drastically different places; it was only making things worse. Here and there lay small piles of gray snow.

Charlie pulled up in the dark sleek Escalade, well-suited for the weather. Between him and Austin, they got her luggage in the back. Finally, she was inside the car with the heated, plush leather seats. Charlie pulled away from the curb and merged with the traffic, all trying to escape the lines at one of the world's busiest airports.

"So, your trip was fun?" Austin asked.

"I loved it."

"I missed you here. I was completely bored." Austin shook his head. "I don't know how you did it with all the dreary snow and nothing to do."

"We kept ourselves entertained," Danni answered. She leaned her head back against the seat as he began to speak.

"Well tomorrow, Chef Johanna's spot is going to be epic! They're going to film at the Japanese tearoom on the top floor of a hotel in Times Square. Erika will be there, she said she wouldn't miss it. You'll see my surprise then."

"Erika's coming for the cooking show? I thought I was going to their offices after..." Danni words dropped, and she turned to Austin, knowing he was behind it all. "What surprise, why all of this? Austin, I am so completely jetlagged. I just want to do the Chef Joanna spot and go home to veg."

Austin sighed and pulled her into a hug. "Danni, it's a surprise, and I can spoil it a little to say now that you have the cosmetics contract, we should branch out. To California, permanently."

What in the world?

"Austin, we broke up, remember? And what about your dad, and the job you have with him?"

"They don't want me there, anyway. No one takes me seriously." Austin shrugged, but she saw the hurt in his eyes. Austin wanted to matter to his father and in his own way, he was searching for where he belonged. "I can work from anywhere, and I plan to show you that we work, Danni. You'll see."

She sat up. "Oh Austin, that's all part of it. You can't just jump in without knowing how your father runs his company. You have to be patient and learn the steps."

"I've been seeing him do it all my life," Austin protested.

"Seeing, not doing. You can't run without learning to crawl," Danni said gently and shook her head. "I don't want to move to California."

"Danni, trust me. I have your best interest at heart." Austin's voice oozed charm. "I just think California is the way to really build on what you have now."

"Why? The cosmetics company is here, so when they need me, I would have to fly across the country," Danni interjected. "I told you. There can't be an *us*. We don't fit like that, and I don't think we ever will. You want one thing, and I want another. We were happier as friends."

"You're tired. We can discuss it after you get some

rest. Tomorrow is a new day." Austin patted her hand. "Everything is planned, and tomorrow you'll feel differently when you see that I'm in, one hundred percent."

"I won't," she said, but he was already going on about who would be at the Chef Johanna Show.

The makeup company had sent promotional goodies, which meant as soon as she'd given him the news, he'd contacted them without her consent. She was too tired to be firm with him, and getting through Thursday would be hard enough. After the party, she would cut ties with Austin. Maybe without her in his life, he could focus on his father's company and take that work seriously. Austin wasn't a bad guy, really; just a little clueless to how reality worked for people without money as a cushion. He was accustomed to having his own way, and it was apparent he didn't often hear the word *no*. Still, there was someone out there who would be perfect for him. It just wasn't her.

The sight of her apartment building was a blessed relief. Exhaustion had her dead on her feet. Austin and his driver helped her get her luggage into the apartment, and he gave her a hug before he left.

"Tomorrow is going to be perfect." He smiled brightly. "Trust me, I'm so happy you're home."

"We are going to talk tomorrow when everything is done, Austin. I mean really have a conversation," Danni said firmly.

"Perfect, we'll put our feet up and have a glass of champagne after and chat." Austin gave a little fist pump. "Tomorrow will be epic, you'll see."

"I'm sure I will," Danni murmured and closed the door behind her.

Her entire body felt like it was weighed down. She left her luggage near the door, locked up, and trudged to the bedroom with her purse. She pulled out her phone to text Amy and let her know she was home. After two words, *home safe,* her cell phone died, because she hadn't had time to charge it on the way from one airport to another.

Finding her charger seemed like a monumental task, so she vowed to plug it in as soon as she woke up. Her landline would take any calls she missed. Danni kicked off her shoes and socks and stripped off the layers of her winter coat and the zip-up hoodie before climbing across her bed. She barely got the alarm set on her digital clock before she lay back against the pillows and crawled under the blankets. Danni was asleep in seconds as exhaustion finally took its toll on her body.

It seemed all too soon the alarm was buzzing, and she sat up bleary-eyed. She trudged to the bathroom and then to the kitchen to find coffee. The blinking light on the telephone of her landline's voicemail caught her eye. She loved that she still had a secondary number directly in her apartment. The phone was a teen favorite from the nineties because, well, didn't everyone still keep a little part of their childhood?

Her parents could never afford one, so when she got her own apartment, it was one of the first things she bought from the vintage thrift shop in downtown Brooklyn. She was just too tired to even contemplate listening to her voicemail and when she pressed the code, Danni wasn't surprised that it was full. Still bone-weary, she leaned against the wall and listened to each message before she could delete.

"Oh, I wish I could go back to bed." Danni yawned around her words.

Danni, are you home safe? I miss you already BFF... Peter, Luna cannot have ice cream, she's a baby...

Anyway, a heads up, your cell is dead, and I think you should know... Dec... A crash sounded and the baby started crying. There was a gurgling sound and silence.

"Dinner plate crashing to the floor, woke the baby, and she dropped her cellphone in Peter's milk." Danni murmured, wondering what the rest of the message was. She would call Amy later that afternoon. It was much too early now. She deleted that and listened to the next message.

Danni, this is your sister Grace. Is this your cell number? Mom and Dad are still in town, they had to push the trip back until January because mom sprained her ankle. Do we need to change the time on your gift for them or can you do it?

"You can do it. Cell number, really, Grace?" she murmured with her eyes closed as she leaned against the wall and went on to the next message.

Grace again, we fixed it, never mind.

That was the last of the messages, and she went into the bathroom. Danni grimaced at her face. She'd have to be flawless with her makeup to hide the tiredness. Knowing Austin, anything he planned would be super elaborate, and she would need every ounce of energy to deal with the day. Danni rushed back into the bedroom and plugged in her cellphone before she jumped in the shower.

Chapter Fourteen

HOW COULD IT STILL BE Thursday? Danni was so jetlagged, it felt longer. The shower helped perk her up and Danni looked at her luggage knowing the task of putting everything away would have to wait. She made herself a cup of coffee and was out the door with the travel mug to the waiting car service. Danni pulled her cellphone from her bag to call Amy, but the call went directly to voicemail. She tried the landline and got voicemail again.

"Hey Amy, I guess the phone volume is down so you and Luna can nap, and I think I heard your cell phone drown in the last message. I made it home, no real sleep because I had to hit the ground running. I'm heading out for my spot on the Chef Johanna show at the Japanese tearoom, Austin has some crazy surprise set up. At least, I told him we can't be together, and I doubt he was listening but after the spot today he will. Your phone cut off just as you were saying something, so um, call me when you can. Love you guys so much."

She disconnected that call and called her sister's number. It rang three times before Grace picked up.

"Hello," Grace said.

"Hey sis, did you get the booking changed?"

"I called you about that a week ago, Danni, but yes, we got it all taken care of."

"You called my landline again, you didn't save my cell number," Danni pointed out. "Also, I was in Alaska visiting Amy."

"She lives in Alaska? Do Black people live in that state?"

Danni shook her head, amused. "The State Trooper Sergeant and his mother are Black, and I saw many different skin tones in Fairbanks and Anchorage, so I'll say yes."

"Sounds cold," Grace said.

"It was, but it was fun."

"Meet any cute guys?"

Danni thought of Declan as she answered. "One or two. How did Mom sprain her ankle?"

Grace made a tsking sound. "Being Mom, of course. We had a little snow, and the boys didn't move fast enough to clean her sidewalk and driveway. She went out to shovel and salt it herself. Ended up twisting her ankle on that four-inch step on the driveway. I told them to get it fixed all summer long."

"How much snow was it?" Danni watched the city go by as she talked.

"Not even two inches. So now she's home with a leg splint on, and they can't leave until January."

"I think the least amount of snow I saw in Alaska was twelve inches." Danni laughed. "But you know Mom, hurry up and do it in her time."

"Are you going to come over for Christmas? I guess we're cooking again." Grace sighed.

"Let's do potluck and make it easier. I can bring

something,"

Her sister teased. "You know how to cook?"

"Says the woman who asked for my meatballs recipe. Text me...on this number which you will save...after I hang up and let me know what to bring."

"Man, you're bossy." Grace laughed. "I'm saving it, lil' sister."

"You may see me on TV today. I got the cosmetics contract and there's some kind of announcement thing on the Chef Johanna show."

"Lead with good news next time, Danni! I am so proud of you! She comes on at two, and we will be watching in the nurse's lounge."

"Really?" Danni couldn't help the surprise in her voice. "You're proud of me?"

"Danni St. Peters, I will *always* be proud of you. We are two different personalities. I'm practical, and you live your dreams. I sometimes wish I had your bravery, but I'm happy with my life. And I am definitely your biggest cheerleader."

Danni took the phone away from her ear to look at it before speaking again. "Hello, pod person, what have you done with my sister Grace?"

"Ha, ha, very funny. Seriously congrats, sis. Live your dreams whatever they may be. See you in a few days."

"See you soon, and thanks, Grace," Danni answered before adding quickly. "Text this number, not the landline."

Her sister's laughter was what she heard before she disconnected the call. There was a huge smile on her face. Her sister was proud, and she felt humbled by that knowledge. But it gave her the boost of energy she needed to perk up for the long day. She was Danni St. Peters. They would expect her vivacious laugh and fun personality to fill the room. Danni would put it all out there, even though her heart was aching. Her sister wouldn't even know she'd met the perfect guy in Alaska.

Her simple dress with the cinched waist and flowing skirt was perfect. It had pockets, and Danni grinned because she had once done an entire video on the merits of pockets in all outfits for women. She paired it with black shoes and a rope necklace that was knotted at the end to form a pendant. Along with her earrings and makeup, she was ready for her guest spot that would also be celebrating her new contract. Life went on in the midst of heartbreak. The world wouldn't stop revolving because she was in love with a man she could never have.

Outside the hotel, the car slowed in front of a crowd of her followers and the press. She had to admit she was impressed with Austin's marketing techniques. When the door opened and she stepped out to the limelight, she felt a bit of panic. Her social media fans wanted selfies, and Danni made sure to snap some because these were people that made *Danni on the Run* a huge success.

There were young, impressionable girls in the crowd, and she always made sure to stop and talk to them. Being a teenager trying to figure out life was hard enough. Danni wanted them to see positivity for every aspect of life, from body image to kindness, so she always stopped a bit longer with the teens.

It was nice to see their parents supporting them. Danni wanted to believe that after all the hullabaloo died down, they'd be in some ice cream shop having a scoop of something yummy together.

"Danni, congratulations on your new spokesperson gig!"

"Danni, are you and Austin Hammond the new power

couple to look out for?"

Questions came from all around as she was ushered inside and to the elevators that led to the Japanese tearoom. The ride up the elevator was silent, and she took that time to center herself. When the door slid open and the hotel host ushered her out, the cheering started. Danni looked around. She didn't know any of these people

She caught sight of Erika and Chef Johanna talking close to the stage where the kitchen was set up surrounded by cameras. Danni made a beeline for that area between the throngs of people and the chairs that were on the main floor. So much work had to go into making a stage in the restaurant and it impressed her immensely. She was just *Danni on the Run*...or at least, that's what she wanted to be. Did she even know what she wanted anymore?

Moving through the crowd, she heard more than one *congratulations* being called out. People she didn't know pulled her in for a hug. Danni's bemused thanks flew unrehearsed from her lips.

"You look fantastic, darling." Austin came up dressed in a gray Armani suit and black tie—dapper as ever, of course. "See, we are kismet. We match perfectly."

"Austin, are all these people from my social media outlets?" Danni asked, looking around.

"Some of them are. I also invited a lot of movers and shakers who can push us higher." Austin took her travel mug and handed her a glass of champagne.

"I thought this was just a cooking show thing?" Danni asked, reversing the process and retrieving her mug of coffee. It wasn't even three yet.

He grinned and took a sip of his champagne. "Look at all the banners, darling, they are all here for you and

Erika is right over there. Let's go rub elbows."

The chef spot was filmed and then Chef Johanna announced the big news. Amidst the applause, Erika came on stage, and it was all done in about two hours. Afterwards, she found herself talking to more people who really seemed interested in what she was trying to do, while others wanted to utilize her platform for their own gain.

Danni was able to nibble on a few canapes, and—thank goodness—one of the waitstaff was able to refill her travel mug. While everyone else drank the flutes of champagne, her mug felt like it was her only hold to reality. She was trying to be a wallflower, but people kept seeking her out, until there was a knock on the microphone, and Austin cleared his throat.

"If Danni St. Peters would make her way to the stage, Danni St. Peters to the stage," Austin said in a teasing tone, causing the guests to laugh.

"Oh boy." Danni breathed out and pasted a wide smile on her face as she made her way through the crowed. An usher was at the end of the stage to help her up the steps and she crossed into the spotlight next to Austin.

"Here she is, everyone, the woman of the hour, Danni St. Peters, and isn't she beautiful," Austin said as he took her hand and kissed it.

An *aww* went through the crowd, and Danni smiled before gently pulling her hand away. "Thank you all for coming."

"This is more than just a party. Danni is fun and genuine. She is making her mark on this world, and she has me at her side," Austin said. "We started as friends, and now I want to make this an official engagement party."

Danni's eyes widened. "What... Austin, what are you doing?"

He pulled out a ring box and opened it to reveal a massive diamond ring. "I'm asking you to be my wife, Danni. This is our next step. Let's make it as man and wife."

No!

Danni heard the gasp of pleasure ripple through the crowd, and her smile faltered. She'd told him more than once that they should be friends. And anyway, this wasn't how she saw *any* wedding proposal, with a bunch of people she didn't know as witness. Austin still wasn't listening. Yet here she was on stage in front of a crowd of at least two hundred people, asking her the last thing she would ever agree to.

She looked out in the crowd and squinted at the back of the room. *Is that...?*

Her eyes had to be deceiving her, or the spotlight blurring her vision. Danni's heart began to race, the ring forgotten. She stepped away from Austin and the lights and looked close to the doorway of the tearoom. *Declan! It* is *him!*

Their gazes met, and she saw the hurt in his eyes, the disappointment. He looked at Austin holding the ring.

Oh no! Please no!

He'd seen Austin's proposal.

"Declan!"

Their eyes met again as Danni began to push through the crowd trying to get to him. *He came for me!* He'd traveled to New York, facing all his issues, for her.

"Declan!"

Danni reached out to him, trying to get through the crowd who were all looking back curiously to see who was there. He turned on his heels and was out the door when she was in the middle of the room. By the time she hit the lobby of the tearoom, he was nowhere around.

No! Nothing else mattered, not the party, not anything, as she frantically punched the elevator button.

A sound of frustration escaped her lips when the elevator stopped on the third floor so people could get on. By the time she rushed out of the downstairs lobby, there was no sight of him, so Danni went out the glass and chrome front doors. People and news reporters were still outside, though not as many as before. Danni ran to the sidewalk, looking back and forth. Declan was gone, and she had no idea where to look for him.

One thing was for certain, though: he'd come all the way to New York for her, and now she would do the same for him. New York wasn't where she wanted to be anymore. This wasn't what made her happy anymore. Her life had changed when she stepped foot on the snowy ground of Auke Bay, and that was where her new path was leading.

"Danni, Danni!" Austin rushed out and put her coat over her shoulders. "Who was that? You left me standing there and just...just ran."

"Sorry." She turned to Austin and even as she spoke, she looked over his shoulder just in case she could catch a glimpse of Declan in the crowd.

"Danni, are you listening to me?" Austin prodded and held up the ring. "You never answered my question."

"No, I won't marry you." She looked up at him as she closed his hand around the expensive piece of jewelry. "We don't love each other. You look at me as an escape from your father's shadow and a way to branch out. But there are no butterflies when you look at me, and my heart doesn't race when I see you." Danni was honest in her words. "You deserve that, and so much more,

Austin. Someone who can help you figure out your life and who you want to be with in this world. A person who will love you and grow with you...but it's not me."

"That guy, he came all the way from Alaska to see you, didn't he?" Austin asked.

Danni nodded. "Yes, he did."

"There's a light in your eyes like a spark of fire that wasn't there before," Austin noted. "Is that what love does to a person?"

"And it's my fondest wish you find someone who makes you feel like I do right at this moment," Danni said.

"Then you're right. We're not meant to be." Austin sighed. "Friends?"

Danni reached up to kiss his cheek. "Always."

With Austin close on her heels, Danni went back upstairs for her coat and purse. Seeing Erika there, Danni knew what she had to do.

"Erika, thank you so much for the opportunity to be your company's spokesperson, but I have to decline the offer," Danni's heart raced in her chest.

"Danni," Erika began. "This is really..."

"I'm in love." Danni beamed. "That is worth so much more than money. I finally found my place in this world and I can't give that up. I think at some point I can find a way for us to work together, so just remember two words. Alaskan Ice."

Erika shook her head with a smile. "Who am I to stand in the way of love? I look forward to hearing from you."

"Thank you," Danni said in relief. "For all of this and Austin you too, I have to go... I have to find Declan."

She started to walk away, and Austin called after her in a teasing voice, "Where to now, Danni on the run?"

Danni turned with a wide brilliant smile and her vivacious laugh of happiness escaped before she called out. "North to Alaska. I'm going home!"

When Declan had gotten to New Jersey, he'd found a hotel so he could crash for a few hours before trying to find Danni. He'd known for a fact he was only a few hours behind her, so maybe he could catch up to her at the swanky hotel address that Amy had sent him.

The low hum of the city seemed to reverberate through him and from the window of his hotel. He could see the tall buildings of the city across the river and the bridge that connected the two states. He was dead on his feet—there was no other way to say it.

The hotel was an easy find, and they even had a good room service menu. Declan needed to decompress and find his center—one of the coping mechanisms he had been taught for his PTSD and the anxiety of being around too many people. Going across that bridge into the city would be the real test because there, people were packed shoulder-to-shoulder on the crowded sidewalks.

There were probably more people in a three-block radius than all of Auke Bay. But this was for Danni and the future he hoped she wanted to share with him. Maybe she would've stayed if she'd known his feelings. Stepping out of his comfort zone to find the woman he'd fallen in love with was like one of the twelve tasks of Hercules to him...but his father always said nothing worth having was easy.

A hot shower was the first thing on the list, and

luckily the hotel had been revamped to a new, contemporary style with standing showers that had no tub. That made it easier for him to get in and let the hot water soothe sore muscles. Feeling semi-human ten minutes later, he came out and was dressed before the knock on the door announced his food had arrived. It was noon, but Declan was able to get a breakfast platter and hot coffee.

He figured if he slept for an hour or two, he'd have plenty of time to get the train into the city. But Amy called with info on where Danni would be that afternoon, so he set an early alarm. Declan, who could ordinarily get by on three hours' sleep, was dead to the world in minutes. His eyes opened wide at one p.m.

He'd slept an hour past the time he wanted to be up. He moved slowly from the bed and got his prosthetic on before going to the bathroom to clean up. In twenty minutes, dressed in a simple blue shirt and jeans and his thick green parka, he was on his way to the train that would take him from New Jersey to New York, and he would find his way to the hotel written on a scrap of paper in his pocket.

New York was never a place he'd thought to visit, and now he was standing outside Penn Station looking up at the massive buildings. Throngs of people moved around him like waves that never ebbed. He checked the paper before he moved from 32nd to 34th Street. Times Square became more crowded, thick with tourists, while large screens and bright lights flashed scenes of the season to encourage people to buy.

It felt like everything was closing in. Like there wasn't enough space to breathe between the buildings, so close together, and the masses of people. Declan controlled his breathing and his anxiety the best he could and the massive sign for the hotel came into view. He also noted the tons of people outside and the cameras.

He entered one of the side doors that led to the main lobby and took off his coat. A former soldier, he knew how to blend in, and he followed other people heading up to the party venue in the same elevator, all the while standing discreetly in the corner. The doors opened, and he kept close enough to the group that he was allowed inside.

The people seemed to get even closer around him, giving him a sense of panic. They milled around, immaculately dressed, laughing too loudly and talking to each other in groups. Declan searched for Danni like she could be his anchor in this new storm. *Did she already leave? Did I miss her?* He couldn't find her, not with all the people, until the man on stage called her name and everyone, including Declan, turned their attention to him.

This had to be Austin in the expensive suit and tie, with the perfect hair, not a strand out of place. Declan ran his hand over his own shaved head. He felt under-dressed and definitely out of place compared to Austin and everyone there. His heart stilled in his chest when he finally saw Danni on the stage. She didn't look like the girl with all the wild curls and barely any makeup from Auke Bay. In New York, Danni's hair was slick and elegant, her dress was perfection, and she was stunning. She also looked twenty thousand times out of his league, and he wondered if this was a bad idea.

Austin began to speak, and when he pulled the ring from his pocket, all Declan's hopes of being with the woman he loved were dashed. He couldn't compete with a man like Austin, who fit in with all this glitz and glamor. Declan was a Trooper from a distant town that not many people could pick out on a map. Austin could give Danni her dreams.

This was a mistake. He had gambled and lost. Even if he'd asked her to stay in Auke Bay, he doubted she would have. Why would she, when she had people here who adored her, including the man who held the ring?

Their eyes met, and she called his name. He heard it easily and saw her move. No, he couldn't stay. The clawing anxiety became too much all of a sudden. Too many people, noise, traffic, buildings...everything. He had to go, had to feel sane, find his footing and head back to Auke Bay.

"Declan!"

He heard his name again, but he kept moving. He couldn't let her see his pain. Why would a woman like her want a man with one leg? He certainly wasn't staying around to see her say yes as this guy slipped the ring on her finger. If he was lucky, maybe he could find a flight out of Newark airport and get back to Alaska, pronto. There was no way he could stay any longer than necessary, knowing she was going to be celebrating her engagement. The elevator door was open and empty. He jabbed the button to go downstairs, and as the doors closed, he tried to breathe.

In less than a minute, he was stepping out into the lobby and walking into the cold evening. It was easy to find his way back to the train station, and in thirty minutes he was heading back across the river to New Jersey, alone. Forty minutes later, the buzzing of his phone in his pocket made him look at the screen as he unlocked the door to his hotel. He answered with a tired sigh.

"Hey Mom."

"Deke, where are you? Are you in New York? Did

you see Danni?" His mother was a flurry of questions.

"I'm in New Jersey again. I saw Danni. Her boyfriend proposed, and I'm coming home." Declan's voice was flat as he spoke. It was the only way to control the heartbreak inside him.

"Oh, Deke. Did she say yes?"

"I'm sure she did," he answered. "I'm on the next flight out as soon as I can book it."

"Maybe if you stay and try to talk to her?"

"And look like a bigger fool than I am now, flying over three thousand miles to see a woman who has the perfect guy for her? I'd rather come home. This was definitely one of my worst ideas."

"Declan Monroe Mathias, it was not a bad idea. You were chasing love."

"When has love ever worked out for me?" He sighed and ran his hand over his head. "Mom, I need to book this flight. I'll see you when I get home."

"Love you, son," his mother said gently.

"Same here, Mom. Bye." He pressed the disconnect button and was on the phone minutes later, trying to get a flight out of New Jersey to Alaska.

Amy called twice, Mateo once, and he ignored all three. He was able to get a flight out since last-minute cancellations always happened this close to Christmas. He could fly out in an hour maybe two with luck, and Declan fully intended not to miss the chance to leave. He had only one pack and shoved the clothes he left on the bed inside it, Declan turned his phone off completely and with soft click of the lock, he left the hotel room to check out. There was nothing else to do. He'd fallen for the wrong girl, simple as that. Back in Auke Bay, he would return to life as normal and try to put Danni out of his mind.

If she came to visit Amy, Mateo, and the kids he would find a way to steer clear of her completely. It made no sense pining over someone he could never have. Heck, he could see the size of that rock from the back of the room. Danni struck him as a person who liked simple and elegant; the ring he would have bought would've suited her delicate hands.

"The ring you would've bought," he muttered to himself. "Gimme a break."

If everything went well, he'd be home and over a few thousand miles in less than forty-eight hours. Declan decided that he would take most of the shifts for Christmas Eve and Christmas Day so Mateo and Jess could have the time with their families. He could grab a plate from his mom and Cooper's place and then focus on keeping the town safe for the holidays.

Anything so he wouldn't be sitting alone thinking about Danni or seeing pity written all over the faces of the people he loved. Maybe he would use this time to revamp his new house, change it up a bit from what his parents originally had. His mother could lease the apartment to their shelter tenant and her daughter, and it would be reasonable enough not to swallow up all her income. It seemed a broken heart led to new ideas, but Declan would rather not feel the tightness in his chest every time he thought of her.

Chapter Fifteen

THERE WAS SO MUCH TO do and consider. As soon as Danni stepped through the front door of her apartment, she had to sit down. *Take a breath,* she told herself, and inhaled deeply while her heart raced. She hadn't been hallucinating; her eyes hadn't deceived her. Declan had been in the back of that room, and now she had to either find him or go back to Auke Bay.

The decision was easy. She knew she had left her heart there and wanted to return. Knowing Declan was there or heading back there was a bonus. She loved her friends, the people she met, the town. And above all, she loved him.

Danni took her phone out, bypassed Amy's cell, and called the house line directly. It had to be around dinner time for Amy in Alaska, so her friend might not answer the phone, but she would hear Danni's message.

Amy answered on the second ring. "Merry Christmas, Azure residence."

"Amy, Declan came to New York." Danni took a deep breath. "But he's gone, and I don't know where."

"Danni! Mateo, it's Danni! I've been going crazy trying

to reach you," Amy said. "Look at your cell, there has to be like ten calls you missed."

"Dang it, I put it on silent." A frustrated sound escaped her. "If I'd known he was coming, I could've met him at the apartment."

"He saw Austin propose, Susie told me," Amy said. "He's on a flight back here. Did you say yes to Austin?"

"Of course not. Even if I hadn't seen Declan, it would be no. Yesterday, I told him we were better off friends, but he just glossed over it, which is par for the course since he didn't want to hear it." Danni explained. "But I saw Declan in the back of the room, and I just knew that I was meant to be with him. I came home and all I could think about was him, you, and everyone in Auke Bay. Amy, I want to come home."

"Then tie up loose ends and bring your tush back to us," Amy said with a laugh. "I can tell Declan when he gets here…"

"No, don't," Danni said quickly. "Let me be the one to surprise him. I think he needs to see he is worth me traveling over three thousand miles for him. I want to be back in Juneau by Christmas Day."

"Oh Danni, that's beautiful." Amy sounded weepy. "You feel those butterflies and your heart knows, doesn't it?"

"It does." Danni smiled, and her eyes misted up.

"But what about the spokesperson gig?" her friend asked doubtfully. "This was your dream."

"Dreams can change. I still have *Danni On the Run*, and our facial products. I talked to them and refused the offer, and hey, Erika said she'd take a look at what we have. None of that is in my heart anymore. Declan is."

"Well, what are you waiting for? Time to make some plans!" Amy gave a little squeal of excitement. "If you can get a flight into Juneau, we'll pick you up."

Danni laughed. "Yes! It's time to put this mind to work to get me there before Christmas Day."

"Hold on. Mateo's getting on the line."

"It might be tough, Danni," he said hesitantly. "There's a pretty big storm coming through, and the airport will start grounding flights soon. Cooper can't even take the Cessna up; the small planes already have no fly orders."

"Oh, no," she moaned. "I need to be there. Maybe you can use the Ski-Doo to get me if I can ger in?"

"Danni, if there's no flight to Juneau, just make it to Fairbanks, we'll get you here," Mateo said. "Leave it to us, I've got family from here to there, we'll get you home."

"Please don't tell Declan. I want to show him my love by standing in front of him on Christmas Day. Mateo, tell Susie to keep him from going off into his little seclusion spot."

"We are on it," Mateo said. "You come on back home, where you belong. I'll lock him in one of the cells at the Trooper Station if I have to."

"I'm on my way," Danni promised.

There was so much to do. Danni took her laptop out and tried to find flights back to Alaska. Everything was booked solid, but Danni wouldn't be deterred. She called customer service hoping to get a miracle. After a twenty-minute hold, even after midnight, she finally reached a live representative.

"This is Jon and thank you for being a valued member of our service," the pleasant male voice said.

"I need a flight to Alaska. I don't care how many stops it makes. I need to be in Juneau on or before Christmas Day," Danni pleaded. "Can you help me?"

"Ma'am, there is nothing open," the male rep answered.

"Please... Jon..." Danni could feel her tears threaten to fall. "I need to tell this guy I love him, and that he is the one person who matters most in this world. He came to New York for me, and things got messed up. He deserves to be loved and to know it. I will cash in all my miles, bounce across the lower forty-eight to get to him in time. Please help me."

There was a long pause on the phone, and then the representative spoke again. "Let me see what I can do. What's your frequent flyer account number?"

Danni rattled off the numbers she had memorized. She heard the fast typing of his fingers on a keyboard and had to remind herself not to hold her breath in anticipation.

"There are no direct flights, but if you can take a flight from New York to Seattle tonight, that will get you into Seattle on Christmas Eve at around 6 a.m. From there it's a flight out to Alaska at 1 p.m.," Jon said. "That flight will get you into Anchorage around four or five in the afternoon Christmas Eve for an overnight layover. The last connection to Juneau around six in the morning." Jon hesitated. "That's a trek, Ms. St. Peters. Do you want me to book it? There's also a travel advisory so flights can be grounded. I can't guarantee you won't get stuck in Anchorage."

"I'll take the risk, go ahead and do your thing, Jon. Use miles, and I don't care how much it costs."

"I wish someone thought I was worth this much trouble," Jon said wistfully.

"I'm sure there is Jon, and they will find you when you least expect it," Danni said with a smile.

Jon cleared his throat. "You are all set, Ms. St.

Peters. Can I help you with anything else?"

"Thank you," Danni said, bouncing in her seat. "Merry Christmas Jon, you have been perfect in every possible way. Have the greatest holiday ever!"

"You too, ma'am, and good luck," Jon said. "Merry Christmas."

She hung up with a sigh, but there was no time to waste. She needed to be packed for tomorrow, taking what she could, though she would have to be back to box up her apartment. She hoped that Declan felt the same way... No, she couldn't think like that. A man didn't cross the country for a woman unless he loved her. Danni knew uprooting her life would, of course, make her parents think she was crazy. But nothing in her life ever felt this right and certain.

She would be at the airport Christmas Eve no matter what. And she could use the rest of Thursday evening and night if necessary, to do what she had to do. Danni piled the suitcases by the door, making sure Declan's gift was nestled safely inside her carry-on. There was no time to sleep or rest; there were two stops to make on her way to the airport. Danni prayed the weather held off until she could get into Auke Bay. After that, Mother Nature could unleash anything she wanted, and Danni would enjoy every flake that fell to the ground.

After a quick shower, she dressed in jeans, a red knit sweater, thick socks, and the boots Declan had given her. Danni had seen Grace in a new light as a caring older sister. Knowing at that time of the night and knowing Grace usually worked the early shifts. Danni took the car service to the family home, hoping Grace would be there along with her parents so she could tell them goodbye. Danni watched the skyline of the city as her car went over the bridge. This would be the last time she saw it for a while, but she smiled at returning to the place she now considered home.

With her luggage in tow, she passed the treelined sidewalks with lights twinkling between the branches. That was one thing about New York: the rest of the year it was all business, but Christmas came around, and people just felt the spirit of the season. Danni went up the steps to the brownstone and pressed the bell.

"Nurse, I think I have something in my ear," Danni teased when Grace instead of her mother opened the front door.

Grace rolled her eyes. "Like the pencil eraser we had to fish out when you were seven?"

Danni winced. "I forgot about that ER trip, but hey, we got slushies out of it."

"And that's when I knew I wanted to be a nurse, so win-win." Grace smiled. "Why are you in Brooklyn so late, Sis? And why do you have luggage?"

"I want to talk to everyone about something." Danni smiled at her sister. "I made a big decision, and I did it for love."

Grace's mouth dropped open, "Yeah, come in. Mom and Dad will want to hear this."

When she followed Grace into the living room, her father raised his eyebrows in surprise. "Danni, what are you doing here?"

"Came to see you and Mom. I heard she decided to be an acrobat," Danni teased. "I also want to talk to you both...if that's okay."

Her father stared at her a moment as if searching for answers before stepping back. "Come sit down, baby girl,"

Her mother was in her favorite chair. The blue velvet ottoman was being used to keep her foot level, with an added pillow for comfort. The TV played her afternoon shows, and the Christmas tree twinkled merrily near the big window.

"Danni!" her mother said her name lovingly as Danni bent to kiss her cheek.

"You guys," Danni teased. "I thought we talked about hanging up those ice skates."

Sandra St. Peters laughed. "Very funny. Those boys were taking forever so I decided to clean the walk myself."

"Mom, it's not jump when you say so, they would've done it," Danni said gently. "Now how long are you going to be a flamingo with only one leg?"

"The doctor said maybe another two weeks." She patted Danni's hand as she sat on the loveseat next to her. "Then we are off to the sun for a month, because this chill is in my bones."

"I don't get why you guys haven't retired down to Fort Lauderdale by now." Danni fiddled with the pillow under her mother's splinted ankle. "I'm sure everyone wouldn't mind Christmas in the sun and a vacation every year."

"Including you?" her mother asked gently.

"Me too," Danni said with a smile.

"Now I know you aren't just here because of my foot." Her mom studied her. "What's going on?"

"I need to talk with you and Dad," she admitted. "You guys may think I'm silly, but I'm in love."

"That's what she told me, too," Grace said sitting down.

Her mother pressed her hand over her heart. "I never thought I would hear those words from your mouth. Tell me everything."

"Who are we talking about?" Her father asked. "What is this young man's name, and does he deserve you?"

Danni laughed. "I think the question would be do I deserve him. He's the state trooper of the town in Alaska where Amy lives. He's a veteran, and he lost his leg in deployment."

"And he's still in law enforcement?" her mother asked.

"You couldn't tell unless you knew him or someone told you, Mom." Danni blew out a nervous breath. "He's amazing and kind. He's the quiet type who doesn't speak unless it's worth saying. He taught me to make a campfire and showed me the northern lights. I got scared about not having that foundation and security you always taught us about, so I came home to take a job. But my heart isn't here anymore, it's there." Danni beamed them a smile. "The thing is, he followed me here."

"Where is he now?" the patriarch of her family asked. "You didn't bring him with you?"

Danni sighed. "There was a bit of a misunderstanding, and he is on his way back to Alaska.... And I'm right behind him."

"What are you saying?" her mother asked.

She hesitated before speaking. "I'm leaving New York and following my heart."

Her parents were quiet before her father spoke up. "Did you think this over?"

"Dad, I saw how much you and Mom put into building your life, nest egg, and raising us," Danni began. "I know you want me to be like Grace and have this all worked out with a safe plan. But that's never been me. I worry about every penny because we grew up not having a lot, and it scared me into coming back here, when what I truly wanted was right in front of me." She watched her father look away as if he couldn't meet her gaze.

Danni continued. She had to, because holding it in wasn't an option. "I never really felt like I fit in with the family. In my mind, I was an aberration because I wasn't like all of you and my dreams were fanciful. I second-guess myself a lot because I was trying to combine who I am with who you wanted me to me. But in Auke Bay somehow it worked itself out, and I met Declan. I understand what I want now, and where I want to put down roots."

"We never meant for you to feel that way." He took her hand and emotion made her father's voice sound hoarse. "You are my baby girl, the peanut. I wanted to wrap you in bubble wrap and keep you safe.... I know I'm stern, but I love you, baby girl, and I want you to be happy."

"Even if it's far away," her mother added and wiped her eyes. "Danni, I have never seen your face glow like this. You came and talked to us, instead of just running away. I'm sorry. Sometimes I saw the hurt in your eyes, and I didn't know how to fix it. I never thought it was us, but now I understand. I wish you had said something sooner, because I never wanted you to doubt our love for you."

"We are set in our ways." Her father picked up where her mother left off. "But our love for you is so great, peanut. I'm sorry that all these years you felt like you were on the outside looking in. We want the best for you and always have. Now, here's my advice."

"What, Daddy?" Danni said huskily, almost in tears at the entire conversation.

"Run toward your new life and to the man you love," he answered. "Don't ever doubt your instincts or your dreams. Live, baby girl, take life on to the fullest and make it yours."

"Oh Dad," she whispered and the tears that threatened to fall slipped from her eyes. "I can't wait for you all to meet Declan. If he will have me."

"He will or he'll have to answer to me." Edward St. Peters puffed up his chest. "I used to be a pretty good boxer in my day."

"Stand down, Dad," Danni said with a chuckle.

"Bring him to Fort Lauderdale when we get settled," her mother announced. "Danni is right. It's time to embrace new things. I'm tired of the city, Edward. The neighborhood has changed, the people have changed, and I want warm sun and sand under my feet. We are going to take one of the many offers on this house and move to Florida."

Ed St. Peters saluted his wife. "Well, yes, ma'am."

"See, that's how it's done." There was a satisfied smug smile on her mother's face. "Now, tell us more about where you'll be living and this man who has stolen your heart."

"Hearing you are in love was not what I expected," Grace finally spoke up, her voice thick with tears. "I feel like I'm losing my little sister. I figured you were going somewhere, but you always came back. Now you're leaving to make a home and a life. When will I get to see you again?"

"You and the male horde will come visit. The boys would love ATVs and snowmobiles. A perfect way to give them an adventure outside the city. I'll come visit, but I need to take this leap of faith, Grace." Danni covered her sister's hand with her own.

Grace nodded. "I know, and I want you to. And maybe I'll finally have a niece..."

"Granddaughters," her mother said excitedly. "We

are severely outnumbered in this family."

"Whoa there, let me see if I get the guy first." Danni laughed.

She spent a bit more time than she'd planned, connecting with her parents and sister in a way she'd never thought possible. These were the people who reared her and loved her. Even at those times when Danni thought they were overly critical, they were in her corner. Rooting for her, in their own way. All she'd needed to do was to talk to them to know she was truly loved and not the black sheep she'd believed herself to be.

The pricing boom for brownstones in Brooklyn meant her parents would be able to buy a wonderful home in Florida and still have a nice nest egg to go along with her father's retirement. By the time she left, they were talking about an Alaskan cruise so they could see the place she fell in love with. Danni couldn't believe how wonderful it felt to truly be on the same page with her parents. It only reaffirmed the choice she made was the correct one. Danni was ready to follow her heart, back to Auke Bay and to Declan.

Chapter Sixteen

"MERRY CHRISTMAS, SARGE!"

People called and waved, and he raised his hand in greeting. In forty-eight hours, he had traveled over six thousand miles and jumped right back into work. As he drove through Auke Bay that morning, the holiday spirit was in full swing. Christmas Eve and everyone was out and about, hustling and bustling with happy smiles while getting last-minute gifts or groceries for dinner. To him it was all a little dimmer; the tree in the center of the city didn't seem as bright, and the bells that chimed didn't ring as clear. It was all because of her. He gambled and lost his heart to the one woman he could never have.

He was back in his apartment after another brutal flight back to Auke Bay from Jersey using Space Aviation. It was a service offered by the military for veterans to find flights, and while it was booked coming to New York, he found a seat easily to home. With no real rest, his already sore leg felt worse. Declan was almost grateful for the pain so he could stay in without seeing anyone and lick his wounds in peace.

He also knew he couldn't hide from the world any longer, and after sleeping for a few hours, Declan got up and put on his uniform. Going to work like any other day would give him the sense of peace and familiarity that served as his foundation. The first hurdle was going downstairs for his customary coffee and coffee cake from his mother—and Cooper, who was now a fixture at the bakery.

"Hey." The bell over the door dinged as he entered.

"How are you, Deke?" It was the first thing his mother said.

"I'm good, Mom. Can we not talk about this and cut out the sorrowful pity looks?" Declan said as he filled his Thermos. "I tried. It failed. I'm home. Things are back to normal."

Declan saw the worried glance that Susie gave Cooper before speaking. "If that's how you want it, Deke, I understand."

He kissed her cheek. "Thank you. Besides, I have a house to renovate."

"Now that sounds good," Cooper said with a surprising amount of gusto. "What are you thinking?"

"Knocking out those walls between the kitchen, dining, and living room. Mom, I think the apartment would work for our shelter guest and her daughter. She can get out of that room and it's a good start for them."

"I was thinking that as well. Maybe by the new year, you'll be done with the house and can move in with..." She bit her lip to cut off her stream of words.

"With?"

"Maybe a puppy! A nice Husky pup—yes, that's it." Susie straightened her apron. "I was always sad we never got you a dog as a boy. Now with a bigger house, you can have one."

"Uh-huh, I'll think on the house plans and the dog." They were both acting odd. "Mateo told me I could use his cabin up near the mouth of the river for a week or two. I'm going to take the time off—"

"No!" Cooper and his mother said simultaneously.

He gave them a curious look. "Um, why not?"

"I mean, it's Christmas, and you'd be alone for New Year's Eve..." his mom said.

"A storm is coming in, and you could be stuck," Cooper added.

His mom nodded furiously. "And you promised to work the holidays so Jess and Mateo could have some time off!"

They both were firing off excuses like a machine gun and looking rather uncomfortable.

Declan narrowed his eyes at them. "What's going on with you two?"

"Nothing." His mother busied herself wiping down the pristine counter. "I mean, you make a promise and that's important."

"Okay," he said slowly. "No parties and no setups, Mom. Cooper, since you are an extension of her now, that goes for you too."

"Deke, we wouldn't dare do a thing like that, not so soon after..." Cooper let his words trail away.

"I'll stick around until the day after Christmas. Then I need some time to myself," he said, covering the top of his Thermos. "This is the only way to find myself again, to remember how I was before she...well, before this whole thing."

His mother smiled. "I know, son, but things have a way of working themselves out. Be safe out there."

He pulled his knit cap over his head and zipped up the thick Sarge's jacket before stepping out the door with a small wave at the occupants inside. It felt like a lifetime, not a span of weeks, since he'd met Danni. Now as he drove through the small town, he saw her in all things. From the bakery to crashing the snowmobile outside the community center.

He needed a few weeks to clear his head. To give Mateo his first Christmas home with his new baby and his family, and to make sure Jess could stay home with her husband, he could wait a few extra days. The window was open to let the cold winter air in, and he could hear the ice crunch under the wheels of the truck.

Hearing the calls of holiday cheer didn't soothe his mood. In fact, it made him that much more anxious to spend time alone. Declan rolled up his automatic window and sighed as the silence enveloped him. He found his favorite spot, one that put him right where he needed to be in case there was an emergency but still gave him the seclusion he needed. At that very spot, he could see the peaks of the mountains with the snow clouds coming in. They were going to be hit hard with snow, and soon. Just looking at the clouds, Declan estimated over three feet of snow would fall over a span of days. He hoped it held off until after Christmas so he could get out to the cabin. Being snowed in out there wouldn't be that bad at all.

He watched the traffic, not that there was much. Every once in a while, there was a truck or a car but the roads on both sides were relatively quiet. Declan took a deep breath, then another, hoping to cleanse the hurt and heartache out of his chest. He kept seeing the image of the ring being held out in front of Danni and the look of shock on her face. Was it happiness or surprise at the proposal, or was it out of left field? He heard her calling his name and it almost halted his steps.

But everyone had started to turn and look at who she had in her line of vision. That had felt worse than anyone could imagine, because it had been like all the people in the city bearing down on him. It had been such a stupid mistake to go there, but the hope within him after speaking with Amy had given him a dream that didn't pan out. He couldn't blame her either, but the ache in his chest worsened thinking about her being married to that guy. He didn't see love in Austin's eyes. Danni deserved so much more, and Declan had thought that would be him. To show her how it was to be loved in the right way.

Mateo tapped on the window, and Declan sighed before rolling it down. "I knew I'd find you hiding out here."

"Not much of a hiding spot, if people can find me so easily."

"Amy wants you to come over for Christmas dinner,"

"So does my mom, so does everyone it seems." Declan shook his head. "Why do people equate feeding a person as a way to stop them from hurting?"

"Ever heard of comfort food?" Mateo teased gently. "Besides, I think Amy and Susie concocted a huge family dinner at our place. Her unpacking at Cooper's house is taking longer than expected."

"Well, that's even more fun." Declan's smile was swift and fleeting. "Here I was thinking I'd be eating French fries alone. Not me sitting around a table with people passing sorrowful looks along with the ham."

Mateo reached in the window to pat him on the shoulder. "We don't care if you say one word while we eat. We just want you to be around people who love you."

Declan let out a harsh sigh. "How do people deal with heartbreak, man? I keep telling myself and everyone I'm okay and life moves on, but I'm not. I haven't felt this emptiness in such a long time. I thought I figured out how to erase that sense of loss but in a matter of weeks Danni showed me I did need someone, and it was her."

"I can't answer that," his friend said in a somber tone. "We all handle it in different ways."

"How did she manage to blow into our world and so completely and utterly devastate me? I swear, I can hear her laughter in the wind, and I just want the pain to go away."

"It gets better, Declan, that's all I can say." Mateo leaned against the outside of the truck. "We have both lived through things that could cripple a man's soul, but yet we're here. I have Amy, and you will have someone to heal you in ways you never thought possible."

"When I was in rehab, after I lost my leg, I saw wives holding up their husbands, teaching them to walk again. They fed them and sat by their sides as they tried to heal. I saw them shed tears, wipe sweat, and fight for every milestone. And I was alone." Declan swallowed thickly. "Right now, I feel much worse, like I lost my chance at the perfect someone because I let the past twist my actions now. I should've acted sooner, shared another kiss, told Danni to stay, anything to have her with me. Now she's engaged to another man."

"Declan, come to dinner and don't be alone feeling like this," Mateo urged him. "We're not expecting any-thing—just you."

"I'm working that day to cover for you guys, so I'll stop in and eat before heading out." That was the only excuse he could come up with as a reason not to stay.

"That's all we can ask, buddy." Mateo gave him a hopeful grin. "Besides, I think the world works out in our favor when we least expect it."

"What is with everyone and this upbeat cloud and silver lining stuff today?" Declan asked, exasperated.

Mateo chuckled. "Haven't you heard? It's Christmas time and magic is in the air."

"Uh-huh, have you people been eating snow while I was gone? Aren't you supposed to be in a car patrolling on the other side of town?"

"Just feel the magic man, let it in and you will see, the miracles of Christmas are all around us," Mateo called out as he walked away and started singing a holiday tune...loudly.

Declan shook his head and opened his Thermos to have a cup of coffee. As he sipped the sweet strong brew with, of course, a piece of chocolate...okay, three pieces of chocolate. He deserved the extra. He thought about all the possibilities. If he'd just opened himself up to what he was feeling, maybe Danni would be with him now. He could be planning a home with the woman he loved instead of spending Christmas alone.

Danni's trip back to Juneau was wrought with problems, and she was on pins and needles every second of her journey. Her flight to Seattle was late, and in those hours from New York to her first destination, she thought she would miss her connecting flight. Of course, Danni knew realistically she had a pretty long wait. Yet anything to mess up the best laid plans made her anxious about what could happen next. Finally, she boarded the other flight to Anchorage and the Captain came over the speaker.

"Thank you for flying with Air Alaska, we are going to try to get you out of here as soon as possible. Our weatherman is forecasting a large storm, and we want to get you on the ground before the bad weather hits. Sit back and enjoy the flight, we have you covered."

Oh no. Danni closed her eyes and prayed that she could get into Juneau in time. *Please give me a miracle, please just one miracle.* It seemed she was jumping from one plane to another for the last few days, but she hoped this would be the last time. She was beyond jet-legged, with only few hours of sleep since Wednesday. Danni contemplated how much sleep she could fit in on every leg of her journey back in Auke Bay. But the very first thing she would do was find Declan and let him know she was his. As the pilot promised, he got them into Anchorage. While she waited for the next leg of her journey, Danni napped in the uncomfortable seats of the airport and ate chips from the vending machine. Her phone rang, and Amy's number appeared on the screen.

Her heart dropped as she answered. "Please tell me you're not snowed in yet, or that Declan hasn't gone off into the wilds of Alaska."

"Declan plans to leave right after Christmas, so he's still here," Amy said. "Currently the weather is holding, and you can still make it in before everything is grounded."

"What if the weather changes?"

"We have a plan for that, too. Susie has a friend in Anchorage who can drive you halfway, and Mateo will meet you there and bring you the rest of the way. We are getting you here for Christmas Day, even if it's dark by the time you get here."

"Oh, Amy. Is this going to work? Does he really want

me there?"

"He loves you. He's hurting without you, and we all see it. So, you're coming to love, Danni, we just need to get you here."

"Tell everyone in Auke Bay to pray hard and keep that weather away, because Danni isn't on the run anymore, she is ready to put down roots," she declared. "Happy Christmas Eve!"

Amy laughed and the baby cried, the cue that it was time for her best friend to get off the phone. "See you soon!"

"Yes, as fast as these feet can carry me," Danni promised and hung up.

A thirteen-hour drive from Anchorage, or a two-hour flight: Danni hoped for the latter. She waited patiently for her flight to Juneau, checking the weather on her phone and listening for the boarding call to come over the speaker system. There was no sign of the sun yet, but it was Christmas Day. She managed to get a hot cup of tea and one of those prepackaged snack boxes and nibbled at her cheese, crackers and fruit. Sitting in a little corner of the almost-empty airport, she could only assume most people who needed to be somewhere were already on their way to their destinations, while she and just a few others waited for a flight to Juneau and hoped a storm didn't keep them grounded.

She took out her laptop to check her site for comments regarding everything that happened the night Austin proposed. She had been in a flurry of activity and her followers needed an update. Her video channel and other social media outlets had blown up with comments and hits, her stats were off the charts.

Did she say yes?

Who is Declan?

She ran right out of there after some guy, Prince Charming, perhaps?

Must be from her Alaska Trip. Danni, we need the Deets!

Spill the tea!

They needed to know, and Danni didn't have a way to set up her tripod, so she just held up her phone to record a brief *Danni on the Run* update.

"Hey guys, I know I must look a frightful mess. Since I landed in New York, it's been a whirlwind, and if you can't tell, I'm not in the Big Apple anymore. I'm in Anchorage, Alaska waiting for my flight to Juneau and then on to Auke Bay. I know there was probably a livestream going from the party, and let me say it first. No, I'm not marrying Austin. We didn't fit as a couple, and it wasn't fair to either of us. Also, I will not be the spokesperson for a makeup brand. I had to make some choices in my life, and that path wasn't for me."

Danni sighed and looked out the window briefly, wishing she was in Auke Bay already, before returning her focus back to the recording. "Maybe in the near future we'll be working together in some capacity, but not right now. Now, who is Declan? He is the man I met in a small town, one who I fell in love with. In the midst of all these new experiences, he changed my socks when I stepped in a puddle. He showed me the northern lights by campfire and shared hot soup. We made the worst gingerbread house in the world, and it was completely perfect. I found the love of a community that's filled with so much culture and togetherness."

She sat back and played with the edges of her scarf from Cooper. "They embraced me and I them, so I'm moving to Auke Bay to everything I hold close in my heart and to a man I hope will honor me by becoming mine. I want to give him my heart and cherish his. So that's my journey, my friends. All roads led me here, and I could not be happier in this small room, hoping the snow stays away for just a while longer. Until I can see his face and tell him I love him and hold him in my arms for Christmas Day, I won't feel complete.

Danni's wide smile echoed the happiness in her heart. "For Christmas you guys, do me a favor? Live your dreams, chase them boldly, jump in the deep end feet first. There will be more from Danni who isn't on the run anymore, but a new adventure begins. Happy Christmas Day."

She stopped the recording and snacked on her meal while uploading to her social media channels. A tired Danni finally boarded her flight. The pilot gave the same information as Amy, the storm was playing nice and holding off for now.

Still, a flight that normally took two hours ended up taking longer so the pilot could get them to their destination safely. She almost wept in happiness when the plane descended into Juneau and the flashing lights beckoned them in.

I made it for Christmas Day! She almost felt like dancing when they could finally get up and grab her bags. Snowflakes and the cold biting air hit her face, but the view outside the airport at that moment was the most beautiful thing she'd ever seen. She was home. Danni looked around the arrival area outside and finally saw Mateo standing outside the family mobile.

"Mateo!" she called out, struggling with her bags as one tilted over on the uneven walkway.

Mateo lifted her in a hug before he grinned. "You made it! Merry Christmas, little sister. You are one lucky woman, you're always ahead of the storm...and again with all these bags."

"Let's thank Mother Nature when we get there," Danni said linking arms with him. "I'm not leaving again, so I need my essentials."

There was a loud knocking on the inside of the window and Amy waved madly.

"Let's get your bags inside." Mateo said, amused. "Get inside before she jumps out."

Danni laughed and got in the passenger door hugging Amy around the seat. "I made it, Amy. I made it home."

"You sure as heck did," Amy laughed and wiped away tears. "We were thinking about every which way we could get you into Auke Bay if the snowstorm hit."

"Where are the kids?" she asked.

"The kids are with Mateo's family at the house," Amy answered. "There was no way I was missing this."

"Well, I'm here now. I'm never leaving again."

Mateo got behind the wheel and slowly merged with the traffic. Soon, she would stand in front of the man who managed to steal her heart without even trying. Around them, pristine, heavy snow was everywhere, bare trees stood out from the stark white, and even the fir trees seemed more laden in only a few days.

Danni felt those butterflies take flight the closer they got to Auke Bay. "Do you know where Declan is?"

"When we came through town, he was parked in front of the trooper station," Amy said.

"Across from the gazebo?" Danni asked picturing it in her mind.

"Yes. Do you want to go to the house and freshen up first?" Amy asked.

"No, take me there. I'm not waiting a second longer."

Amy reached back to pat her knee. "We're almost there."

Danni pressed her hand against her stomach when the car made the turn to the familiar main street. The snow began to fall, soft, thick flakes that floated lazily from the sky.

"You okay back there?" Amy teased.

"I'll be fine," Danni said and heard the tremor in her own voice.

She saw the knowing glance passed between Mateo and Amy before he picked up her hand and kissed it. They understood. They both stood in this very moment years ago when love was new and unsteady, like a newborn fawn. Danni stared out the window as the gazebo came into view. The memory of holding his hand as they stared at the northern lights flashed in her mind. Decan was there now. His knit hat with the trooper's emblem was gathering flakes of snow as he loaded emergency supplies into his truck.

Declan looked up with a curious expression on his face when they drove up and parked. Of course, he probably wondered why his close friends were in town on Christmas morning. Then Danni stepped out, and in one crystallized, still moment, their gazes met. His eyes widened in surprise. She walked toward him, slowly at first until Danni was running towards him, her future, everything, through the snow that had picked up just a bit, and their eyes never broke contact. He opened his arms to catch her, and Danni knew she would never fall again.

"You're here," Declan said huskily.

Danni nodded. Tears clogged her throat for a moment, making it hard for her to speak.

"But why?"

She cupped his smooth ebony cheek. "For you. Why did you leave? I called out to you."

Declan turned his head away. "I can't give you what Austin can. I can't give you those lights, cameras. You looked so amazing. How could I compete? I'm still learning to be a whole man with only one leg. How could I..."

"There was never a competition. Before I even left here, I was yours." Danni turned his head so she could see his eyes. "Declan, without even trying, you took my breath away, and I knew I would never be the same without you. If you had said stay, it would have been a done deal. But I didn't know if you wanted me, if what I felt was real. So, I left even though everything in me was screaming for me not to. But you came for me, in a city that had to have caused your anxiety to rise...you braved all that for me. I'm here now, and if you'll have me, I'll love you for a lifetime and beyond."

Declan took her lips in a fierce kiss, one that sealed them together under the mistletoe still hung in beautiful green bundles tied with a red ribbon. When he lifted his head, a wide grin spread across his face, making Danni shake her head in amusement. Behind them was the Auke Bay Christmas tree that signified so much to everyone there. One day their ornaments would be part of that tradition. Declan pressed another soft kiss on her lips.

"Does that answer your question?" he asked in a low voice. "I love you, Danni St. Peters."

Danni let her laughter of happiness ring out as clear as Christmas bells. Declan hugged her tight while their friends and family looked on, and she laughed again as he swung her around in his arms.

Chapter Seventeen

CHRISTMAS WITH THE WOMAN HE *loved.*

Declan shook his head with amazement, replaying their kiss in his mind and holding her in his arms. Danni had left with Mateo and Amy to go back to their house, and he would see her tonight at dinner. For the next few hours, he had to make sure that Auke Bay was secure because they were going to get slammed with snow and everything would be closed down. Unable to resist, as he stood on the deserted rise over his small town, a shout of delight escaped him, and he pumped his fists in the air.

Heck yeah! He had gotten the girl.

His smile was wide as he got back into the truck to head back into town. She was waiting for him, so Declan moved quickly to complete his tasks. One of these was to make sure that certain areas had the items they needed. That meant the community center needed to be stocked with food and warm blankets in case power went out and some residents had to stay there to be warm and safe.

He made hot coffee for the large Thermoses, put

sandwiches in the fridge, made sure the generator was primed and ready, and opened cots. He placed blankets and pillows at the foot of twenty emergency beds. Before he left, he made sure the emergency code placard was on the door so anyone could enter in an emergency. The system would notify him if anyone showed up, and he would get in his truck that could handle a few feet of snow to go check on them. There was still one thing he had to do.

Declan parked in front of the small artisan jewelry shop and went to the door and knocked. Sam Bellevue and his wife Petra were artists who traveled art fair circuits in the summer selling the jewelry they made in the wintertime. They used many natural stones they harvested themselves from the rocks and cliffs of Alaska, and the three-story house had their small storefront on the bottom while the other two floors was their home. It took a few minutes before Sam opened the door, and a look of surprise crossed his face. Sam, who had to be around forty-five, was dressed like Santa, probably for his family.

"Sarge...um, what are you doing here? Something wrong?" Sam pulled his fake beard out from under his chin to ask.

"I know it's Christmas, and I am so sorry, but I need a ring," Declan said in a rush. "Like an engagement ring."

"I don't have anything like that, with diamonds and stuff. We use semi-precious stones and silver, mostly," Sam said. "I could order one from Anchorage, but it'll take a few weeks..."

Declan shook his head and grinned. "No can do, and I think she would like something from the town, created here. She refused diamonds, and I'm not going to show them to her twice."

Sam grinned. "Come on in, then, let's get you set up."

Declan stepped inside and looked at all the glass cases with different jewelry from necklaces to bracelets. Sam and Petra were skilled in Celtic knot work and intricate designs. He was sure he could find a beautiful piece that would be perfect for Danni. He was still wondering if he was dreaming since this afternoon when she stepped from the car.

At that moment, he had been trying everything not to think about her, so much so that when he saw Danni, Declan was sure she was a mirage. Hearing her declare her love was the most cherished gift she could ever give him. Now it was his turn. At dinner that night, he would ask her to be his wife.

"Here are a few choices," Sam said coming back with a case in his hand. "We've got some Aurora Borealis quartz, red garnet...."

Declan looked at the rings nestled between black velvet, and his eyes settled on a ring with a cluster of smoky green gems. He could swear tendrils of dark blue moved through the stone. The thin band looked like it was braided with three strands, and the entire thing was simple and elegant.

"This one, what's this?" Declan pointed.

"An Alaskan Jade." Sam smiled and took it from the case. "This cluster is very rare. We barely find any of it each season. Petra made this and she calls it Snow Magic. It's made for elegant hands."

"That's the one," Declan said instantly. "Do you have a box?"

"I have everything you need," he said with a quick grin.

Sam went to work dressed like Santa and in a way, he was because Declan got exactly what he needed on

Christmas Day. With the ring box sitting heavy in his pocket, he made sure that Auke Bay was safe and secure before heading home to change for the celebration with family and friends.

The snow was definitely coming down. The lights of the season gleamed through snow-covered bushes and roofs that were now pure white while each chimney he passed had lazy curls of smoke going into the sky. Declan parked his truck by the roadside since Cooper's truck was already in the driveway. His boots sunk into at least six inches of snow, and he knew before the night was over, it would be double that.

Excitement filled him as he walked quickly up the driveway to the steps that led to the front door. When Declan knocked, Danni opened the door with a wide smile on her face.

She took his breath away. Her hair was a mass of curls again, and she wore silver earrings in her ears. Danni was dressed in a red knit dress with black tights and those too-big boots he gave her weeks ago. Why did it feel like a lifetime ago...like his life had been moving toward her for months or years instead of a few weeks?

"Hi," he said feeling like a shy teen all of a sudden.

"Hey, Deke," Danni answered just as shyly and took his hand to lead him inside. "Come on in, everyone is waiting."

"Listen to you with the nickname," he teased, stepping inside.

"Look who's here!" Mateo said loudly and embraced Declan. "Merry Christmas, brother."

"Merry Christmas," Declan answered. It was a little disconcerting with all the attention, feeling the way he did about Danni, and so many people around offering love and embracing the warmth. But Danni met his gaze, and he found his center in her eyes. Declan assumed he would always be a little hesitant in certain situations, but together, he had no doubt they would be able to traverse life and whatever it brought.

Everyone talked and laughed, and conversation was loud and happy. Amy bounced the baby, and then Danni took her to coo at the small face wearing a red silky headband and a tiny red dress to match. Mateo's family came back with more food, and the celebration got bigger as dishes were placed on the dinner table. There was so much food that every counter space had a dish, pie or bread.

"You look happy, Deke," his mother said with a smile and handed him a glass. "Aren't you glad you didn't go off to that cabin alone?"

"So that's why you didn't want me to go—you and Cooper knew she was coming back!"

"Whatever do you mean?" She gave him that innocent look he knew so well.

Declan embraced his mother and whispered in her ear. "Thanks for keeping me here, Mom, and for holding on to that miracle even when I couldn't."

"To see this happiness on your face, I would do it all over again." She smiled up at him. "Go take Danni a glass of wine. Dinner will be on the table soon."

Declan made sure she didn't feel his pocket. His mother wouldn't be able to stop the scream of happiness and would start crying immediately. He took the glass of wine to where Danni stood by the fireplace.

"Wine." He handed her the glass.

"Thank you," Danni said. "Don't look now, but they keep watching us and smiling."

Declan chuckled. "It's like a chaperoned first date with lots of people."

"Second date. Our first was the campfire over Auke Bay," she teased. "I'm glad to be here... with you."

He took her hand. "I'm glad you came. Look at us, traveling thousands of miles for love."

"Would you change it?" Danni asked.

Declan grinned. "Not one bit."

"Let's sit and eat," Amy called out.

"This is amazing." Danni took his hand as they walked to the table. Amy and Mateo had added the mahogany extension to make the table longer so it could fit everyone. "I swear, even George was happy to see me."

Declan chuckled as he pulled out the chair next to him for her.

Mateo did the blessing for the meal and looked around with a huge smile. "We are so blessed to have family and friends here on Christmas Day. The snow may be thick outside and the winds cold, but the warmth within these walls will sustain us for a lifetime. Let's enjoy our meal."

It was time. Declan cleared this throat. "Before we eat, can I say something?"

"The table is yours, brother," Mateo said.

He cleared his throat. "I don't say much..."

"No! You're kidding, you are such a jabber jaws when I talk to you," Mateo teased.

"Hush." Amy slapped at his forearm lightly.

Declan shook his head and continued. "All of you have been in some way a part of my healing since I came back to Auke Bay. I thank you for that, for your patience, kindness, and friendship. I found out that all of you were directly involved in bringing Danni back home to us, and for that I am eternally grateful. You brought the woman I love back to me when I thought I'd lost her for good."

He turned to face her and took her hands. "Regardless of if it's me saving you from snowmobile accidents, teaching you how to fish, or wiping frosting from your face, I want to spend the rest of my life with you. Christmas in Auke Bay became so much more to me because you're here."

He reached into his pocket and pulled out the box and heard his mother give a soft cry of delight.

"Oh!" Danni covered her mouth with her hands and tears shimmered in her eyes when she looked at him.

"He's going to propose!" Amy squealed and clapped her hands.

"Shh, let the man do it," Mateo said.

"Danni St. Peters, my world tipped off its axis when you came into my life. Hearing your laugh healed my soul, and looking in your eyes, I can see a future I never thought I'd have." He opened the box to reveal the ring. "Do this broken Army crew chief the honor of becoming his wife. I will cherish you for the rest of our lives."

"Yes," Danni whispered and nodding frantically. "Deke, it's all the way yes! It doesn't matter how long we've known each other. Our hearts know."

He put the ring on her trembling hand as their close friends and family clapped in support and joy.

"Declan," his mother said gently and when he looked in her direction, she pointed upward with a tender smile on her face and tears in her eyes.

He looked up. Above him and Danni hung a sprig of mistletoe, and he knew his mother had put it there.

"Really, Mom?"

"Whatever do you mean, dear?" Susie said, not so innocently. "Kiss your fiancée, son."

Declan cupped her cheeks and kissed her gently, sealing Danni's acceptance of his marriage proposal and feeling like the luckiest man in the world.

"And on that note, let's definitely eat. We have so much to be thankful for and to celebrate!" Amy said and gave Danni a wink. "Butterflies."

Danni's laugh rang out. "Butterflies times ten."

He had no clue what the secret was between two best friends, but without Amy he wouldn't have met his soulmate. As the potatoes were passed and he placed a slice of one of the roasted chickens on her plate, Declan knew this was the first Christmas, one of many to come with Danni by his side.

"I thought you had a goose for Christmas dinner this year?" Declan commented. "Weren't you picking it up from your dad's?"

"He's in the yard. His name is Henry now," Mateo inclined his head towards Peter.

That set out a round of laughter around the table and Danni leaned her head against his shoulder. Declan kissed the top of her head... *Perfection.*

Epilogue

One year later....

HOW THINGS HAD CHANGED IN her life, Danni mused as she sat at her desk looking out the big bay window that graced her office built by her husband. Each time she looked at the ring on her finger and the word flitted through her mind, she smiled. A sense of contented happiness filled her. This time last year, she was learning her place in Auke Bay.

Now she was as much a fixture there as the gazebo that was in the center of the square. The tree was already up, and this year she and Declan had added their own ornament that he'd made and she'd painted. A small plane with six thousand miles and a heart carved into the side. Danni painted it yellow and white to signify Cooper's plane bringing her to Auke Bay.

They'd been married just before Valentine's Day, weeks after Susie and Cooper took their vows. Danni had stayed with Amy and her family until the wedding, and then she and Declan had lived in the apartment over the bakery while he renovated the house. Danni had helped in that aspect as well. Coming home covered in drywall dust from sanding or with speckles of paint was the most fun she'd ever had in her life.

She chronicled everything in her new revamped platforms, *Danni, Love from Alaska*. She had gained more followers along with the interest of her original fan base as she tackled not only living in Alaska but being a new wife. The hilarious episode when Declan was teaching her how to fish in the summer was all people talked about for weeks. Danni also wrote articles now. She'd been approached to be a contributor for a magazine, and she jumped at the chance.

The makeup company Danni had made a connection with ended up being the marketplace for Alaskan Ice. Danni helped Amy with the recipes for the skin care products, and when the weather warmed, they started her own backyard greenhouse on the acreage of land that was part of their home. Amy bloomed, and Danni watched Declan change as well.

He laughed more easily, and together they grew more in love. She talked to her mother, father, and sister more frequently—almost every week. And her parents had made the move to Florida. Danni had gone from feeling like she wasn't part of a family to being connected in more ways than one. She and Declan visited her Mom and Dad in Florida while Grace was also there, and they finally got to meet him.

"What do you think of my parents?" she asked Declan one night as they walked on the beach at sunset.

"I like them. Your dad reminds me of my father. We talked about books and golf. He seems to have taken a liking to it since they moved."

"Golf, huh," Danni said with a laugh. "I never would have thought of my dad as a golf man."

Declan held up his fingers. "He has two sets of clubs."

"Well, they adore you." She leaned her head against his shoulder. "Like I do."

"We should go to Disney World," he said suddenly.

Danni laughed. "Declan, you hate crowds. Do you know how many people go to the theme park?"

"But you're with me." Declan kissed her temple. "We're going to Disney World while we're here."

And they certainly did. Together, they rode rides and ate ice cream, then watched the night parade of lights as fireworks broke in the sky. One of her favorite memories was seeing him look completely embarrassed wearing her mouse ears. Yet she snapped the picture anyway, and it was saved in her phone. With her laptop opened and one of the first snows of the season packed outside, Danni didn't miss New York or her old life. This new path had so many twists and turns, it always kept her guessing. A secret smile crossed her lips. It wasn't done yet because another surprise awaited them as a couple.

"Deep in thought?" Declan asked from the doorway.

She looked at him and smiled. "Good memories."

"Finished the article?" He stepped in the room with her coat.

"Yep, and I hit send. I also did the invoicing for Amy, so I am done with work until after Christmas," Danni said brightly as she closed her laptop and stood.

Declan helped her into the thick coat. "Then we should go. Ed and Sandra will be arriving soon."

"Wonder how they fared in Cooper's plane?" Danni mused. "You know, the authentic way to get into Auke Bay,"

"Well, he's not flying anymore, so probably great," he teased. "I think they'll be flying out of the Juneau airport on the way back home."

"Hey, leave Coop alone. He's the best pilot ever," she said as they walked to the door. "I'm telling."

"Tattletale." Declan kissed her temple. "Get in the car, woman."

They had purchased a small SUV in the summer and now with the snow tires on, it was ready for the winter weather that would hold on to Alaska for at least nine months.

Declan opened the passenger door and helped her inside. "Are you okay?"

"I'm fine," she said with a laugh. "You need to quit doing that."

He closed the door and got in on the driver's side. "That's not going to happen. Be prepared, it may get worse."

"Oh boy," Danni murmured.

Their home was in the opposite direction from Amy's, so they would come through Main Street from another way. As they passed, it was a familiar sight, with the lighted garlands and other decorations being hung for the festival in the coming weeks. They passed by Baker's Dozen, and her new mother-in-law and Cooper were outside pasting holiday stencils on the windows.

Declan slowed and rolled down the window. "The both of you, do not get on that ladder."

Cooper laughed. "We got caught by the Sarge."

"Barry is coming out to do it," Susie called. "He's doing handyman work now." Barry was one of the new students who worked part-time at the bakery. "Love you both. Can't wait to meet your parents, Danni." She blew a kiss at them.

"See you soon. Love you too," Danni waved and called back.

"How do you think they'll react?" He cast a quick glance her way.

"Hmm." She tapped her chin. "My mom will cry, your mom will join in, more than likely Cooper as well. Amy will scream, which in turn since Luna is in the vocal stage will activate her screams. Mateo will slap you on the back repeatedly, and Peter will run around. Questions and general chaos will ensue, then lots of hugs."

Declan's laugh was a lovely baritone that instantly made her smile. "I think you pegged it just about right."

The car passed by the one lone baby boutique that graced Auke Bay and the owner was hanging red and silver tinsel stars between the tiny pink and blue booties that hung in the window. Christmas was in the air again. They had made a full circle around the sun, and her life had been blessed each and every day of it. Danni glanced at the store window in the rearview mirror once more as they drove on by. Declan took her hand and squeezed it before kissing her knuckles gently.

Danni pressed her other hand against her stomach and whispered. "Next Christmas."

The End

Super-Simple, Amazing Chocolate Cake

In *Mistletoe in Juneau*, Declan owes Danni an apology. So he walks into his mom's bakery and asks her for "a really good cake recipe—as simple as you've got." His mom gives him this one. He's a little doubtful about the "secret ingredient"—mayonnaise—but the cake is delicious, and Danni forgives him immediately. Even if you're like Declan and don't have any baking experience, this moist chocolate cake will win anybody over.

Prep Time: 15 minutes
Cook Time: 25 minutes
Serves: 16

Ingredients

CAKE

- 2 cups all-purpose flour
- 4 tablespoons unsweetened cocoa powder
- 2 teaspoons baking soda
- 1 cup sugar
- 1 cup mayonnaise
- 1 cup cold water
- 2 teaspoons vanilla extract

CHOCOLATE FROSTING

- 1 cup unsalted butter at room temperature
- 6 cups powdered sugar
- 2/3 cup cocoa powder
- 1/2 cup heavy cream
- 2 teaspoons vanilla

Preparation

1. Preheat the oven to 350°F.
2. Grease two 8-inch round cake pans and dust them lightly with flour.
3. Sift together the flour, cocoa, and baking soda in a small bowl.
4. In a separate bowl, mix together the sugar and mayonnaise, then beat in the water and vanilla.
5. Gradually add in the dry mixture and mix well.
6. Pour the batter into the prepared pans and bake for 20-25 minutes or until a toothpick inserted in the center of the cake comes out clean.
7. Make the frosting while the cake is baking.
8. In a work bowl with an electric mixer, cream the butter. Sift the sugar and cocoa powder together and gradually add to the butter, beating well after each addition. Add the cream and vanilla. Beat

until well blended and fluffy.

9. Remove the cake from the oven, remove the layers from the pans, and place them on wire racks to cool.

10. Frost cake.

Thanks so much for reading *Mistletoe in Juneau*.
We hope you enjoyed it!

You might like these other books from Hallmark
Publishing:

A Gingerbread Romance
Sweet Tea
On Christmas Avenue
Christmas Charms
An Unforgettable Christmas
Wrapped Up In Christmas

For information about our new releases and exclusive offers, sign up for our free newsletter at
hallmarkchannel.com/hallmarkpublishing-newslet-
ter

You can also connect with us here:

Facebook.com/HallmarkPublishing

Twitter.com/HallmarkPublish

About the Author

Dahlia Rose is a *USA Today* bestselling author. She was born and raised on the Caribbean island of Barbados and now currently lives in Charlotte, North Carolina. Her life revolves around her five kids and her husband and longtime love, an honorable retired Army veteran. With over seven dozen books published, Dahlia has become a reader favorite. Her novels feature strong heroines with a Caribbean or African-American culture, showcased in the vibrancy of her words. Books and writing are her biggest passions, and between the pages of her books, she hopes to open your imagination.